MIST OF THE KING

THE MAKING OF SUZANNE

REX SUMNER

Published in November 2016 by

MyVoice Publishing
www.myvoicepublishing.com

Copyright © Rex Sumner 2016

The right of Rex Sumner to be identified as the author of this work has been asserted by him in accordance with the Copyright, Designs and Patents Act 1988.

Cover and interior artwork by Maria Gandolfo.

All rights reserved. No part of this publication may be reproduced, transmitted, or stored in a retrieval system, in any form or by any means, without permission in writing from the publisher, nor be otherwise circulated in any form of binding or cover other than that in which it is published and without a similar condition being imposed on the subsequent purchaser.

ISBN 978-1-909359-53-6

Note: this is a work of fiction. No characters are based on actual people, alive or dead; policies and actions of countries and governments depicted bear no relation to actual historical fact. Customs of various people are from the authors imagination and have no bearing on actual customs of any people.

Contents

Acknowledgements	III
Harrhein	IV
Dramatis Personae	VI
Historical Notes	VIII
Three Little Girls	1
Feeding the Dragon	3
A Bouquet for a Queen	19
Thief in the Night	29
The Harvest Ball	39
Reputation	51
Healing	60
Strollers	71
Training	84
Spiders	104
A New Court	125
Politics	138
Betrayal	153
Champion	168
First Blood	178
Ashes	187
Missing	201
The Wagonmaster	213
About the Author	233

Mistress of the King

Acknowledgements

My thanks to the many people from whom I have cheerfully liberated not just their names, but often their description and characteristics. This helps me present more rounded characters, and to remember that there is no such thing as a bad guy. Everybody tries to do the right thing from their own perspective.

My readers asked me for a sequel to In Search of Spice. It's coming. However I like to write short stories to develop each major character, so I know how and why they act. Suzanne's short story took on a life of its own, and when I found I had written 150,000 words with no sign of ending, I realised I needed to get it out quickly.

I wrote 40,000 words in three days over a forgotten Christmas and I am eager to finish the second part, where new characters forced themselves into the pages and lit up the story with their antics.

The second part, Mistress of the Gods, will be finished shortly - it is in editing - and then I will complete the third part, Mistress of the Kingdom, before the sequel to In Search of Spice, provisionally entitled In Search of Solace. Keep an eye out on my Facebook page.

Special words of thanks to my family, my lovely wife and my boys who each in their different ways make me proud.

Rex Sumner
Ubud, Bali 2016

Harrhein

Over the past five hundred years, the kings of Harrhein consolidated the kingdom by conquest, bringing Fearaigh and Galicia into the country, while waging a ceaseless war with the northern tribes.

Coillearnacha stayed separate, with another race, Elves, occupying the western shores. An uneasy truce prevails, with frequent raids from both sides of the border.

No one knows what happens in the far north. Expeditions founder on the enmity of native peoples, but Hardenwall stands as a bulwark against the Uightlanders with an insatiable taste for the fat cattle of the Hallowed Fields.

To the east lie the islands and peninsulas of the warlike Spakka, who delight in raiding Harrhein and capture every ship they can, while in every other direction lies limitless ocean.

To break free, the people of Harrhein need to make a deep sea vessel and sail over the edge of the world. First they must ensure the safety of the Kingdom.

This volume recounts setbacks... Internal intrigue, Spakka invasion and a king desperate for a male heir.

Susan wants to be queen, to the malevolent horror of the Church and nobles, who disapprove of her base-born origins, her intelligence and her singular lack of piety.

Dramatis Personae

Galicia

Mr and Mrs Taylor
Roger Browne
Abigail – a friend
Lord and Lady Sol, Duke of Galicia
Lady Alice of Galicia
Viscount Fabian of Galicia
Colonel Devran
Viscount Richard of Galicia - Ricky

Orb and Sceptre Playhouse

Mary Sidney
Will
Ben
Kit
Harry

Court

King Richard Starr
Lady Durrant
Lady Irina Sarl
Treste – servant
Chamberlain Douglas
Marcia Henderson
Lucinda, Duchess of Westport
Lord Gower
Sir Timothy Brown

Pathfinders

General Roberts
Lancepesard Andy Russell
Sergeant Craig
Colonel Donnell
Corporal Donald Riggs
Corporal David Brand
Sergeant Murphy
Captain Rogers

Church

The Venerable Reinand
Lady Belvedere
Count Rotherstone
Bishop Roseton
Bessin

Historical Notes

Throughout this novel you will find little snippets of information. The vast majority of this is quite true, relating to European cities in the 15th century.

Streets did get so muddy you could lose a boot - not a shoe, mind, but a boot, for the mud could reach to the thigh. The smell must have been indescribable, for there were no sewers; leather was made by soaking the hides in urine - stale urine - and the favoured rubbish tip was the street. Lavatory too.

Combined with this, people believed washing to be dangerous...

Medical care was in flux, as the millennia old knowledge of herbs was decreed by the Church to be pagan and herb women burnt as witches, leaving priests in charge of health. They believed in the power of prayer, with a good dose of bleeding to go with it. Harrhein's Church is not so universal, allowing herbalism to flourish.

The Church has an interesting history, with heavy involvement in politics from the start and a morality very different from the one we see today. Nunneries in the early middle ages supplied ladies to nobles as mistresses, passing back influence and information to the Church. The Seminary referred to in this story has a very real base on historical fact, though whether boys were also trained I do not know.

Many of the characters in the novel are based on historical figures. Many are not. Have fun working out which is which. Some of the historical events on which something is based come from up to 500 years before or after.

The military organisation is described with some accuracy. At the time there was no rank insignia, nor regiments as described here. Most soldiers were the gentry, who spent all their time practising their craft and disdaining the merchants and farmers whose success they 'taxed'. And come warfare, the poor farmers were required to turn up, barely trained, as cannon fodder while the gentry had a good time, though at the time of this novel the situation is somewhat advanced from this.

Senior titles were coming into being, General, Colonel and

Major, while a professional telling them what to do might be the Sergeant General, for example. The rank of Lancepesard was an early rank derived from Italy, which in due course evolved into Lance Corporal. Sergeants derived from Latin via French, meaning one who serves, servant, and no doubt started out as the manservant of the noble who raised the army and would pass on his orders.

The dances described in Court are from the time, before such dances as the Waltz. It seems strange that in a lusty time where sex and infidelity were the norm, you did not hold your partner.

For long periods, love was considered most important and you were never unfaithful to your lover in your heart, though you could dally where you wished and marriage a political convention. Even in the lower classes, marriage was for financial gain: a field, a mill, a herd. The higher nobility could indeed help themselves to the wives of lower ranks - a custom which seems to exist to this day...

I have not tried to make people speak in the English of the time, but as if they were speaking today. I have used modern swear words though I take care not to use those we know have a modern origin, such as 'crap'. On occasion, I present potential origins of some of these words. Twat may surprise you, and is indeed a leap of intuition on my part, coming from the name of a people, perhaps forerunners of the tantric arts.

It was a violent time and a violent age. People took what they could, and you needed guards and friends to prevent that including you. Strong women abounded, whether ruling their little kingdom directly, or through an ineffectual husband or being skilled at arms. The latter tended not to be beautiful.

The Victorian Era, epitomising the strength of one woman, has changed not just history as we know it, through the re-writing of history, but our attitudes and morals.

This is another interpretation of small aspects of our history. I am but an amateur dabbler, so make no claims to being correct, but my word, it is fun!

Mistress of the King

Three Little Girls

This book opens with three short stories, prequels to the main event, giving you the reader insight into major characters.

They feature little girls - very different girls, but with one thing in common. Strength of character. These stories are prequels to this story, and two of the little girls appear in this book, while if you have read In Search of Spice you will enjoy discovering of Sung Bai Ju's origins.

These stories prepare you for the main event but make no mistake. This is not Young Adult fiction but mature reading, red in sword and passion. You may expect to see your emotions go in different directions and that is intentional - you cannot enjoy the good times if you haven't been through the dark valley first.

Remember these early characters, those in the second two stories. You will meet them later.

Mistress of the King

Feeding the Dragon

In the Ancient Kingdom of Sung, an old monk slept in the afternoon sun under a plum tree. Ju Qua woke with a start, rubbing his forehead and finding it sticky. He gazed in disbelief at the half crushed plum that had woken him.

"I brought you rice, Holy One," came a small piping voice, and he looked up into the innocent eyes of an urchin, proffering a bowl to him.

He took the bowl, taking in the child, dressed in rags, barefoot, black hair cut roughly like a down-turned bowl and intense black slanted eyes looking at him with a disturbing lack of guile.

"You should not sleep under a ripe fruit tree, Holy One."

Suspicion flared through him, along with incredulity. Surely this child would not have dared to throw a plum at him? And why was he not scared of the monk? Did he not know who he was? And he presumed to give him advice! Where was his respect for the aged?

"Do you know what I am, boy?" Ju Qua's voice was rough and gravelly, sounding unused.

"I am not a boy," said the child with deep scorn. "You are a fighting monk, from the monastery of Sindalar. Is it true you have a dragon?" A barely perceptible leaning forward betrayed the girl's interest and the monk was astonished.

"Why are you not afraid, girl? Where are your friends?"

"They think you will feed them to the dragon. I am the only one brave enough to feed you," she boasted.

The monk was silent for a while, and ate the rice, chewing the required thirty times for each mouthful as he watched the girl from under his brows. Scooping the rice up with his right hand, he formed it into a ball, dipped it into a piquant sauce and flicked it into his mouth with his thumb. The girl waited, a stillness in her that caught the monk's attention and he studied her aura with care. Strong and robust, without weakness, and even; light colours in the main but with plenty of red and a definite black streak coming out in places, indicating ruthlessness and the ability to kill. Oh, interesting!

He sent out a mental probe, exercising care and gentleness as he intruded it into the childlike mind. Which snapped shut like the jaws of a tiger, fangs bared in protection. It would take a mental battering ram to get through that, he thought, which would probably destroy her. For the first time, expression flitted across the girl's features, as she looked sternly at him.

"You did something," she said with indignant accusation.

"So did you. Do you know what you did?" asked the monk.

"I ... pushed?" she said, uncertain.

"You did," he confirmed with a nod. "Why are you not scared I will feed you to the dragon?"

"It is a story," she said with the deep annoyance of one subjected to many such stories. "One that isn't true but is supposed to stop me from doing what I want to do. None of the other stories are true, why should this one be true?"

"Tell me one of the other stories," said Ju Qua.

"If you go too close to the river, a water horse will rush out and grab you, pull you into the river and drown you."

"Why?"

"So it can eat you. I think the story is to stop stupid people falling in the river and drowning."

"Did you stay away from the river?"

"No, I went to see the water horse and fell in. I am the only person in the village who can swim."

This statement came as the monk was swallowing some rice, which in consequence went down the wrong way and caused a fit of coughing. When he recovered, he wiped his eyes and accepted a stone flask of tepid tea from the girl, who had not moved.

"What will you do," he asked, "in the coming years? Will you marry and be a farmer's wife?"

She snorted like a delicate foal. "They are too stupid. No, I shall make my parents sell me to the brothel in Sinkian. I will be their best courtesan and go to the capital."

The monk nodded as he considered this information. It could be the most advantageous career plan open to a young girl of intelligence and he wondered that at so young an age she had already mapped out her future.

"You know what happens in a brothel?" he asked.

"Last rice harvest I went with my father to Sinkian. While he talked to the merchants, I went to the brothel and spoke to a pretty girl. She told me everything. That was when I decided. I don't want to be a farmer."

"And the capital? That is where you will go?"

"When I have learnt the skills of singing and playing music, of massage and the body, only then will I be ready. I will make myself the best," she said, with grave determination.

Ju Qua nodded with a straight face. "The best, so you will become a courtesan for the Emperor?"

"No," said the little girl, indignant. She stuck out a bare foot, perfectly formed and exquisite. "My stupid mother thought I would be a farmer. She didn't bind my feet. I can never have lilies, so the Emperor will not want me, for I can never advance beyond the sixth rank." Lilies are the term for feet bound at birth on girl babies, so the toes are crushed and maimed and the feet never develop properly. It was considered a mark of great beauty in Sung.

The monk blinked at her feet. He thought the binding of girls' feet to make them sway when they were older a disgusting, effete practice that summed up much that was wrong in Sung.

"The dragon will not care," he said, for the first time making the mistake of not asking a question. "He will think your feet very tasty."

"How do you know it is a male dragon?" The girl pounced on this trivial opening. "Does it have a big baz-baz?"

"A what?" said Ju Qua, uncertain at this new term outside his experience, before deciding he didn't want to know. "He says he is a male dragon."

"Why doesn't he eat you?" she asked, happy to turn the tables on the monk with a stream of questions.

"He's my friend," said the monk with an evil smile. "He knows I bring him tasty virgins to eat."

"I will be his friend as well," said the girl with determination. "I will be able to bring him more virgins than you can. Why do dragons eat virgins anyway? All the stories say they want gold and virgins, but it doesn't make sense. The courtesan explained to me that the mandarins don't like virgins, they want skilful girls, so they break the barrier in training."

"Well," began Ju Qua, again wrong footed by this extraordinary child, and then changed his mind about what he would say. He wanted this girl. Perhaps the most potential in any he had ever found in his recruiting expeditions for the monastery. It was time for action. "I have finished eating. Come, take me to your father and I will negotiate a price for you." She was a jewel beyond price, he knew, and perhaps there would be others in the village who shared her abilities.

*

The following day he set out for the monastery, cutting short his trip in his eagerness to get the girl back. He had accepted two other girls, pressed on him by eager parents, who followed him with lowered heads and dejected body language, tears pouring down their faces in silent misery. The girl, meanwhile, skipped along in front of him, chasing a vibrant, cerulean coloured locust across the rice fields.

She returned from a successful chase, handing him a locust while she spat out the legs of another and cast a judicious eye over her friends.

"Do you have rope?" she asked. "I think we need to tie them up at night to stop them running or killing themselves."

"It won't be necessary," said the monk with finality.

She walked beside one of the girls, bigger than her, and prodded her with a hard finger, under the ribs. The girl flinched.

"We mustn't go too fast, or she'll lose weight and won't be tender for the dragon," she announced. Her victim shrank into herself and moaned. The girl returned to the monk and proceeded to walk backwards in front of him.

"My name is Wu Gui." She announced.

Turtle, he thought, no doubt a snapping one. "I shall call you Nu Hai." Nu Hai means girl in Sung, and in particular refers to a serving girl.

"Nu Hai? You just call me serving girl!" she cried, her indignation rising into an instant storm. "I shall call you Shanyang Fen as you don't seem to have a name."

He bristled outwardly, inwardly chuckling. "You have no respect for your elders. You will not call me goat shit. You may call me Shifu, Honoured Master."

"We have an old man in the village who was always stupid and now drools in the sun. He has never done anything in his life to earn respect. Why should I respect him, Shanyang Fen?" She twitched effortlessly away from his staff as he aimed for her buttocks.

"To think anyone managed to live into his old age, in a village with you to look after them, deserves respect," he began, but she forestalled him by twirling and running off to a nearby pond, shouting something over her shoulder. He consoled himself with the thought that soon she would be exhausted, and then worried that he would have to carry her. They had many leagues to go today.

Fifteen minutes later she was back, beaming from ear to ear and covered in mud, soaking wet.

"Look!" she cried in triumph, brandishing her hand for them all to see. "I got a full handful, all four!"

She had four large dragonflies on her hand, each with the wings trapped between her fingers and the legs waving soulfully in the air. Having displayed her prowess, she released them carefully, ensuring each one flew away undamaged. She laughed at Ju Qua's expression.

"We have no skillet to fry them, Shanyang Fen. I will catch more for you when we stop for the night."

The path forked and with an unerring sense of direction she took the left fork. The monk started to take the right fork, not intending to say anything.

"This way is better," she said.

The monk stopped and looked at her. He knew both ways were the same distance.

"This way we spend the night at the village of Seventh Happiness. The water is very good and the people are friendly; we will eat better. So says Wu Yang, the merchant, and he is always concerned for good food."

"When did he say that?"

"Two months ago, he came with the news that you monks were searching for dragon food. He warned everyone to hide their daughters. I decided then to come with you and asked him the best way."

"Why would he talk to you?"

"He says that he ends up overpaying my father when I distract him and the best way to get rid of me is to feed me to the dragon.

He has been telling my father to do that for years. I like Wu Yang."

The monk found himself following her during this conversation, and in due course they approached the village of Seventh Happiness. Wu Gui stopped at the travellers' shrine overlooking the village, and he overheard her talking to the other two girls as he went in to meditate.

"Clean the stone there under the tree. The Shifu will sit there while he eats. Make up a bed for him under the travellers' roof, using those long grasses from beside the river. Make sure they are dry. Ting Lah, you have good hands, you will massage him when he finishes praying and I will come back with food from the village."

Indeed, on completing his meditation he found a beautiful grass bed made up for him and the girls sat him on that while one washed his feet and the other worked the knots out of this shoulders.

As he enjoyed this unexpected attention, he noticed a procession coming from the village; Wu Gui bringing at least a dozen people with her. Somehow, she had managed to obtain a jacket, silk if he wasn't mistaken, and looked terribly important. She stopped the villagers outside the shrine and arrayed them in front of the stone, making sure they all averted their eyes from the monk, who watched in some astonishment.

Wu Gui came under the roof and inspected the monk with critical attention, checking his ears and nostrils to ensure the girls had cleaned them. Ju Qua did not find the inspection in the slightest bit respectful, but was too fascinated in her plans and machinations to object, and allowed himself to be escorted to the stone under the tree.

Wu Gui had appropriated his staff, and now stood at his right and thumped it down on a stone, making a solid sound and the audience shake.

"The Guardian is ready. You may approach and show your respect."

The humble monk was careful to take control of his ch'i and ensure no leakage that would betray his amazement at the spectacle of the village head man, who only the previous year had ignored him while pushing past him in the street, now throwing himself prostrate and gabbling words he couldn't make out. It was clear they were some sort of apology, though, and a promise of better behaviour in the future.

He raised a hand to stop the babble, and he felt Wu Gui's ch'i pulse from beside him as she interrupted.

"The Guardian says enough. Retreat and put forward the candidates."

The headman scuttled backwards and four awed children, freshly scrubbed, came forward and bowed before the monk. He blinked at the sight of children never seen before, but examined their auras. Each was strong, bright and even, no blackness but the streak of red that indicated intelligence. He beckoned them forward and laid his hands on their foreheads, each in turn. He skimmed the surfaces of their minds and was pleased. He noticed that two were boys, unusual for parents to present. Settling back, he prepared himself to speak when he was interrupted again.

"They are acceptable. Just." Wu Gui's voice had taken on an ethereal tone, and from the corner of his eye he could see the force of her ch'i as a beacon shining from her. The peasants must have been able to see something as well, because they prostrated themselves on the ground. "They may spend the night with their families and be here at dawn. They will serve the dragon and protect you in your homes. Go."

Adults and candidates both shuffled backwards, bowing several times in the process, till they felt far enough away to turn their backs without giving offence.

Ju Qua watched them go, then turned on Wu Gui, to find her slumped to the ground, her fingers releasing their hold on his staff. He grunted and took her wrist, feeling the slow, cold pulse of ch'i exhaustion. He trickled a little of his ch'i into her.

"Sit, girl and rest. The others will bring you food."

She glared at him. "Do not call me girl, Shanyang Fen. My name is Wu Nu."

He was taken aback that she was now called Beauteous Lady instead of Turtle. "I thought your name was Wu Gui?"

"I changed it to suit my new role as Trainer and Polisher of Goat Shit into Guardian of the Dragon and the People." She struggled to her feet and issued peremptory instructions to serve herself and 'the Guardian' and to bring her a stool.

Ju Qua noticed she was served first and hid his delight as she first had him put to bed, then ensured both girls were tucked up comfortably on beds of grass the other side of the roofed area. She knelt beside them and he listened, fascinated, to her answering their questions.

"Honoured Auntie, how will you stop the dragon from eating us?" This, from a girl at least a hand taller.

"There is no dragon, Little Sister. It is just a story to frighten people into giving food and money to the monastery."

"Why do they want us in the monastery, Honoured Auntie?"

"Think, girl, how many monks does this monastery have? Very few. They need more. We are to be monks."

Ju Qua was delighted with her reasoning and the girls reassured.

"What does a monk do, Honoured Auntie? Will you or this old monk teach us?"

Wu Nu sniffed in mighty if pretty disdain, managing to convey the exact amount of disparagement. "This old monk is a fighting monk, a Guardian monk. He will protect us from bandits and I will help you with your lessons."

"What will we learn, Honoured Auntie?"

"You will learn to think, for you will need to come to the villages and help to dispense wisdom and justice. You know how little there is of both. Now, sleep, for I want you awake before dawn to clean my jacket. See, I shall put it here where it is safe. I must be wearing it when the villagers come with breakfast and our new recruits. May the Dragon's thoughts send you miraculous dreams."

Ju Qua was astonished and realised the girl was older than his first assumption. He was still astonished several days later as they filed up the winding path from the valley to the imposing carved stone monastery on the mountain top. Theirs had been a journey of grace and triumph, gaining recruits from every village, willingly fed and looked after at every stop. Wu Nu had stopped even checking for his opinion when selecting the recruits and the only part of his role she had not usurped was leading the morning and evening exercise rites. She clearly adored these and leapt into them with delight, questioning him with close attention on the purpose of each one while relishing the martial flavour.

He wore a new orange robe. He had new sandals that actually fitted. He didn't remember being so well fed, nor so pampered.

It was clear there was a need in the countryside for the guardians Wu Nu promised the credulous villagers, for which they had been rewarded with clothes, food and recruits, and he thought the abbot would see it worthwhile to fill this need.

Even so, he worried as they neared the gates and would have slowed the procession, but Wu Nu had taken the pole position in her silk jacket. The little girl reappeared as she stared up at the soaring spires with a big grin on her face.

Ju Qua prepared his speech to the door monk and hoped there would be sufficient accommodation for all the recruits.

The great gates swung open with ponderous deliberation as they approached, with no sign of a person operating them.

Revealed in the middle of the outer hall stood a lady. Ju Qua's heart quailed as he recognised one of the reclusive female monks unique to Sindalar.

Her face was heavily powdered to make it glaring white with bright scarlet lips and black eyes, her hair tied into a tight bun with two sticks thrust through it. She wore a high blue silk jacket with voluminous sleeves that made her look very young and small, with a golden skirt that covered her legs and feet. She glided forward.

Wu Nu walked straight up to her and bowed deeply. The Lady returned the bow and spoke. "Welcome Novices. Long have I waited for you. The years grow weary, the dragon is hungry."

Wu Nu beamed. She started to speak, but was cut off. "Girls will come with me." The Lady turned and glided away. Wu Nu followed her, trying to imitate the glide, and the other girls trailed along behind, some looking back. The Lady's enigmatic greeting awakening the fears Wu Nu had laid to rest.

Their path wound through corridors into the open air and into a small village behind the monastery. A low stone building proved to be a dormitory, with numerous hard cots.

"Place your belongings on a bed, wash and go to the dining hall. You will eat, and then meditate. This afternoon you feed the dragon."

The girls didn't quite panic, but they all looked at Wu Nu.

"It is a story, a test," she said, taking off her precious jacket and folding it neatly on a cot. She stripped off her white cotton shift, went into the wash area and started to pour frigid water over her head, ignoring the Lady while cataloguing her charges. "Look! There is soap! Ayee-ah! The water is very cold so high on the mountain. Ting Lah, come wash my hair, then I will do yours."

The girls flocked into the wash area, some still watching the Lady out of the corner of their eye.

Through the veil of her short wet hair Wu Nu examined the Lady. Her aura was strong and even, golden with hints of red. She thought about how the monk had tested her mind and flinched. She realised the attention had been sufficient to cause her mind to reach out and the Lady had smacked her errant thought down and back into her.

The girls were chattering away, mainly about water temperature and how wonderful the soap was, but Wu Nu could feel their nervousness seeping through their ch'i. She checked her own, and projected a calming confident ch'i, pleased at this new skill learnt from the monk without his knowledge.

"Look at the Lady, girls," she called as she came out of the wash area and rubbed her body and hair with a cloth. "Once she came here just like us and see! The dragon did not eat her. It is a test, and to pass it we must be like her."

The Lady did not move or show expression, though Wu Nu had the impression that she was being studied, perhaps with ch'i. Wu Nu pulled on the white shift that was laid on her bed, frowned at the simplicity and shrugged into her beautiful jacket as well. She stood watching the Lady as Ting Lah came running over with a comb and brushed her hair. One by one the girls completed their ablutions and came to stand beside Wu Nu, staring at the Lady.

Anyone else would be unnerved, but the Lady stood serene till all were ready, gave them an extra minute to underline her authority and led them to the dining hall.

A fragrant soup waited for them, with some steamed vegetable dumplings and rice. There was a low table with no chairs or cushions.

Wu Nu collected a bowl of soup and two small dumplings in another bowl. She seated herself on the table in front of the Lady and subjected her to an intense and obvious scrutiny while she ate. On consuming the dumplings, she sipped her soup and raised her eyebrows at the subtle taste. She slurped the soup, loud and polite to show her appreciation, all the while not taking her eyes off the Lady.

"What is the next rank after novice?" she asked.

"Student," replied the Lady, her eyes on the horizon through the window.

"What rank are you?"

"Wisdom," came the answer, a ghost of a smile barely visible.

"What is the top rank to be achieved?" Wu Nu had learnt the benefits of asking questions.

"Sung Bai Ju," answered the wisdom. "The Chrysanthemum of the Country, the Flower of Death, Protector of the Realm."

"Will we meet her this afternoon?"

"It is more than one hundred years since the last Sung Bai Ju walked amongst us."

"Why are you not promoted?"

"You looked at my aura, Little Novice. You did not see black. I can never be a Bai Ju."

Wu Nu considered this, and hitched her right heel higher into her lap, brow wrinkled with concentration.

"There is black in my aura."

The wisdom looked at her with interest. "We cannot see our own aura. How did you know that, Little Novice?"

"I didn't. Until now." She paused to let the wisdom see the trap into which she had fallen. She handed her dirty bowl to Ting Lah for washing without thinking and scratched her head, considering what to probe next. The other girls were listening to the conversation with fascination, while eating and cleaning up. The wisdom made no pretence of not watching her now, a glimmer in her eyes which might have been amusement or respect.

Wu Nu turned and looked at the other girls. They had finished clearing up and were standing around. "It is time for meditation," she said, clapping her hands. "We will meditate in the garden there," she pointed out of the window. "The Wisdom will come for us when it is time to be tested." She led them out to the garden leaving the wisdom smiling in serene dignity as she sought oneness.

*

Ju Qua stood proud and tall in his new robe and sandals by the small arena. It was a bowl in the mountain, with a spring in one corner where a little well and shrine to the water god nestled in the lowest part. The shrine was the intricate, carved head of a dragon, with the jaws wide open, each tooth portrayed in sharp and savage splendour. Numerous little paths crawled round the mountain and00 into the depression, granite rock interspersed with little rock flowers, each in its own pocket of soil.

Behind him, seated on suitable rocks, were the five boys he had brought back, each in a new robe. They would be trained as fighting monks. Around him stood every single monk from the monastery. All gathered to see this testing. A strong candidate, lots of girls, unheard of numbers. Rarely did a recruiter bring back more than two.

Ju Qua preened in the glow of their admiration and, in some cases, envy.

The girls arrived, led by Wu Nu, already in a perfect glide while the wisdom followed behind her, hands hidden in her sleeves.

Wu Nu spied him across the little area. "Shanyang Fen!" She waved. "Are my boys doing well?"

Ju Qua gave a lordly nod of his head to acknowledge the girl's respect to her guide and mentor, before noticing the other monks' smiles. His world and satisfaction collapsed as he replayed the conversation and realised he had been called Goat Shit in front of every person in the monastery and, worse, had acknowledged the name.

Wu Nu took her girls over to the dragon shrine, and arrayed them in front of it, seating them on the ground. The wisdom walked into the shrine and retrieved several small clay dishes, simple oil lamps. She placed them on a flat rock and started to light them, going into a light trance as she did so.

She started out of the trance as Wu Nu took the taper from her and took over lighting the lamps. "Allow me, Wisdom. It will allow you to start the ritual in a more relaxed mind."

The wisdom smiled with a fixed glare, sat on the stone dragon's tongue, cleared her mind and started to meditate, chanting in a low tone as she did so.

Behind her, Wu Nu placed the largest lamps in the stone dragon's eyes and more in the nostrils. The dragon appeared to come to life. Wu Nu gestured at her awestruck girls, who went into the seated position and picked up the wisdom's chant. Instead of joining them, Wu Nu took up a position slightly to the right of the wisdom, where she cast an impression of such importance, with her novice's robe covered by her jacket, that an unprecedented amused murmur rustled around the assembled monks.

The wisdom came to a stop. She opened her eyes and looked without seeing over the group. "First the Reading Test. Step forward those who can read and write."

She was taken aback when all the girls arose and stepped forward. It was unusual for girls to be able to read and write, but Wu Nu had chosen for cleverness, and clever girls could, especially if they aspired to become a courtesan where it was an important skill. In recent times the recruiters only found the dullards. Wu Nu's promises to the peasants had produced a very different class of recruit.

Wu Nu felt a draft of ch'i coming from the dragon's throat and saw another wisdom appear, dressed in identical fashion to the first wisdom but built a little larger. She carried some scrolls in her arms and came out of the dragon's throat, making it apparent that this was, in fact, a tunnel. Wu Nu's interest peaked, especially as she realised the flow of ch'i was huge, clearly from a powerful, spiritual person and not the second wisdom as at first appeared. Without conscious thought, the call of the ch'i too much to resist, she pushed past the wisdom, following the flow of ch'i. Down the throat of the dragon.

Seeing their leader disappear, her girls, clustered in front of the wisdom for the reading test, followed. So did the boys, jumping down from their seats into the shrine.

Ju Qua managed to restrain the boys, with the help of his fellow monks. The wisdom was not so fast and watched helpless as the girls pushed past her and her fellow wisdom, rushing down the tunnel. The real test was just to detect the flow of ch'i, not to find its source.

It was dark in the tunnel, but Wu Nu went downwards on the run, as fast as her tunic allowed, immersed in the massive flow of ch'i. The girls caught up with her and nobody stumbled or fell, for the floor of the tunnel ran smooth with the erosion of years. Somehow, the source of the ch'i sensed them coming, for it cut off and Wu Nu felt bereft. Too late for them to stop, though, for a light was visible at the end of the tunnel.

Wu Nu burst into the sunlight and stopped, the girls arrayed behind her, looking into a beautiful meadow. Green grass rippled down to the banks of a laughing stream tumbling down one side; wildflowers winked from the green waves as a zephyr of wind fluttered through the grass. Sheep and cattle grazed along the bank of the stream and lying on a large rock in the middle of the meadow was an enormous lizard, basking in the sunlight.

A large, domed head was at the end of a long neck, now raised to allow eyes bright with intelligence to study them. A solid body with a swollen belly, huge back legs and front legs that looked more like arms and seemed to end in fingers. A crest ran down the back of the lizard, becoming a magnificent sail down the centre of his back. Predominantly yellow-green over most of the body, the sail was a startling gold with red and black patterns, and his throat the vivid blue of a babbler's egg.

"That," said Wu Nu in tones of wonder "is a dragon."

He looked nothing like the drawings, paintings, images and models of dragons that appeared in their daily life, but all the girls knew they were looking at a dragon.

Wu Nu set off across the meadow towards him without thinking, almost in a trance and able to feel the ch'i seeping from the dragon. Reluctant, the girls followed. They trod on the odd bone as they went, many of which looked distinctly human. The girls slowed, one gave a little scream, as they stopped a few paces into the meadow beside the first skeleton, but Wu Nu didn't notice. She was entranced. The two wisdoms appeared in the entrance to the tunnel behind them and watched, making no attempt to interfere.

The dragon fixed Wu Nu with a basilisk's unblinking eye as she approached. Wu Nu slowed, and started to speak, the same words she used when stalking any of the multitudes of animals she spent hours catching.

"There's a pretty dragon. What a lovely skin you have, so colourful and beautiful and I adore your sail. Don't worry, I won't hurt you." She held her hand out towards the dragon for him to sniff, coming to a halt several yards away.

The dragon relaxed, its crest drooping down and it stretched in the sun.

"You look nice and warm, my beauty, and with a big full tummy. Would you like it rubbed? We're good at rubbing tummies."

Astonishingly, the dragon rolled on his side and lifted his legs to allow access to his tummy. Wu Nu climbed up the rock and started to rub.

"Oh, there's a horrid tick in your armpit, no, there's lots of them! Not to worry, we will get rid of them. Uggh! The big ones bite!" She turned and gestured at the girls, standing near the entrance to the meadow and close to the exit. "Come on girls, what's the matter? Come here!"

The girls didn't move. An actual dragon, despite Wu Nu's assurances to the contrary, was scary.

This didn't occur to Wu Nu, who wasn't scared of any animal in the first place and secondly could feel the ch'i now pouring out of this dragon. She *knew* it was friendly. She stamped her foot.

"What's the matter with you? It's just like a big buffalo that you work with in the fields." The dragon raised his head and looked put out at this invidious comparison. The girls shivered, and began to inch forward under her scorn. Wu Nu shepherded them over the recumbent dragon with a stream of instructions. "I want this dragon checked all over for ticks and injuries. Ting Lah, go and tell the wisdoms that we need oil and rags to polish him and some alcohol to clean the wounds of the ticks. Make sure you get it, go with the wisdoms. Poon Wah, I know it is his bottom, but it still has ticks around it! Look, more than anywhere else. Get rid of them."

While the dragon enjoyed the ministrations, he did not expect to have his cloaca cleaned and tried to move his tail back to obstruct access. Wu Nu thumped him on the head.

"Stop that! You are very dirty there and we must clean you. Ting Lah!" She shouted at the girl running across the meadow. "We need hot water and soap as well! And knives! We need small daggers for the big ticks. Wu An, she will not be able to get it all, go and help her."

She grabbed the nearest foreleg and inspected the limb critically. "Hmmn. We are going to need a rasp, or file. These talons are in poor condition. Stop that!" she barked this last at the dragon who tried to pull his foreleg back. "Wisdoms! What a bad name for them. Stupids would be much better. How could they let this dragon get into this condition?" She muttered under her breath so not even the other girls nearby heard her.

"They're scared of me," said a small voice in the back of her head.

"Was that you?" asked Wu Nu in astonishment, looking the dragon in the eye.

"Yes. It is long since a human could hear me properly."

"Why don't you speak? That would be easier, everyone could understand you then."

A long, bright orange tongue flicked out, gently gliding over her face. The girls gasped, as from the corner of the eye it seemed the dragon bathed Wu Nu's face in flame.

"My tongue is for smelling and sensing. It cannot make sounds."

"Do you understand us when we speak?"

"Oh yes. You I understand from far away; I hear your thoughts, so loud. I have been waiting for you. Others, only from their words."

"How long have you been here in this valley?"

"More years than you can comprehend, child. From here I have guided the country since it was very small."

"Where are your attendants?"

"They died and have not been replaced. Only two remain, and they don't know how to groom me. They can feed my mind; they are librarians and read me stories. It is hard to understand what is happening in the country for we get less information now."

Wu Nu looked at the dragon. "You are the Abbot, aren't you?"

"Yes. My name is Sung. This is my country. I am its protector. You are welcome in my monastery, Wu Nu"

Wu Nu smiled at the dragon, basking in his warmth and the bright sun.

"My name is not Wu Nu, it is Sung Bai Ju."

The dragon butted her with his huge head, knocking her off the rock, to land on her bottom in the grass. "Not yet, little novice, but with proper training we might make something of you."

--ooOoo--

A Bouquet for a Queen

As the new King and Queen's coach rolled down the High Street of Bresol, lined with a cheering populace, a little girl squealed with excitement as she drummed her feet on her father's chest.

"Susan! Stop that," he said, "or I shall put you down."

Susan tried to contain her excitement and waved her red rose in a frenzy. The ceremony was so exciting! The new queen here, in her hometown! Oh!!!! She couldn't wait to see the clothes she would wear and the sparkling jewels; already her fevered imagination bedecking herself in the same outfits and regalia.

Irritated at a thorny rose thumping on his ear, her father gripped her hips and eased her down in front of him, ignoring her struggles.

"Daddy!! Now I can't see anything!" Her little face glared up at him, cornflower blue eyes furious in a cute face framed by blonde ringlets. She turned and was off, lost in the forest of legs and the crowd.

"Quick, stop her," said her mother. "Oh, where has she gone now?"

"I don't damn well care," said her father, having found blood on his ear where a thorn had pierced it. "She'll be safe enough and will come home later."

Susan found herself behind the crowd, unable to see the street. She ran down an alley, skidded as she turned left into a parallel street and raced to the square at the end where King Richard and Queen Rose would dismount from their carriage. The mayor was waiting to greet them on a wooden stage erected that morning. The best view could be found here, where they should have waited, but her stupid parents left home late, at the last minute, and now couldn't get close through the crowds. They knew the importance of today to her, how special to see a real live queen up close and personal. The tailors in the shop took the day off so they had plenty of time to get there.

"Nincompoops!" cried Susan in fury, her new favourite word. Very naughty, she wasn't allowed to use it at home. There was nobody to hear her now, as she rushed into the square and found herself behind the stage, unable to see the street. For a moment, she wondered what to do, despair rising. The crowds were thick on both sides, but she noticed a hole in the cloth over the stage, right at the back, unnoticed and unwatched. The moment she saw it, she made a beeline for it. About to duck inside, the unguarded shop to the right caught her eye. The shopkeeper was standing on a table in front to see over the crowds, and behind him were arrayed his wares. Flowers.

A lovely, wicked idea formed in her mind, and Susan sneaked over to the shop, lifted a large bouquet of roses from a bucket without a sound and shot back under the stage. She rehearsed words in her mind as she made her way forward. With relief, she saw that the front of the stage, too low for an adult, was not wood but also cloth, in royal blue. Not even sewn up, but hanging in folds. With care, she eased herself to an overlapping join in the cloth and peeked out.

Immediately in front of her was the great armoured back of a soldier, fierce shiny studs sticking out of the leather, giving her shudders right down to her shoes.

Looking left and right, more soldiers lined the way, keeping the crowd from pressing too close to the Royal Carriage advancing up the street. Oh! It was nearly here, it was stopping! Susan's heart was in her mouth, but she was determined this would be her moment. She remembered last year when that mealy-mouthed, ugly girl, Lord Smallacres' daughter, had presented flowers to the old queen mother. She tried to remember the girl's words, something about from the town.

Pushing further through the cloth, she saw small shoes tipping over the edge above her, and heard impatient tapping as well. *'Another girl,'* she thought, *'some lord's daughter. I must get in first!'*

The coach came to a halt, and the footman took the steps round for the queen to dismount. Susan saw this and acted. She prodded the soldier on the right leg and shot off to the left as he turned the other way, hearing his muttered curse behind her. Another soldier moved to block her and she was conscious of the king looking at her as the queen stepped down from the carriage.

She feinted to the left and dived between the soldier's legs, years of street games with other children paying off. The soldier struggled to bend down far enough to grasp her, but he was prepared to stop adults and his despairing grab was just too high, his fingertips brushing the back of her dress. Susan raced to the carriage, seeing the queen looking down at her. She waved the roses at her as she tripped and went headlong low into the queen's pink dress, spattering mud onto it, causing a great massed intake of breath from the watching crowds.

"From the people, Your Majesty!" she squeaked, out of breath, from where she lay entangled in the folds of dress at the queen's feet and holding the bouquet of now sadly damaged roses up in her general direction. "We love you!"

A large hand grabbed her foot and a soldier jerked her up by the feet, holding her upside down, as he removed her, while his officer came up, starting to apologise with a nervous tremor in his voice.

"Stop!" The queen's word froze the men, her voice like liquid steel in red velvet. "Give me the girl."

She squatted down in the street, unmindful of the dirt on her long satin dress, and pulled the girl from the soldier, turning her upright and looking into her face. Her heart melted at the sweet little face looking up at her with adoring eyes.

"Am I in trouble?" asked Susan, clearly unable to imagine any punishment that wasn't worth it. "I just wanted to see you close up and give you some roses, to show we love you."

Giving in to impulse, the queen kissed her. "No, darling, you aren't in trouble," she said, looking deep into her eyes. "Thank you very much for the flowers, I really appreciate them. Would you like to stay with me for a little bit?"

Dumbstruck, Susan nodded and the queen picked her up, perching her on her hip as if she were a common farmer's wife, jauntily sticking her hip into Susan's weight in a very un-royal-like manner. The crowd roared with approval. She waved to them and smiled at her husband as he descended laughing from the coach, his love for his scandalous wife plain for all to see. He held out his arm to her, and she took it and they walked towards the stage, Queen Rose sashaying in dramatic style with Susan on her hip.

There is no laid down rule on the correct etiquette when the queen picks up a child, so the waiting dignitaries did what they always do in the face of the unknown. They ignored Susan. Except for the little girl, slightly older than Susan, who eyed her with curiousity, before curtseying in grave and perfect manner to the queen.

"Welcome to Bresol, Your Majesty, on behalf of the people," she said, concentrating hard on getting the words correct. She handed Queen Rose another bouquet, larger and finer than Susan's which was now in the coach. The queen accepted the bouquet, adjusted Susan and leant down to kiss the girl on the cheek. The assembled dignitaries shuffled with unease at this further flagrant breach of protocol.

*

Susan woke in the dark and panicked, wondering where she was and why it was so soft. After a moment's energetic struggle with a huge, enveloping grizzly bear, she discovered her opponent to be an eiderdown. A candle guttering on the mantelpiece cast just enough light to create scary shadows around a room, full of rich furnishings. Oh yes, she was in the duke's manor house, staying with the queen! What a wonderful day. The queen had kept her close by throughout, even sitting beside her at a sumptuous feast, where she had eaten things she didn't know existed. She liked grouse, it tasted so much nicer than chicken. She wondered if she would be able to eat it again.

She didn't remember going to bed, and guessed she had fallen asleep and to be packed away.

Now she was hungry, and didn't feel like sleeping any more. She watched the shadows with care, the now friendly eiderdown tucked up under her chin where it provided solid protection from the evils abounding in the night. After five minutes of prolonged study, she was unable to see anything hiding in the shadows, which left the possibility of a bogwart under the bed. She wasn't sure if a bogwart could get into a manor house, but didn't think it worth the risk of putting her feet on the floor.

She pushed down the eiderdown and stood up on the bed, pausing for a moment to 'Oooh' quietly at the beautiful nightgown she was wearing. Holding to the bed post, she could reach out with a foot to stand on a chair which brought the mantelpiece in reach. In moments she had the candle on the floor, then with supreme cunning dropped her head over the other side of the bed to discover nothing at all except for a large chamber pot.

This needed to be extracted and examined. Beautiful roses decorated the sides, and for a moment she wondered if this could be the queen's chamber pot? Well, it definitely had to be used, so she pulled up the skirt of her nightgown and hopped on, smiling at the musical tinkling sound she made. There were some cloths instead of rags for wiping, and she hesitated before cleaning herself, worried they were too fine for the use she required. Desperation and the fear of soiling the nightgown decided her, and she dipped a cloth in the washbowl.

With one need relieved, she was aware again that she was hungry, which surprised her because she had eaten so much. She tried to see out of the window, shuttered tight with a small crack, preventing her judging how long till morning from the pole star. Finding a pair of slippers at the foot of the bed, she delighted in pulling them on. Oh, what a wonder! Warm and snug, made from wool, she could dance across the wooden floor without making a sound. Which she proceeded to do six times just because she could.

She found two candelabras each with three candles, which she lit from the single taper and explored the room with care, delighting in a clever cupboard with clothes hanging in it, none of which fit even though she tried them all on. She thought this very special, as she thought all clothes had to be kept in a garderobe where the fumes from the night-soil would kill the moths that ate the wool.

The room soon palled, and, heart in her mouth, she eased open the door and looked onto a corridor.

It was lit with candles, which caused her to wonder at the expense and she tried to calculate how much it cost but the sums were beyond her. A lot, she thought with envy. Nobody was in sight, and she didn't recognise the corridor. Surely she wouldn't be far from the queen? She slipped into the corridor, the door opening just for a moment. She needed to find the queen, who might wake in the night and want Susan. Determined, she set off, keeping in the shadows for she suspected evil people like guards would try to stop her getting close.

Within a few minutes she was lost. It didn't help that she daydreamed of herself as a queen, in beautiful robes, with jewels and a crown. She was beginning to think it might be nice to find a soldier after all, as surely they would help her find her room again, when she heard a scratching, skulking sort of noise. An evil, illicit, dastardly noise.

Peering round a corner, she saw a stair coming up from below, and the noise was from something coming up the stairs. Gathering her courage, she eased forward to look through the railing from the other side of the stairwell. Her breath stopped and her heart thudded in her chest.

It was a witch.

A witch with long straggly grey hair, a curved, pointed nose like a crow's beak almost meeting a bony projecting chin, but the killer evidence sprouted from her face. Warts. Big ones, with hairs sprouting out of them. Susan shuddered in horror.

The witch came slowly up the stairs, holding something in one hand with her other hand protecting something in her pocket. Susan considered this, before understanding. Of course! Her familiar. She wondered if it were a toad, and looked aghast at the warts, wondering which one the witch used to feed the toad. She bet it was the huge one by her right ear, it looked bigger than a nipple.

The witch reached the top of the stairs and turned to come round towards Susan. Susan shrank back into an alcove, slipping behind a curtain with no more noise than a mouse. Fascinated, she watched the witch go past, and realised she was muttering under her breath. An incantation! She was saying a spell, probably to keep the guards from seeing her.

Susan wondered what the witch was doing in the manor, and realised with a start the witch would be after the queen. Witches always went after queens and princesses, gave them poisoned apples and such. Duty warred with fear for a moment, and but Susan knew her mission, girded her loins for battle and set out to follow the witch, her mind racing over different options.

She decided the best thing to do would be to find a guard. He would sort out the nasty witch! Chop her head off and squish the familiar toad.

She kept well back from the witch, letting her go round a corner then hurried up to peek round the bend and see where the witch was heading. A guard! But the witch was doing something. She was standing in front of the guard, muttering, and then she gave the guard something.

Mechanically, the guard took it and ate it. He did nothing about the witch, just stood there, wooden, as if she didn't exist.

"Be-spelled," breathed Susan, so fascinated she forgot to be afraid. She had heard about it in stories, but never seen it happen. The guard seemed oblivious to the witch, who shuffled past him through a door which Susan recognised now as leading to the queen's chambers.

Her heart raced, the queen would be in danger. About to run down the corridor, she stopped herself, realising the bespelled guard would catch her and stop her from warning the queen. She slipped behind the nearest curtain and found that it covered a long window. She was able to climb up onto the window ledge and walk along it, dodging vases and ornaments as she did so and hoping there were no bogwarts outside to see her through the glass.

At the end of the window, she peeped out and found she was only half way to the guard, but there was another window. She scuttled across to that one and emerged just yards from the guard. Easing along on her woollen, slippered feet, she inched past his back into the corridor he guarded.

The witch was opening the door to the Queen's Bedchamber, peering in! Any moment she would cast a spell, maybe turn the queen into frog or a bird!

Without thinking, but uttering a piercing war cry, Susan hurled herself along the passageway and into the back of the witch's legs. The witch fell forward, cracking her head on the floor with a nasty thump and Susan scrambled up onto her back, pinning her down and crying out, "Run, your majesty! It's a witch! Quickly, while I have her down, run!"

King Richard erupted from the bed, stark naked, grabbing for his sword, scabbarded by the bed. With smooth precision, he unsheathed the sword and stood in the defence posture of a trained soldier, while he searched the room for enemies with his eyes. Queen Rose sat up in the huge four-poster bed, her mouth a perfect 'O', her eyes wide and with the sheets clutched to her neck to protect her modesty. The guard came crashing down the corridor and burst into the room.

The witch started to struggle, still not in control of herself and started to buck Susan off.

Susan saw the sword in the king's hand and shouted, "Sire! Take her head off! Quick, before she can say a spell!" She pulled back a little, wary of getting blood all over herself. Who knew what a witch's blood would do to you? It would probably burn.

She saw the king relax out of the corner of her eye, fixed on the witch. She was aware that the guard had stopped behind her, and she wondered if he was still bespelled, or if the noise had broken the spell. She flinched, half expecting his sword to jab her in the back. The king was making a strange noise. She flicked a look at him, then looked again.

The king was laughing.

He was sitting on the bed, sword across his knees, laughing like mad while looking at the witch and Susan. Queen Rose was scowling at him in irritation.

The witch was starting to shout, making incomprehensible sounds and spitting blood from her mouth where her lips had smashed against the floor. She pushed Susan off and started to pull herself up by the corner of the bed. Susan prepared to leap on her again, when the queen shouted at her.

"Susan! Stop that at once! She is not a witch!"

Susan stopped her leap, just in time and stared at the queen. Not a witch? "But," she started to say, and the queen over-rode her.

"Get out, I'll sort this," she said first to the guardsman, who left at speed; nothing in the rule book or in his experience helping him know what to do.

"Richard," she said to the king, "stop that and go and help my aunt. Get her to a healer. Susan, come here."

The king sheathed his sword, pulled on a robe and moved towards the old lady, who was now standing, looking at her bloodstained hand with horror, and feeling over her ruined face. Her nose looked as if it might be broken, and was pulsing blood. As the king reached her, she looked up and saw Susan taking disconsolate steps towards the queen, head down. A look of hatred flashed across her face.

"You little bastard," she screamed in fury. "Look what you haf dun to ma dose!" Her speech was obscured by the injury to her impressive proboscis. "Flogged," she continued, "I want her flogged to an inch of her life! I want to see the white of the bones coming out of her back! She'll regret doing this to me, the little bitch! Flogged! I will wind the whip meself!"

She advanced on Susan, blood dripping down her chin, her long grey hair loose and tangled around her head. Susan screamed, all her earlier bravado gone, and ran to the queen, throwing herself onto her and hiding her head in the queen's armpit. The queen put an arm round her, with the other hand rescuing the sheets dislodged by Susan's need for reassurance.

"That's enough, Aunt Mary. I am sorry for your injury, but the girl thought she was doing the right thing. Please go with Richard and get your nose sorted, you don't want it getting infected."

"Damn my bloody nose," screamed Aunt Mary in fury but with extreme accuracy. "I want that brat flogged, flogged this instant! I want her locked up! She's a damn menace, attacked me she did, I tell you…. Richard, let go of me! I won't go, damn it!" But she allowed herself to be dragged away, protesting recriminations on the cowering Susan as she went.

The queen turned to Susan and sighed. Susan lifted a tear-streaked face and said, in a woebegone voice, "I am so sorry, Your Highness. I followed her through the manor and saw her bespell the guard. I thought she was attacking you. I didn't know she was your aunt. Will you become a witch one day as well?"

The queen sighed again and hugged her.

"No, darling, I won't. Mary isn't a witch. I know she looks like one, I've often thought that myself, but I promise you she isn't. She's just an old lady. And tomorrow you will need to apologise to her. She will be over her anger by then, and will find it all very funny. She's a lovely person, really."

Susan thought that highly unlikely but was sensible enough not to say anything. At that moment the king returned, came over and ruffled her hair.

"Ah, girl, that was glorious," he said. "Funniest thing I've seen in ages. Made the whole trip worthwhile. I've half a mind to let Rose adopt you after all, if only to see Mary's face every time you appeared at dinner. You were wonderful," and he chucked her under the chin, "but don't go round attacking all the ladies–in-waiting. Some of them look even more like witches."

"Richard, you are not helping," the queen glared at him. "Now

Susan, dry your eyes, everything is all right. Get me my robe, there it is on that chair, and I will take you back to your room."

*

Susan waved as fast and as hard as she could, tears streaming down her cheeks, as the royal coach went down the road. The queen's white handkerchief was no longer visible.

"Mummy, can I go and stay with the queen in the summer when she is back from her trip? Please, please, please! She said I could be a lady in waiting."

Her mother smiled at her, while flashing a worried glance at her husband. "We will have to see, darling. It is not easy travelling at the best of times, and Praesidium is a week away."

"The queen will arrange it, Mummy, I know she will! She loves me and I love her so much. She wanted to keep me, but the king said she couldn't steal me from you." Susan was still staring after the coach, oblivious of how her words hurt her mother.

"I would have happily sold you," said her father, rubbing at his ear with a wince. where the rose thorn scratch had become infected, so the ear throbbed big and red. "If he'd asked the price, it would have been cheap."

His wife smacked him on the shoulders half-heartedly. He ignored her glare demanding support. "We will see in the summer, darling, when she sends a message. We can't presume so we must wait."

She forestalled Susan's retort by wrapping her in a big hug.

"When I grow up," declared Susan, extricating herself from her mother's embrace. "I'm going to be a queen!"

Thief in the Night

The knife gleamed from under the chair and Andy grunted in satisfaction. He'd been looking for it for the last hour and had been retracing his steps, trying to find where the strap on his belt had broken. As he leant down under the armoury table to pick it up, his senses screamed at him and he banged his head on the heavy oak table.

Repressing a few choice swear words, he sat down in the chair, muscles tensed for instant action, and with meticulous care inventoried the room using sound and scent. The dark hair on the back of his neck was rigid, chafing the uniform collar and he knew he wasn't alone.

Nothing.

His senses were never wrong, and had kept him alive many a time in the past. He adjusted the wick on the oil lamp he carried, took off his belt and placed it on the table, removing the various weapons and laying them close at hand. Picking up the belt, he examined the frayed strap, holding it closer to the lamp and twisting it this way and that, using the movement to scan the armoury, working out where the enemy could be hidden.

He grinned to himself, realising he was enjoying the threat of combat. He had spent the last two months helping out in the armoury, recovering from a spear thrust through the thigh, taken during a night melee up on the border, from a hairy Uightlander. The man's halitosis had been appalling as he screamed his guts up with Andy's sword in his belly.

Behind the spear rack, he decided, the only place with enough room to hide a man.

Andy balanced the knife on his hand, inspecting the narrow space below the rack for feet while wondering if he could still throw the knife. He used to be damn good, hitting a target the size of a hand at twenty paces nine times out of ten. But then he'd been a basic squaddie with time for the daily hour's practise you needed. Somehow he doubted he could do it now. A lancepesade didn't have the time. He pulled out the short sword, stood up and walked to the rag bin where he pulled out an oily rag and started wiping the sword down while pacing down the passage. He wasn't a tall man, but tough and wiry, fit with a moustached face that the girls rather liked.

Tensed and keyed up, he swung the sword to the ready position as he rounded the end of the rack. Empty. Damn. And he'd alerted the bastards now.

"All right, shithead, so you know I know you're here." He spoke with slow and venomous precision into the darkness. "Why don't you come out and grovel to me, because if I have to come and find you, I'll chop you into little pieces small enough for a fucking dog to eat." He smiled, pleased with himself. The Uightlanders didn't like dogs.

Something slithered at the back of the room, a whisper of sound so light he almost missed it and his backside clenched into spasm. A wave of horror washed over him and he backed towards the lamp, swallowing. Nothing human could make so little sound. Not up here. Thoughts of ghosts drifted through his mind and tried to lodge there. He shook his head, reminding himself he'd been there for two months and nobody had seen a damn ghost.

'The little people,' his subconscious whispered to him. *'You've not left them a gift. Your mother taught you to leave them some cream. All these years you've ignored them, now they are coming for you.'*

"I don't believe in faeries and demons," he whispered to himself and gripped the sword tighter. "I'm Lancepesade Andrew Russell; I've stood in three shield walls and killed eight men that I know about. I'm posted to the Royal Pathfinders, the elite frontiersmen. I'm a good soldier. No thief in the night can scare me. It's hiding at the back of the room because it's scared of me. Of Andy Russell. It knows how dangerous I am."

He smiled to himself, feeling much better, grabbed the lamp in his left hand and stalked the back of the room.

A tiny scuff came to his ears, from above, and his eyes widened as he realised the intruder had climbed the old racking at the back. Slight movement caught his eye and he saw a dark shape jump from one rack to another, up near the ceiling, astonishingly quiet. It was half the size of a man and he had to quell his fear sharply.

Time for cunning. He walked towards it. It froze. He shined the lamp into each nook at ground level that he passed, never looking up. He went under the shape and his skin crawled, expecting it to land on his back while his unconscious chittered about sharp teeth and claws.

As he came directly beneath it, he reached up, found an ankle, grasped it and pulled. With a squawk and a desperate ineffectual scrabbling, the shape came off the rack and into his waiting arms.

He dropped the lamp with care and tried to restrain the bundle without stabbing it with his sword, but a heel smacked into his guts and the bundle sprawled onto the floor, revealing itself in the lamplight as a small boy. Which leapt to his feet and took off. Andy dropped the sword and took off after him, spitting with anger that a child could so scare him.

The boy was agile, slipping round racks as Andy closed in, once ducking under his arm. At ;last he made an expected dash for the door and Andy dived full length to grab his legs, knocking the boy to the ground.

Where he turned into a whirling mass of legs, claws and teeth, scratching, kicking, biting.

Andy pulled back his fist and smacked the kid hard, and had the satisfaction of seeing his head bounce off the floor. The kid went quiet. He stood up, grabbed the shoulder and pulled him into the lamplight to inspect, while rubbing his injured thigh where of course the little bastard had kicked him.

In the lamplight, the boy was revealed to be about ten, a shock of ragged red hair and a big pointy nose making him look like a mouse, no, a rat. Not starved, unlike many of them, and he wondered how the bloody Uightlander had got into the fort. Especially now with the heightened security for the King's visit.

"Speak Harrhein, do you boy?" he asked, shaking the kid as he saw the eyes flutter. The boy looked up at him, with beady, malevolent eyes, radiating hatred.

"Stealing what you can find, hey?" Andy continued, feeling the quality of his thick shirt and rubbing it with his hands. "You were lucky to find something this good, this small up here. Now, what were you after from the armoury? Huh?"

The kid glared at him, his left eye beginning to disappear in the swelling Andy's fist had caused.

"Bastard fucking savages," muttered Andy, his thigh hurting. Keeping the kid restrained with his left hand, he reached over for a coil of light rope. Flipping the boy over, he swiftly and expertly tied his hands together and put a noose round his neck. He hauled the boy to his feet and jerked the noose.

"Ah, you might not speak the King's language, but by God you know the feel of a noose, hey boy? We'll have you dangling from the ramparts by noon, I reckon. Ugly little shit that you are, you won't scare anyone but maybe it will stop more kids coming in."

Now the boy responded. "Pig fucker!" he hissed. "Your mother shagged goats to make you, that's why you smell so bad, you're so ugly and can't grow a proper beard! Ducks! You fuck ducks because your rotten prick is so small."

Andy rocked back on his heels and grinned. "So you do speak Harrhein. Straight out of the gutter. That explains how you got into the fort, anyway. Live here, I reckon, make your living by thieving."

The stream of invective didn't stop, and Andy grew tired of the inventive list of animals with which he enjoyed sexual congress in more and more peculiar ways. Sighing, he shoved a rag in the boy's mouth and tied it down, finding the sudden silence rather enjoyable. He tied the noose to the table and proceeded to clear up the mess they had made in the armoury, at the same time double checking that there were no more boys hiding around. He had to admit that he found the boy's courage admirable - most boys came in gangs, it was unusual to find one alone. He told the boy as much.

"If you weren't a fucking Uightlander, we'd let you join the regiment as a drummer. Got guts you have. One day you might even make a soldier."

The beady eyes glared at him and the boy made horrid noises from behind the gag.

Andy finished clearing up, and dragged the boy out of the armoury. As he locked it, he noted that the mortise moved more cleanly than usual and a close inspection proved it had been recently oiled. He looked at the boy with more respect and searched him with attention. Inside the hidden pouch was not only a small leather oil bottle, but a selection of keys.

"Wonder who you stole these from," he muttered. "Somebody will be on a charge."

*

At the guardhouse he passed the boy over to the Duty Corporal who locked him in a cell without removing the gag. The corporal refused to wake the Duty Officer and Andy was told to come back before the watch changed to have his report taken down by a scribe.

*

Next morning Andy had finished with the scribe and was joking with the outgoing watch, when the Duty Officer came rushing in, white and looking harassed. Several guards started bobbing up and down behind his back - junior officers were renowned for panicking, and a legendary Regimental Sergeant Major was reputed to have said they bobbed and weaved like a virgin with her first prick, a saying that had quickly passed through the army.

"S-s-s-sergeant," stuttered the excited officer. "Get the men on parade, quickly now! We have an emergency."

"Of course, sir," said the sergeant calmly, face straight and grave despite all the soldiers behind the officer now bobbing up and down and grinning. "What seems to be the trouble?"

"The Princess has disappeared," wailed the officer, "on our watch too! She has probably been kidnapped by Uightlanders and we'll have a ransom to face!"

The soldiers stopped bobbing and looked concerned. This sounded like a genuine problem for which they might even be held responsible.

"Princess, sir?" asked the sergeant with the calm and placid demeanour reserved for panicking officers. "I'm sure we can track her down in no time. What does she look like? Perhaps she went dancing in the Officers Mess?"

Andy suppressed a grin. The Officers Mess was tiny.

"Dancing? Don't be ridiculous. Turn out the guard and the next Watch as well. We're going to have to search the fort. The Princess is far too young to dance. She was sent to bed straight after supper last night and hasn't been seen since."

Something in Andy's guts turned over and the world spun. His face ashen, he listened as the sergeant lined up the guard for the officer to address.

"The Princess Asmara is missing and we have to find her. Men, I am relying on you. She is not just the Princess of the Realm, but the Crown Princess and only Heir. It is of Paramount Importance that she is found safe and well immediately. If we've lost her, well, I'll be cashiered and I'll make damn sure you all spend years breaking rocks in a punishment battalion! You will search the whole fort! You will search the dungeons! You will search the bed-chambers! You will go through the town, you…"

"Sir," interrupted the sergeant, "do we have a description of the girl? I am sure one of the Watch will have seen her last night."

"Description? What do you mean? She's the Princess, isn't that enough? Haven't you seen her?"

"Nossir, we've been on the frontier a while, sir, and we don't get to see many princesses up here." Like most things, the sergeant's irony went over the Duty Officer's head.

"Oh, well, she's eleven years old, very beautiful, red headed and… what's the matter?"

Every head had turned to look at Andy, who had dropped his cup of tea.

"Let me just go to the cells a moment, sir," said the sergeant with as much tact as he could muster and went towards them, with the Duty Officer following behind him.

"Cells? Cells? Why would we look in the cells, it's not exactly where she would choose to - OH MY GOD!!!! Your Highness, I am so sorry, I had no idea you were here, I'll get you out immediately, um, sergeant, it's locked!"

"Yessir, it's a cell, sir."

"Well get the fucking key! Oh, I am so sorry, Your Highness, I didn't mean to swear in front of you, we'll have you out in a moment, oh, your poor face, what has happened, I will be with you in minute, I am Second Lieutenant Peter Purcell, your rescuer from this terrible ordeal, get a move on soldier, open the door! Oh, Lord, somebody has tied her up! She's gagged! She has a noose round her neck! Her eye! Oh, the king will have us on the frontier tomorrow, quick, sergeant, get those bonds untied, CAREFUL WITH THAT KNIFE! There, Your Highness, I have you now, I shall take you straight to your father, no we must fix your face, where is the medic? SERGEANT! GET THE MEDIC! CAN'T YOU SEE THE

PRINCESS IS INJURED YOU FOOL!"

"The medic has been sent for, sir, as has her maidservant who will come with clean clothes. Ma'am, if you would like to step into the Duty Officers' Quarters, we'll have somebody attend to you shortly."

"Thank you, sergeant, and if I could have some water followed perhaps by some hot tea and bread, that would be wonderful." The voice was sweet, melodic and childlike. Over his devastation, Andy tried and failed to compare it with the filthy ranting he'd received during the night. He slumped against the wall.

As the door to the Duty Officers' Quarters closed, Purcell turned and hissed, "Who is responsible for this outrage? I want him locked up instantly!"

*

Andy was marched into the Great Hall by the Regimental Sergeant Major, at 120 paces to the minute, twice normal speed. He was brought to a halt in front of the head table and stood at attention, fixing his gaze on a point about two feet above the king's greying head. King Richard, a powerful man with his daughter's red hair and a prominent nose jutting forward aggressively, gazed at the soldier with interest.

The princess, dressed in a demure green frock, sat on his left with a piratical cast to her looks, brought on by the immense black eye and huge swelling on her eyebrow. She grinned in delight at the sight of Andy and pouted when he didn't respond.

Andy stood in misery. Purcell had spent a good half of an hour telling him that the automatic penalty for striking a member of the royal family was death and speculating on how sentence would be carried out. In consequence, he had resigned himself to his fate and spent the day contemplating his life. Mentally, he had apologised to his parents for the disgrace he had brought on the family. He regretted that he hadn't managed to bed Mariestty that summer, and hoped that Molly wasn't pregnant if he was going to the gallows.

There was silence in the great hall as the king examined Andy. The king had over ruled the general, who had wanted a public trial in front of the soldiers and threatened to resign his commission if the king went over his head to punish the boy. The general sat fuming to the king's right, while to one side of the hall was a long table at which sat several officers from the fort garrison, including Purcell. Opposite them was another table at which sat soldiers in total contrast to the garrison officers, like a row of dowdy sparrows opposite parakeets.

They made Purcell uncomfortable. They were men from the Royal Pathfinders, who had appeared just before the hearing, come in and taken the table in silence. Purcell looked at them and sniffed, they hadn't bothered to change and their clothes bore the evidence of hard riding. He was sure he could smell them from across the hall and sniffed again.

A scarred brute met his eye, and Purcell felt a desperate need for the toilet. The fellow didn't even wear insignia so he had no idea what rank the man was. None of them wore insignia, damned confusing, and Purcell couldn't understand why they were permitted in the room.

Mentally, he rehearsed his story again, ignoring the Pathfinders, checking that his rendition showed himself in excellent light and would crucify this sorry excuse for a soldier. He thought he could draw it out for a good half an hour, and already imagined the congratulations he would receive in the Mess that evening. Why, if he played it well he should get that promotion, not before time!

The king broke the silence. "So, boy, how long have you been a Pathfinder?"

"Two years, sir," snapped Andy, although confused by the question.

A bejewelled flunky that Andy hadn't noticed stepped forward. "The prisoner will call the king 'Your Highness' and only speak when spoken to."

The king waved his hand in irritation. "He's one of my soldiers. It is an honour to be called sir by a Pathfinder. We're on the frontier and don't need your bloody Gallic tomfoolery." He glared at the courtier who retreated indignantly.

"I spoke to Bobby earlier." He nodded at one of the dowdy soldiers. "Told me your record. Said you did well at Meadowsweet last year."

"Sir, thank you sir," said Andy a bit more slowly, as it came to him that 'Bobby' was General Lord Roberts, Commander of the Royal

Pathfinders, and he flicked his eyes to see his Commanding Officer and staff sitting in a row without expression. Even his sergeant was there, staring at him. He shrank at the thought of the trouble he had caused his boss. Somebody must have ridden to tell him straight after his arrest and he wondered who, even as he thought that it was three hours ride to the camp.

"I read your report from the guard record," continued the king. "Fine report, what I would expect from a Pathfinder. Clear and to the point."

Purcell's dreams crashed around him. It hadn't occurred to him that a stupid soldier would think to make a report, and he hadn't checked the record. Quickly he tried to prepare an edit for his story.

"You are very wrong on one point, though, boy," said the king with great relish. "I was married to her mother, you see." The king sat back in his chair and stroked his beard to hide his grin at Andy's confusion.

"I, I don't understand, sir," stammered Andy.

"She's not a bastard. You called my daughter, the Crown Princess of the Realm, a foul-mouthed, ugly little bastard. In writing."

"Sir," said Andy in a faint voice, as a gasp ran round the hall and a brief mutter from the garrison officers. The princess sat up straighter and beamed, her pride at this apt description self-evident.

"From your report, this was shortly after you clouted her to cause these injuries." The king waved his hand at his daughter who angled her face to make sure that everybody could see the damage. "Very precise blow," mused the king. "Not hard enough to cause permanent damage, just enough to stop her struggling. Deliberate or accidental?" He barked this last straight at Andy, who was too confused to reply.

"I think it was deliberate," said the king as Andy failed to speak, "based on what I hear about your skill with weapons. So, boy, what should I do with you? Striking a royal personage hard enough to mark them like this? You know what the penalty is?"

"Sir," replied Andy, "Permit me to lead the next Forlorn Hope."

A Forlorn Hope is a suicide mission, the first into an attack on a defended position, to open a crack that other troops can pour through. Very few soldiers survived, but there were always volunteers for them. Survival and success meant promotion to Lieutenant.

"A soldier's answer, but I think not," said the king, smiling. "I have negotiated with your commanding officer for your detachment, Corporal Russell."

It took a moment for Andy to realise that the king was talking to him and had got his rank wrong.

"You will spend the next six months as Master of Arms to the princess, Corporal Russell, responsible for her training and expertise in all weapons. The appointment is pre-dated to yesterday." A rustle of conversation went round the hall.

"Perhaps you should be aware that the Princess' Master at Arms is of course exempt from punishment should he hit her."

Rex Sumner

The Harvest Ball

"Roger," squealed the beautiful young woman walking down the street with her rather dowdier friend. She rushed across the street and threw her arms around a man walking the other way, dressed in the dark blue uniform of the Galicia Guards.

He looked in perplexity at this ravishing girl busy hugging him. Light dawned as puzzled recognition came into his even featured face.

"Susan?" he said with disbelief. "Little Susan Taylor? My word, you have grown into a lovely lady."

"Oh, Roger, how wonderful to see you!" She released him and turned to her friend as she came across the street, eyes alight with curiosity. "Abby, it's Roger who used to take me to Praesidium to visit the queen." She turned back to Roger, holding his hand tightly, and took in the blue uniform with its yellow piping down the trousers, the crowns on each shoulder and the empty right sleeve. "Only a sergeant major, Roger? You promised me you would be a colonel by now. And in the Guards, I am surprised." She touched his sleeve gently and said in a low voice, touched with gentleness and compassion. "What happened?"

His eyes went flat and bleak. "Spakka are incredibly fast. I thought my training good enough to stand against them with a sword, but their axes go straight for your arms. Broke my sword and took my arm." He stopped for a moment, remembering the sweet little girl riding pillion on his horse, brave, always cheerful and pretending her legs were not rubbed raw from gripping the horse's flanks. "I am lucky. Most don't survive, and King Richard granted me this administrative post with the Guards as a pension. Arrived last week."

"Administration? So you are in charge of your own time. Excellent, you are now going to take Abigail and myself to tea at the Queen's Tea House and tell us all about the frontier." Susan turned Roger around, slipped her arm through his left, trapping him, and marched him off, laughing, while Abigail tripped along beside her.

The tea house was a brand new establishment in Bresol, copied from one in Praesidium, and the fashionable place to stop and pass the time of day. Susan took control, ordering for Roger, which was useful as he had no idea about any of the drinks or sweetmeats. She was all vivaciousness at first, bubbling happily with Abigail until they were no longer the centre of attention for the other habitués.

"Were you there, Roger, when the queen had her accident?" Susan's voice dropped very low and cracked, unshed tears misting her eyes.

Roger dropped his eyes to his plate. "No," he said, his voice turning dead and dour. "I was on leave. You know how she was on a horse, the risks she would take. It was just bad luck. All of us in the Royal Guard were very upset and I think we all volunteered for the frontier. We all felt guilty, damn, the king did too."

"I never got to see her baby," Susan's eyes did drip now. "Oh, Roger, I miss her so much."

"Please, Susan, I still don't talk about it." Roger pulled himself together and with clumsy and obvious tact, changed the subject from the queen's unfortunate death in a riding accident. "So tell me about Bresol. I shall rely upon you for the gossip, and to know to whom I must be polite and who I must avoid."

Susan took the offered chance, and Roger found himself surprised by the range and depth of her knowledge. He said as much.

"Ah, Roger," she smiled, "I may have been very young, but the queen taught me so much. Not only how to talk and act like a lady, but how to listen and find out what was happening. We ladies have our own sources and often know the soldier's orders before you do!"

Roger looked at her again, and was struck by how beautiful the little girl had become. He wondered at her status, thoughts of his own future and family surfacing for the first time in many years.

"I am sure you do. Now, tell me, am I in serious trouble for taking up the time of you beautiful ladies? Will some arrogant young lord come and challenge me to a duel for the temerity of taking tea with his betrothed?"

Abigail giggled, and launched into a long description of the young cloth trader's son who was her current beau, and whom she was expecting to speak to her parents at any moment. As she tailed off with a contented smile, Susan was looking at Roger, her smile a sad one.

"My father has pushed several boys at me, but I have refused them all. He thinks that at sixteen I should be married, and I fear that next year he will insist."

"Huh!" Abigail snorted, her coarser accent in marked contrast to Susan. "You have ideas above your station, my girl. You should encourage that Wayne, he will have a good business in leather, you mark my words. Her trouble," she leaned forward and tapped Roger on the knee, "is she wants to be queen!" She brayed with laughter, causing other diners to look at her. "Queen Susan! That's what we call her."

"You want to marry King Richard?" asked Roger in surprise.

"Don't be silly," said Susan in resignation at the old joke. "It is just what they say when I speak in the proper manner."

Roger had a sudden insight into the way Susan's life had been irrevocably changed by the queen's attention. The creation of hopes and dreams that were impossible to realise in their structured society. He remembered the little girl wanting to be a queen like her heroine and felt sad for her.

"In that case, you will make an old man very proud if you will be my partner to the Harvest Ball, which I understand is in a few weeks. I may be short a wing," he said, self-conscious, suddenly appalled at his forwardness and finding himself shy and inarticulate, "but I can still dance a bit." He couldn't look at her, couldn't take the refusal he knew was coming and turned to call for his bill and go before she could speak.

"Oh, Roger," she said, care and understanding in her voice, "you're not old. You are barely thirty, and I am sure you still dance beautifully. I remember seeing you dance all those years ago. You were very good. I would be honoured to go with you to the Ball."

Abigail stared, speechless. She did not dream of going to the Ball, the most she could hope for was selection as a serving girl.

It was Susan's turn for insight, seeing that the Spakka axe took not just an arm, but career, confidence and future. She wondered if they did not make a fine pair, as she was well aware that she no longer fitted into society.

*

Susan's father not only gave permission for her to attend the Ball, but saw opportunity. His contacts in Praesidium sent him the latest fashion designs, and his seamstresses produced a stunning dress in the light blue cotton for which he was famous. Susan was delighted, and spent hours doing up her hair in the manner of Queen Rose. No longer in fashion, but she did not care, and built up a great edifice complete with glass beads woven through, catching the light as if they were jewels.

Her complexion needed no adornment while she mixed cochineal with beeswax to redden her lips. Helping herself to dyes from her father's workshop, she created the dark azure coloured wax she wanted to line her eyes, pleased with the way this highlighted the cornflower blue. It also made them huge, and she didn't think anyone else would be doing that in high society.

She found she was quite wrong, as she came through the great doors into the grand reception room in the mansion of Lord Sol, the Duke of Galicia. All of high society used make up - even some of the men. The older women in particular, vainly trying to stave off the depredations of age. Susan's make up was perfect: nicely understated and elegant, in comparison to Lady Sol who 'oohed' dramatically over Susan, remembering when she went to visit the queen.

Susan accompanied a proud Roger to join other officers. She was aware they were joining fighting soldiers, and he was not the only one minus a body part. They were smart enough, to be sure, but nothing compared to some of the officers resplendent in gaudy atrocities who made certain they were a good distance away from the despised fighters.

A slim, spare lieutenant colonel with greying hair fixed her with an unblinking eye which she realised with embarrassment was glass, and switched her attention to the real eye as he spoke after being introduced.

"Welcome, Susan. But would you not prefer to be with the fashionable set?" He indicated the gaudy officers, whom she now noticed were not only considerably younger but also surrounded with young ladies in the latest fashions, though none as modern as her own.

"Thank you, colonel, I prefer reality to illusion," Susan answered without thinking, turning her attention back to veterans. Several smiled and a couple even snorted with laughter.

"Ha. I like your lady, Browne," the colonel nodded to Roger. "You must bring her to more events." He appropriated her from Roger, tucked her hand into the crook of his arm and led her towards a bar. "Let us see if we can find something suitable for a young lady. I believe there are some apple juices, but if I am not mistaken there is some rose water which you may prefer." The twinkle in his eye told Susan he knew exactly who she was and she warmed to him.

Unlike many of her contemporaries, Susan's experiences visiting the Royal Court made her aware of the different soldiers. The only regular soldiers employed were the Royal Guard and the Royal Pathfinders. Barons raised their own little armies, creating their own impractical uniforms, often designed by the baron's wife, which they captained along with a couple of lieutenants and an ensign to carry the flag. The counts ruled counties and oversaw several barons. They took the title of colonel. They borrowed veterans from the royal regiments, and these officers, usually despised until called to war, were the trainers and administrators, with the ranks of sergeant major and lieutenant colonel. These were usually the only full time soldiers in the regiments, which otherwise only came into being when called upon by the kng.

The women of the few regular soldiers were fierce and proud, disdaining make up and wearing sensible clothing. Yet they warmed to the lovely Susan and welcomed her into their midst, telling her tales of managing on the frontier while their men fought. In a very short space of time, Susan found herself with an understanding of what it was like to be a soldier's wife, and she rather liked it, certainly more than being a tradesman's wife, as her father planned.

An elegant young woman appeared at her elbow, and with a smile to the soldier's wives, begged Susan away to speak with Lady Sol. The girl was friendly, and told Susan she was Alice, the youngest daughter of Lady Sol.

"I didn't like you when I first saw you," she smiled. "I was waiting on the stage to give the queen flowers when you ran out from underneath me."

"Oh, I remember," said Susan. "I saw your shoes and was determined to get there first."

As they made their way towards the ornate window where Lady Sol presided, a young man pushed in front of them, his eyes taking in Susan with rather an insolent manner. Susan felt her hackles rise. He was handsome enough, with slicked back dark hair and brilliant blue eyes, immaculately turned out in a scarlet and blue uniform. He carried a light sabre with a jewelled hilt, indicating he was a full colonel, which was quite ridiculous considering his youth.

"I don't believe we have been introduced," he began with a slight lisp marring an otherwise perfect accent. "I am Prince Fabian of Galicia, it is a great pleasure to see such divine beauty at our poor reception." Susan realised that this was the son of the Earl of Galicia, descendants of the kings who had ruled Galicia before it was absorbed into the Harrhein kingdom.

Susan instinctively started to curtsy, and then stopped herself, feeling something was wrong. Alice glared at Fabian.

"Fabian, she is only a girl and doesn't need your sort of trouble. Go away and stay away from her, do you hear me?"

Fabian smiled, and touched Susan's arm, where it was bare at the wrist. His touch tingled. "I merely thought the lovely Queen Susan would like to meet a real prince." He turned away, a scarlet cape swirling from his shoulder as a flush spread across Susan's face.

"Oh dear, why does what we say when we are little children come back to embarrass us?"

"Susan," said Alice, urgency in her tone, "Fabian is my cousin and he's a bad one. Don't trust him at all."

"I didn't know there was a prince in the country, let alone Galicia." Susan found herself whispering.

"He claims that as we're descended from the royal house of Galicia, from before we became part of Harrhein, he's entitled to be called a prince. It's not recognised by anybody except his friends. He is just saying that to impress you, he's really a viscount."

"Ah, Susan dear, there you are." They had arrived in front of Lady Sol. "Come and sit beside me, I want to introduce you to all the right people. Alice! I want you to be friends with Susan and take her to your parties." Both Alice and Susan tried to speak but it was like trying to dam a river. Lady Sol kept right on talking, introducing Susan to her friends, telling her about each of them, including some rather personal details, and enlarging on her plans for Susan's future. Nobody seemed to mind, all smiled at Susan who was in some shock. Lady Sol was just telling one of her cronies that she had searched for Susan many times, and she would continue the excellent education started by the late Queen Rose, when a trumpet sounded from by the doors.

"Ah! Supper time! Excellent, I was beginning to feel rather peckish. Susan, I want you sitting beside me."

"She can't, mother," interjected Alice. "It's a formal ball, the settings are laid out and can't be changed. She needs to go in with her partner."

"Don't be ridiculous! I am sure I can arrange it, where is the butler? Oh, hello Jack old man, are you taking me away?" Lord Sol arrived with a smile, chucked Susan under the chin and whisked his wife away, still protesting that she needed the butler.

Susan promised Alice that she would see her later and headed back to Roger. As she neared him, she felt a hand grasp her elbow and restrain her forcefully. Turning, she found herself looking into the blue eyes of Viscount Fabian, uncomfortably close.

"Wouldn't you like to dine beside me, my dear?" he smiled at her.

"No thank you, I have a partner." She didn't smile and felt panicky, so Roger's arrival was welcome.

"Leave us, soldier, you are not welcome," said Viscount Fabian.

Susan grabbed Roger's hand and spoke before he could. "Sergeant Major Browne is my partner, thank you." She tried to turn away and move towards the doors through which couples were streaming, but the viscount's hand restrained her.

"He was your partner," said the viscount. "We shall trade, shall we not, Sergeant Major?"

To Susan's horror, Roger looked worried and uncertain; he hesitated. Susan didn't.

"We certainly shall not." She shook her arm free of the viscount's grasp. She glared at him, for some reason finding Roger's uncertainty imbibing her with anger and a steely resolve. "I would have expected a prince to understand about honour."

Head high, she dragged Roger away. "What is the matter with you?" she hissed once they were out of earshot. "Why didn't you stand up for me?"

"He's ... difficult," said Roger.

"Difficult, hah!" said the Colonel's wife who appeared behind them. "He's a damn menace who does his best to stop us doing our jobs while ruining the men. Pretends he's in charge of the whole bloody army. All the same, Roger, we had best hide Susan. I don't trust that man." As they approached the table, while Roger and the colonel checked the seating arrangements, she whispered in Susan's ear. It appeared that the prince didn't like career soldiers and was quite capable of ending Roger's job here in Galicia. The colonel's wife thought this would be a good thing and Roger could go to a fighting regiment, but it would be a black mark on his record.

Roger and the colonel returned after a bit longer than expected. It seemed the prince had bribed a servant to change the seating arrangements, and it had taken some time to discover the correct order. To Susan's relief, they were sufficiently far from the head table that they could neither see nor hear the viscount.

The meal was a pleasure. Susan was careful not to eat too much from the many dishes, but even so, she felt stuffed. She noticed early on Roger avoided any dishes requiring cutting, sticking to food he could get into his mouth with a fork or spoon. When some boar came past, he looked at it with wistful longing and was surprised when Susan took a large slice. She cut it into small pieces and slipped them onto his plate with a conspiratorial wink.

Wine was served, the first time Susan had drunk it. She didn't like it much, but the colonel's wife persuaded the serving girl to find her a light Varn Valley white, which she found delicious. The noise levels rose as the meal progressed, and at the end, while Susan was wondering if she could cram in another spiced grape, Alice collected her, saying it was time for the ladies to retire to prepare for the dancing.

In the next room, Lady Sol called her over to where she was enthroned in a large stuffed chair while a servant waved a fan over her. She grasped Susan with a sticky hand and pulled her down onto a stool beside her. Susan stared at her other hand, which held a glass with a clear liquid in it, like none of the wine. Lady Sol saw the look, and insisted Susan try it.

"Gin," she boomed, while poor Susan choked feeling her throat was scoured clear. "Wonderful stuff. Makes boring men interesting again." She roared with laughter at her own joke. "Now, then, young Susan, I think we must find a suitable man for you. No, no, we can do better than your major. Nice man, but he's not Galician, is he? No family either. I think young Ricky would rather fancy you. What do you think Alice? What's that? Fabian? That bastard! Listen to me my girl, you're to have nothing to do with him, do you hear? If he bothers you, come and see me, I'll see him off."

She swigged her gin, subsiding to fume at the thought of Fabian laying hands on the lovely Susan. Alice managed to sneak Susan off the stool and away.

"We're just going to repair our make-up, mummy darling," she called as she pulled Susan out of reach of Lady Sol's snatching hand.

Alice took Susan to another room, where a number of younger girls were touching up their make-up and hair. Susan was an instant success for her waxes, and they all wanted to experiment. In return, they gave Susan the lowdown on all the available men, everyone adding a warning about Fabian. At the same time, Alice made sure Susan knew enough of the dances to be comfortable, and the girls recommended various men for different dances. A few men they placed out of bounds. Susan wasn't sure whether to trust them; she knew her own friends would colour their words to improve their own chances, but these girls were older and, in her opinion, prettier than Susan.

Music started, causing the girls to pour out of the room while at the same time the men appeared from the dining hall. Some of the men had drunk far too much wine and were weaving. Susan found herself swaying to avoid a few wandering hands as she made her way to Roger, who smiled at her.

"Ah, my sweet princess! May I have the honour of this dance?" He bowed deeply.

"It is my delight, oh handsome prince," she curtsied in pretty perfection, oblivious to the looks her youth and vibrancy attracted.

It was a formation dance, the Sinkapace, quite complicated, but they joined a group that included Alice, who winked at Susan and mouthed 'follow me' at her. She did, and managed quite well. The next dance was a Galliard and she felt Roger tense, knew he was preparing to sit down. Instead, she untucked his empty sleeve from his belt and held it in her left hand while firmly putting his left hand on her waist. She smiled in wicked anticipation at him and the music started. They careened around the floor in fine style, Roger freed from his earlier reluctance.

The colonel insisted on trading partners and taking her for the next dance, on the completion of which a strange young man in a not too outlandish uniform politely asked her to dance, which she accepted. This was the cue for a number of different men to drag her onto the dance floor until she became tired enough to sit down at the table, where Alice and two other girls joined her. She saw that Roger was drinking with his friends.

Just as she was thinking it was time to re-join the throng, a cheerful voice spoke from behind her. "So this is the delightful Susan?" She turned to find the youngest man she had seen so far, really a boy, grinning at her. He had fair hair parted on the side, bright blue eyes and a little scar at the end of one eyebrow. Her heart lurched at the sight of him.

"Auntie Val sent me over. She insists that you dance with me. I am not to take no for an answer!"

"Well," said Susan with a smile, trying to conceal her feelings. "In that case it seems I have no option."

'I'm Ricky," he said, beaming, while Alice and her friends all smiled. He whisked her off towards the dance floor, then paused and looked quizzically at her. "I don't suppose you know the local peasant dances? You know, the ones where they move rather faster than this boring old stuff?"

"Sure," said Susan. "I'm pretty good at them too."

"Great, we'll give them something to talk about, shall we?" He stopped by the bandmaster and whispered in his ear. The man nodded, and on completion of the current dance, the band swept into a rousing tune, a hornpipe. The elderly dancers who were perambulating at a snail's pace hurried from the floor while the younger generation flocked to join in.

Susan allowed Ricky three dances in a row, most unseemly, but she didn't care. She did feel guilty about Roger, and went back to him after the third dance. He was pleased to see her but she was alarmed at how much he had drunk. With regret, she suggested that they should perhaps leave, as she wasn't sure how to handle him. He agreed, and she excused herself to visit the garderobe. Alice was dancing, but she asked one of the other girls, Mary, to accompany her. Mary knew the way, and led her to the one reserved for the ladies. She stopped, and pulled Susan into a recess hidden by a curtain.

"Watch," she whispered in Susan's ear.

Fabian came running down the corridor accompanied by two of his friends. Keeping quiet, they watched him go to the ladies' garderobe, and Mary led Susan to another one, taking care not to be followed or make a sound.

"I've been keeping an eye on him," she said as they walked. "Don't trust the bastard."

Neither did Ricky, who came rushing down the corridor in response to Fabian. He insisted on accompanying them, to make sure they were safe and unmolested, as he put it. He stayed with Susan as Mary went into the room, and she didn't resist as he pulled her into an alcove. He put his arms around her and looked deep into her eyes.

"I've never met anyone like you," he whispered, the scent of spiced wine sweet on his breath.

Susan could feel tremors running up and down her back where his hands rested gently and couldn't speak. Her eyes dropped to his mouth, her lips parted slightly and she let out a tiny moan as he leaned forward, hesitatant, before he kissed her when she didn't pull back. His lips caressed hers, cautious. Time seemed to stand still as they stood, unmoving, bodies slightly apart with just their lips touching. Her first kiss.

Susan jumped as the door opened and she pulled away, going in as Mary came out, smiling at Susan's flustered state.

As they walked back to the ballroom, Ricky asked her to dance again.

"I can't, Ricky. I would love to, but I fear my partner has drunk a little too much and I should get him to take me home while he still can. Besides, I don't think it would be correct to dance with you again, when I am here with somebody else."

"There is a dance next week end. I insist on taking you, but I won't let you dance with anybody else," he said unsmiling, with a steely determination that caused a tightness in her belly which she didn't understand, but it didn't stop her nodding. She didn't trust herself to speak.

"I'm not sure I can wait that long to see you again. Tell me where you live, so I can visit."

He left her before Roger could see them, with a quick press of her hand, and went to find his friends, no longer interested in dancing, his head swimming with thoughts of big blue eyes. He wanted to tell them of this gorgeous girl, with her slim figure and wonderfully translucent skin and a smile that lit up the room.

Roger staggered as he got up, holding the table for support, and the other veteran soldiers decided to leave at the same time. They went and paid their respects to Lord and Lady Sol, who beamed at Susan and insisted on wrapping her in a bear hug and planting a sloppy kiss on her cheek.

As their small carriage went down the drive, Roger just in control, Susan thought it was the happiest day for a very long time.

The other officers peeled off onto different roads, and Susan waved to them, sitting close to Roger, admiring the way he managed the reins with only one hand. She felt sorry for him, but realised now that she could have a glittering, golden future of her own as long as she was strong enough to go for it. She didn't quite know who Ricky was, whether he was above her station, but she could already feel herself married to him.

Hooves sounded behind them, and Roger moved the carriage to one side to let the horseman by. The horse slowed and came along side. Susan came out of her reverie, smiling, expecting to see Ricky. However it was Viscount Fabian grinning at her, his lips twisted into a cruel smile.

He leaned past her and slammed his steel shod walking stick onto Roger's head. Roger slumped without a sound. Fabian reversed the stick, slid it into a holster and with his arm freed, jerked Susan off the carriage and over across the front of his saddle. She started out of her shock, screamed and began to struggle, whereupon he punched her hard on the side of the head. A flash of pain and the world went dark.

Reputation

She woke in the dawn, in a light drizzle, cold, wet and in a world of pain. She ached all over, and hard cobblestones dug into her tender flesh. Moaning, she staggered to her feet and looked around, recognising the street. Barely conscious, she started out for home.

Susan tried to take stock, having difficulty in remembering. Her hair hung in rat tails down her shoulders, one of which was bare and she had to hold up the strap to keep her just budding breasts covered. The shoulder was sore, and when she felt it, a sharp pain stabbed through her, the fingers coming away with a smear of blood. Examining the area, she found almost a circle of small punctures. She couldn't work it out, befuddled, and slowly realised there was a similar pain in her left breast. Holding the dress away from herself, she looked down and saw another circle around the nipple, blood oozing from a deeper hole at the top. Puzzled she angled her breast up slightly and drew a breath in horror. It was a bite mark.

She staggered on, trying to take an inventory of her hurts. She realised there was sensation from lower down. She had blanked all feeling away. A raging sea of agony occupied the space her groin should fill, fire extending deep inside her. She missed a step as the pain hit home, and stopped while she blanked it off, strapping it away in her mind, with small success.

Uncomprehending, she struggled along, a vague awareness of early workers beginning to appear. First somebody went past and she heard them laughing. Another went past, she saw the dress, and the woman, must have been a woman, muttered something. It took her several yards to work out that the woman had said 'whore' as she passed, and several more to realise that she had meant her, Susan.

She stopped then and cried, before continuing at a slower pace. Another woman cursed her and told her to get out of decent streets, to stay where she belonged. She limped on, her sight coming back and showing that her beautiful blue dress was a mass of dried blood from the waist down.

At last her door was in front of her, and she slipped inside, unaware of the angry looks from neighbours in the street.

She dragged herself up the stairs to her room, collapsing on the bed. After a while, she gathered her strength, sat up and looked in the mirror. One eye peered through a swollen slit, already turning blue. Her beautiful blonde hair hung lank and dark with dirt and water while red wax smeared around her mouth, making her a parody.

Wincing, she drew off the remains of the dress, wondering where her underclothes were. There was too much blood to see the hurts, so she took her drying cloth and made a painful way to the washroom. It was too much effort to start a fire and heat water, but she drew some fresh water from the well in the courtyard, her face contorted with the effort of pulling up the bucket in the rain.

As she squatted on the floor, dabbing at her hurts with a damp cloth, the door opened and her father walked in, tucking in his shirt and blinking sleep from his eyes. She pulled the cloth over herself to cover her modesty.

"Daddy," she sobbed, "I've been attacked." She held her arms up to him and he took a step towards her, face slack in shock. Not a demonstrative man, he hadn't even touched her in the three years since her mother died and now he couldn't bring himself to give his daughter the comfort she needed.

He backed away, leaving his daughter and only child desolate on the wash-room floor. He left the room, muttering, "I'll get the herb woman." Susan cried again, deep racking sobs, for several minutes before returning to her attempts to clean herself.

Twenty minutes later, most of the blood was gone, and she was discovering new hurts when the door opened and the herb woman came in, with no sign of her father. Mother Adkins took charge, inspecting Susan with a critical eye, soothing her and cleaning her delicate areas. She put Susan to bed and gave her a cup of healing tisane, made from the herbs in her sack.

Later in the day, Susan awoke to a firm knock on the door and heard her father answer. She listened to the voices.

"Morning to you, gentle sir. I believe you are Mr Taylor? Susan's father?"

"Yes, that's me."

"My name's Colonel Devran. Met your daughter last night. Charming girl. Called to check she is fine and reached home in one piece."

"She's only just come home. Somebody has hit her and she is covered in blood." She could hear the anger in her father's voice, but he was also deferential to his superior.

"I am sorry to tell you that her escort came home this morning, alone, in his carriage. Horse brought him home, he couldn't, because he was dead. Somebody bashed his head in. I need to talk to your daughter."

A memory flooded back into her mind, the dark night, the hooves beating, the stick going past her and striking Roger. That cruel grin, the hand dragging her onto the horse. She sat up in the bed and screamed.

Staggering to the door in her thick woollen night dress, she opened it and went to the head of the stairs, looking down at her father with the colonel framed in the open door.

"Fabian," she said, "it was Fabian. I saw him hit Roger before he hit me." She cried again and collapsed to her knees. "I will give evidence," her eyes gleamed with passion and hatred. "I'll tell Lord Sol what happened."

Colonel Devran sighed. "I am so sorry, my dear. But you will not be believed." The colonel wiped a tired hand over his face. "Viscount Fabian is spreading a story that you propositioned him at the ball, that you were in fact a prostitute hired by Roger, his disabilities preventing him from finding a decent woman. I see now how it will go. He will claim that your monger will have struck Roger, and will have beaten you."

"But, but, Lady Sol," stammered Susan in anguish, "she will speak for me. She warned me about Fabian. And Alice, and Mary. Oh, Ricky! He will help me!"

Colonel Devran cleared his throat uneasily. "Master Taylor, may I come in. There are things I must tell you that are best not said in the street."

"What? Oh, yes, of course. Come in, sit down. Mother Adkins, would you be kind enough to make us all a hot tea? My daughter? A prostitute?"

There was a clatter of hooves outside, the door flew open and Alice blew into the room. "Is it true?" She asked. "Let me see you." She stared at Susan for a moment, before leading her to sit at the table in the kitchen where she sat beside her, putting her arm around her. Susan sank into the comfort. "Who are you?" She asked the colonel.

"Colonel Devran, ma'am, ex Pathfinder, now Guardsman."

"Ah, yes, you were there last night. Her partner was one of your men?"

"Yes, ma'am. Are you aware that he came back dead in his carriage, his head stove in from a club?"

"Didn't know the details. They don't matter. It was Fabian, I'm sure. Now we need to sort out the story and what we are going to do."

"Do?" said Susan. "We'll tell Lady Sol. She doesn't like him."

Alice looked at her. "Do you like Ricky? Love him, if it isn't too soon."

Susan's eyes welled up. "He's the nicest boy I've ever met. What is he going to think of me now?" She sobbed, great racking sighs from the depth of her being.

Alice waited until she was more composed. "We all love Ricky. He's like my little brother. And he fell for you big time. What do you think will happen when he finds out what Fabian has done?"

Susan looked at her, not knowing what to say or think. It was Colonel Devran who broke the silence. "Oh, hell. He hasn't a chance, but he's an honourable boy. This is getting worse."

Alice's eyes flicked to him, then back to Susan who didn't understand. "Susan, if Ricky sees you like this, or hears what happened, he will challenge Fabian to a duel. And then he will be dead. He will lose, Fabian doesn't like him."

"But, but, Lady Sol, won't she punish him so Ricky doesn't need to fight him?"

"Fabian's mother is her sister. She was arriving at the mansion as I left. She will have breakfast with my mother and after that she will believe Fabian's story. I am sorry, but your reputation is ruined."

Susan's father wasn't following. "What do you mean? Susan is a prostitute?" He looked at her in horror then buried his head in his hands. "What have I done? I don't deserve this."

Susan, however, had understood everything. "Ricky mustn't know," she said and her eyes brimmed again. "I can never see him again, can I?"

"My business," interjected her father in his own world of misery, "it'll be ruined. Nobody will buy fine clothes from a man whose daughter is a *prostitute.*"

Alice shook her head, her voice soft and gentle. "No, darling. It would be best not. And you need to leave Bresol."

Colonel Devran cleared his throat in anger, catching Alice's attention while Susan wept in a different agony. "This is all very well. I understand you wishing to protect your friend. But Viscount Fabian is guilty of rape and murder. The murder of my good friend and colleague, to facilitate the rape of this child. He must be punished."

"And how do you expect to achieve that, Colonel?" Alice said, her voice tired and choked with anger. "Do you expect to bring charges before Lord Sol? What witnesses do you have? Will they stand up against the weight of feeling Fabian will bring against Susan? Do you want to put this child through that?"

"Gallic nobility," grated the Colonel. "You make me sick. Always an excuse, isn't there? Doesn't matter that one of you is an animal, you'll all rally round and protect him. Well, it's not going to wash this time, girl. I will see him hang."

Something roiled in the depths of Alice's eyes, as she ran an eye up and down the Colonel with disdain. "Of course you may do as you see fit, Colonel. But I am fascinated as to how you expect to hang the future Earl of Galicia? Where do you expect to find a court that will carry out such a sentence? Why, even if you took him to Praesidium and found proof enough to convict him, the king could not have him hanged."

"A military court would."

"Only on the frontier, and you know perfectly well that Fabian will never go near the frontier. Colonel, please see sense. A dreadful crime has been committed. One for which we can never get justice. All we can do is try to lessen the hurt of those affected."

"You will find, madam, that no real soldiers will serve in Galicia after this. I shall be resigning forthwith, if he is not punished. Moreover, so will all my officers and men. Furthermore, the king will not find a single Pathfinder prepared to come here in the future, until Fabian is punished or dead."

"That is worthwhile, sir, and will have more effect than anything else you can do. Believe me or not as you wish, but I am on your side and would love to see him dangle. He is a disgrace to the family, an embarrassment to us all."

"Well, you give your precious Fabian a message from me." The colonel leaned across the table and whispered so low it was a hiss. "Roger had a lot of friends. He was a good soldier. There are men who owe their lives to him, yes, and officers too. When, not if but when, I tell them what has happened, I can think of at least three officers who will travel to Galicia and challenge Fabian. Each and every one of them are better fighters. That's just the officers. The men will try to get here first, with their bows and field craft. He won't know what happened, as the arrows come from nowhere, and nobody will find a thing. But you'll know, girl, and then you can tell his precious mother, that the Pathfinders look after their own."

Alice sat straight, and the ghost of a smile flitted across her face. "I shall enjoy passing that message, Colonel, both of them. You will find yourself a better friend of Galicia than you may imagine. Don't send the officers. Too open and obvious. I prefer the arrows. Afterwards, you may find an invitation to return, Colonel, or should I say Sergeant Major General?"

"I want to be there." They had forgotten about the others. Susan stared at them, though her father was looking at his shoes while Mother Adkins sat with bright and beady eyes, like a jackdaw seeking opportunity, taking in all this marvellous gossip. "I want to watch him die. I need to watch him die."

Neither the colonel nor Alice knew quite how to respond, this vicious hiss redolent with a depth of hatred unsuspected and unnatural in a young girl.

The tableau was broken by a knock on the door. At the second knock, Mr Taylor pulled himself to his feet and answered the door. They could not see the person there, but heard his voice, which kept them motionless.

"Mr Taylor? I am Francis Vermeer, the personal representative of Prince Fabian, our glorious future Earl. I am sure you are a loyal citizen of Galicia."

From the silence, Susan's father was not capable of speech; however, he must have given some form of assent, for the voice continued.

"Our prince enjoyed the company of your daughter last night. He appreciates her very much and congratulates you on the way you have raised her. He looks forward to enjoying her company on many occasions in the future. However, he is well aware that she incurred an unfortunate injury while with him, and would like to make this small contribution to help with the costs of her recovery."

Susan gasped and started to struggle from her chair, while the voice went on in remorseless and agonising detail.

"In addition to your daughter, the dress she wore found much favour with our prince, who proclaims it a perfect setting for such a jewel. He is most impressed by your work, and would like to commission similar dresses for his mother and sister to wear at the next ball. I am also instructed to enquire if you would be interested in supplying the uniforms for the regiment."

Susan was staggering towards the door. "No, daddy, you mustn't take the money! Don't you understand what it means?"

Her father backhanded her as she approached and she fell to the floor, hearing his words in a dim recess of her brain.

"Thank you, Master Vermeer, I am delighted that my poor services are so appreciated and of course I would be delighted to dress his family and the regiment. When would be a good time for me to attend for the measurements and discussions? And of course, my daughter will be available for the Prince as soon as she is recovered, which I am sure won't be long."

"Excellent. No time like the present. Please attend the quartermaster this afternoon at, shall we say, 3 o'clock? I will confer with Lady Galicia as to when you should attend and inform you of her pleasure. Good day, Master Taylor."

"Pleased, good Gentle Sir, pleased. Have a good day." Mr Taylor shut the door, a happy smile on his face. He stepped over Susan as if she wasn't there on his way back to the kitchen where his other guests sat around the table, expressionless faces taking in the smug, satisfied and pleased expression he wore.

"Thank you, madam and sir, for your concern for my daughter. I will be able to handle the situation now, thank you." He made a minute but unmistakeable gesture towards the door. Alice rose without a word and left, her horse's hooves drumming at speed, quite illegal in the city. Colonel Devran was slower, stooping an unobtrusive hand to squeeze Susan's shoulder as he left with a venomous glance at Mr Taylor.

*

Three days later Susan's body was healing, with the resilience of youth, while her heart still lay in broken ruins. She was beginning to hate her father. He invited three prominent madams to inspect her, discussing at length in her hearing the best way to market her body. All too nightmarish to fully understand.

Mother Adkins visited daily to check on her improvement and brought her news. The town was atwitter at the news one of the veteran officers had taken a prostitute to the ball and that Lord Sol had insisted on their all resigning. This the reason given for them all leaving the duchy. There was no news of Roger's murder, while Viscount Fabian received a promotion, now the General of the Galicia Guards with no mention of those to fill the vital ranks of Lt Colonel and Sergeant Major, the ranks to restrain his military naivety. Viscount Richard had amazed everyone by leaving to join the Pathfinders, saying he would join as a private soldier if they would not take him as an officer. And everyone was jealous of her father, who had won the contract to supply uniforms to the Guards. Already the newly-installed doorbell rang with a constant stream of callers seeking work or gratuities.

Yet if she so much as appeared at the door, fingers would point and abuse would come.

Susan wanted to die.

It was late when her father returned that night. He was drunk. She listened to him moving around downstairs, heard the drink gurgle from bottle to mug. His footsteps echoed down the wooden passage as he came up the stairs, pausing outside her room. The door creaked open and he lurched in to sit on her bed, his weight causing a creak and making her slide towards him.

"Well, lass, I've sorted your future. Good one too! Mrs Heather is sending a carriage for you tomorrow, you are going to stay with her while she teaches you the trade." He breathed heavily as he looked down at her, ethereal in her beauty, blind to her misery. "Think you owe me something for fixing you up," he said, alcoholic fumes washing over her. "It's long since your mum died. Your duty, it is, to take her place."

With that, he threw back the thin blanket and yanked up her nightdress, flinging it over her face and running his hand over her body. Susan went into shock; she couldn't believe this was happening, it was a dream, a nightmare, couldn't be real. Pain lanced through her, coming up from her breast and she realised he was kneading her. Right on the part-healed bite, starting her from frozen indecision. Anger rushed through her. Bastard! Always he made life difficult, drove her mother to an early grave and now this. She groped one handed under the bed for the empty chamber pot, brought it out and swung it up. His mouth biting at her breast lent strength to her arm and she screamed in anger as she slammed the pot onto his head, shards flying everywhere.

He collapsed on top of her, a dead weight, and she wondered for a moment if he was dead, realising she didn't care. Now what to do? She was NOT going to become a prostitute. She wondered who she could go to for help. Abigail she discarded immediately - the girl had not come to visit and anyway she knew that Abigail didn't like her. Alice would help, she thought, but was not sure how or where to find her. Maybe the Colonel was still here, he would help her, without a doubt. Yes, the best choice.

Decision made, she pushed her father off to fall to the floor like a sack of grain, dressed as fast as she could in sensible trousers and shirt with walking shoes. A last thought made her raid her father's desk where she found a pouch heavy with gold and silver coins. In haste she packed a sack with essentials, fearing he would stir, took a walking staff and slipped into the night, pausing only to hug the cat.

Thirty minutes later, she stood by a soldier who was knocking on a door. The guard on the military compound had not let her go to the colonel's house alone. The thought she might be an assassin gave her the first smile in three days. Colonel Devran answered the door, and regarded her.

"Just in time, girl, we leave in the morning. We've had a bed waiting for you these last three days."

Healing

Susan stepped through the snow with care not to freeze her blue woollen socks as she came to the green plank door, almost reaching up to the scraggly thatch above it. It was a woodland cottage, out of place here in the middle of Praesidium, the capital. She knocked twice and went in, as instructed in the invitation. Blinking in the gloom, she made out the shape of a woman sitting at the back of the room, a table in front of her with a pot of tea and two cups.

"Punctual," said the woman, "I like that." She poured a cup of tea, the scent of chamomile filling the room, and pushed it towards Susan. "Sit."

Susan sat. This was a job interview. After arriving in Praesidium three months earlier, she was conscious of being a drain on the Devran's meagre resources. She needed to contribute and her father's money would not last much longer. This invitation was unexpected and she didn't know what it was for. Suspicion crawled up her spine, trust long since burnt out of her.

A cat leapt onto her lap, and she jumped, and then stroked the cat, its purr loud in the silence.

The woman chuckled. "That's the first test passed, girl. Can't abide people who don't like cats. Now, I know a lot about you, girl, more than you might think. Got all sorts of people telling me things, I have. Never know what will be useful. Here's some free advice - change your name. Too many people know about Susan Taylor."

Susan sipped her tea and waited, keeping quiet. She didn't speak much these days, sadness still etched into her heart.

"Speak to me in a Galician court accent."

"What is the employment that you offer me, madam?"

"Well, that was just about perfect," said the woman, who Susan could now perceive was not as old as she had first thought, perhaps late forties. "Now Praesidium court, followed by Fearaigh country."

Puzzled, Susan demonstrated the different accents, and mimicked some people she knew. The woman made her walk up and down the room in different ways. She started writing notes on paper.

"Well, this has been fun, but I would like to know what is going on," drawled Susan, who realised she was enjoying herself. "And perhaps you would introduce yourself?"

The woman smiled and went over to the window, looking out. For the first time, Susan was able to see her properly. A pleasant face with a long nose, small mouth and chin. Dark, intelligent eyes and carroty-red hair set off a pale complexion unmarred by scars or spots, which indicated a good upbringing. And she could write.

"Call me Mary, Auntie Mary if you want. Two nights ago you were at the Rose, watching a play. The Drowning Man. I wrote it. Thinking of having you as an actor."

Susan's heart beat faster. She had loved the play. "There are no women amongst the actors. Never have been."

"None writing the damn things either. Time to change that, don't you think lass?"

"Yes," said Susan with abrupt decision. "I can do this."

"We'll pretend you're a boy at first, then as your tits grow they will suddenly realise you're a girl, but by then they will love you. Too late for anyone to object. Now, what are we going to call you? Something Gallic, I think. How about Delamere, Sam, no Sebastian Delamere."

"Delarosa," said Susan softly, "for the queen."

"Excellent," said Mary, going to the door. "Harry!"

A broad shouldered young man with very short hair came to the door.

"Yes, Mrs Sydney, I'm here." He spoke with a cheerful wink to Susan.

"You're to escort Susan home today and in future you will escort her when she comes for her lessons, until we sort out lodgings. She is to go nowhere in Praesidium without you as a guard and you are to tell nobody anything about her. She is our secret."

"No problem for the next month, anyway." He smiled at Susan. "I'm training for the Royal Guard and put a spear through my arm. Bit clumsy, I'm afraid."

"Get along with you." Mary pushed his shoulder. "Be back tomorrow just after dawn. I don't want her walking the streets in the dark."

*

Three weeks later they walked along Highside, the main thoroughfare with its firm cobbles. Susan looked with worry at a grey sky pregnant with rain. She pulled her cloak tighter and cursed the light sandals she wore.

"Has it been raining today, Harry? I'm not wearing good shoes for the mud." Praesidium streets were dreadful in the rain, except for the cobbled Highside and the Royal Mile.

"It'll be a right bastard," said Harry, delighted at the prospect. "Been pouring down most of the day. We won't go down Tanner Street, their pits will be flooded into the street and the smell awful."

Susan shuddered. The leather workers steeped the raw hides in urine for a week; she hated taking that route in any weather. She regretted the Devran's lived so far away from the acting company's theatre, really a converted inn. She thought that she would soon take up Mary's offer to live there, though she noticed Mary didn't. She knew she had a husband somewhere, and rather suspected he was a baron.

They turned into the entrance of Randall Street and Susan stopped in dismay. The mud was thick, and she saw the people walking down the street smeared up to their thighs. She moaned, knowing she was going to lose a shoe to that glutinous, smelly horror, foul with the contents of chamber pots thrown from the windows.

"Don't worry, Duchess," said Harry, using the nickname she hated but he insisted on using. "I'll keep your lily-white tootsies clean and fresh." He swept her off her feet, one arm round her shoulders and one behind her knees. She squealed in outrage, but he pulled her up high and her arms went round his neck to keep from falling.

"That's the way, Duchess, hang on now and I'll have you home in no time." He strode off down the street making light of the mud, oblivious to Susan's growing panic. She closed her eyes, trying to quell the awful feeling of dread and horror that came from his touch. She panted, head turned into his shoulder where he wouldn't notice. With her eyes closed, a memory she didn't know she possessed came back to her, of being carried like this by Fabian. As the memory continued like a bad dream, she forced open her eyes and shook her head, refusing to let it continue. Closing her mouth, she allowed herself to feel Harry's arms and hands holding her. Slowly, deliberately, she relaxed her muscles, feeling the tension slide.

Harry was bantering with stallholders now, as they went down Woolmarket, and she became aware of her surroundings, holding onto happy emotions while she fought her personal demons. She used the emotions as a wash to flush round her soul, clearing out the poison that fermented there all unknown, in that deep wound she had scabbed over.

Harry strode out of Woolmarket and King Street was dry, so he gently swung her down. She clung to him for a moment, then, daring her emotions to rebel, she deposited a chaste kiss on his neck.

"Thanks Harry, that was sweet of you."

"Blimey, Duchess, what a carry on! Don't you worry, girl, I'm here to look after you." Harry gave her a funny look. She had never even touched him before, and he was aware of why. It hadn't occurred to him when he had picked her up, and it was too late when he realised why she was gripping so tight, her body as tense as a bow string. Not knowing what else to do, he had ignored it, but noticed the softness return just before he set her down. Still, he hadn't expected the kiss, and wondered if he should carry her again as they approached another lot of mud.

Susan was laughing now at a man trying to sell her some apples, gleefully pointing out a worm crawling out of one, to his intense annoyance. She bought some hazelnuts from a young girl, a regular who knew her by name, and warned her the mud was thick.

"Not to worry," said Susan. "I've got my own horse!" She slapped Harry on the shoulder.

"Horse? That's a rum donkey if you ask me," said the girl, and other stallholders joined in, with one offering to push some grated horseradish up his rear.

"That'll make 'im move, Duchess," said the man with a grin on his crooked face. They all called her Duchess along the route, and she was friends with most of them.

Harry picked her up and went into the mud again. This time Susan kept her eyes open and didn't flinch. She was pleased with herself. She looked with close attention at his neck.

"Your skin is very white, Harry," she said, noticing a lack of boils and spots.

"No it isn't," he replied. "It's clean. I'm from Fearaigh, we wash there, not like you smelly lot."

"Its winter, Harry, you catch a chill and die if you wash. I do wipe my face though, with a damp cloth."

"You're still smelly, though, beginning to smell like a Praesidium girl now, not a Galician."

"Mary doesn't like me using perfume," said Susan, considering the issue. She'd never thought about washing and smells. "Do you wash in the winter, then Harry? Why aren't you sick?"

"Sure. Back home we're in the bath every day, but it's harder here in the city. I pour water from the well over myself instead."

"That must be freezing! Not every day, surely?"

"You get used to it. Most days, I do, if I've been sweating for sure." Harry slipped and recovered, squeezing her tighter.

*

With the spring rains getting worse, Susan moved into the inn, going back to the Devran's for the occasional weekend. She had a room to herself, a tiny one in the attic. She loved it, feeling warm and safe, decorating it with spare blue ribbons that reminded her of Queen Rose.

She was becoming very good as an actor, with a natural talent. She learnt several parts, and was gaining a reputation as a young boy who made people laugh. She found learning the parts easy and enjoyed listening as Mary, Will, Kit and Ben argued about the plays as they wrote them. Often they would take it in turns to act out a part in the manner they thought it should go, or make Susan try different things. Very quickly she realised that her knowledge of clothing and make-up exceeded all of theirs, and she was making valuable contributions. This earned her a slight increase in shares. She didn't get a wage, but a share of the proceeds. She was still a secret, hidden away whenever a patron came to call, but then so was Mary.

Harry came in one day with a letter for Susan, an invitation for dinner from the Devran's, whom she hadn't visited for a month. As she was reading it, Ben came in, taking off his coat and hanging it up by the door.

"Heard the news?" he said to the room at large.

"You ate enough at lunch?"

"The widow Harrison is with child?"

"You bought somebody a drink?"

"You know that playboy prince in Galicia?" He ignored the jibes and continued. "Susan, you must know him, what's his name, Prince Fabulous or something?"

"Fabian," said Susan in a flat monotone. "Yes, I know him. What's he done now, killed someone in a duel?" She felt a tremor in her stomach, worried he had killed Ricky.

"No, nothing like that. Silly idiot got himself killed in a hunting accident."

"What?" said Susan, staring at him, her face blank.

"Arrow right through the belly. Was on his own except for his friend, who shot him. Friend says it was an accident, but they still hung him because he tried to run away. Mind you, from all I hear there is a party still going on in Galicia, particularly Bresol."

"I wasn't there," breathed Susan, "they knew I wanted to be there."

"What's up Sue?" said Will. "You look upset, did you like the guy?"

"I HATED HIS BASTARD FUCKING GUTS!" She screamed at him. He shrank back, shocked at the suddenness of the eruption. "They promised I could be there when they killed him." She burst into tears and ran up to her room, while they sat back in amazement.

"Fabian accused her of being a prostitute," said Mary into the silence. "Why she had to leave Bresol. There's a rumour that he raped her and made up the story to clear himself, killed her boyfriend too."

"Well," said Will. "I reckon that's no rumour, now. Explains why she smacked you so hard when you pinched her, John." Nobody laughed, and Mary closed the book in which she recorded the plays they discussed. Kit poured Ben a drink and filled up the other glasses.

"That girl has some interesting friends," mused Ben. "Notice she thinks he was killed. Might be a good idea not to get on the wrong side of her."

"I'd better make sure she's alright," said Mary, getting up and leaving the room.

*

Colonel Devran eased the cloak from her shoulders and hung it on a peg without saying a word. He opened the door to the parlour and gestured for Susan to go through. She went through the door, her back rigid, her emotions in turmoil and unsure what to say but desperate to share her feelings.

Two strides into the room, she started to greet the colonel's wife when she recognised the other man in the room and stopped dead.

"Ricky," she gasped and sagged into the nearest chair.

*

The meal was over, and the awkwardness faded. She was feeling good towards Ricky, and thought he still felt something about her. The colonel passed Ricky a fortified wine while his wife served tea.

"Tell me what happened," Susan said with simple and undeniable fervour.

Ricky's eyes went to the ceiling as he remembered. "When I first joined up I was heartbroken. I really thought you were what Fabian claimed, his story seemed to stack up and make sense. I just had to get away from Galicia. Then this story went round the regiment, about Browne's death and what really happened. I was so angry. I was going to leave and go back to Galicia, but the sergeants caught me and the captain gave me a good going over. They told me what they were going to do. I was told I could come along, to show them the way. I know all the forests. So I was on the team. Colonel Devran briefed us."

"You knew I wanted to be there," Susan stared at the colonel, who nodded.

"Wouldn't have been possible," said Ricky, staring into the fire. "We were led by this half Elf, Grey Fox, who was a bit contemptuous of me, didn't really want me along. And it was tough. Hard to keep up with them. I thought I was fit and found out I wasn't. We spent a week in the forest, shadowing them while they hunted. Grey Fox didn't let me near them, said I was too noisy. Me, the woodsman. We collected their arrows after they fired and lost them. They never knew we were there."

Ricky paused and sipped at his wine. "Grey Fox caught this wild boar, a sow with piglets. Alive. She wasn't very happy, but he managed to keep her under some sort of control. Wouldn't have believed it. I had to hold the pig while he went into the woods with some of the others. We waited for hours. Pig kept eating roots I had for her and bit me if I stopped scratching her. Seems Grey Fox managed to make a boar trail that led them towards us. When they were in the right place, Grey Fox made a sound like a piglet in distress."

Ricky shuddered and looked at his arms. "Damn pig went mad. Ripped herself out of my arms and charged off through the bush, straight at that bastard Fabian. Of course she didn't care about him, but he was in the way, between her and her piglets. Fabian rushed at her with his sword and Grey Fox shot him through the belly with one of Vermeer's own arrows. Let it off at the same time that Vermeer loosed. Even Vermeer thought he had shot him. Nobody knew we were there."

Ricky trailed off, looking at the fire.

"In the belly?" asked Susan. "I would have shot a bit lower." She spoke with no hint of levity, just venomous hatred.

Ricky blushed. "Grey Fox was going to put it through his heart. I asked him for the belly shot, so the dying would be hard. It was. We could hear him screaming in agony a couple of hours later as he the life went out of him. I thought it would make me feel better. It didn't. Seeing you does, though." Ricky blushed.

Susan looked at him, feeling tears welling up, then the dam broke and her emotions broke free, washing away the poison and horror still enmeshed in her soul. She cried, deep racking sobs, and buried her head on Ricky's shoulder when he enveloped her in his arms. He stroked her hair, wondering what to say and fortuitously saying nothing at all.

*

"How do I look, Mary?" asked Susan. She was wearing a pretty, flowery dress and trying to see herself in a small mirror. She pulled at her hair, nervous and convinced she needed to dress again.

"You are gorgeous, darling, you always are," said Mary. She had helped Susan buy the dress, delighted with her romantic interest. Ricky was taking her out this rest day; the first opportunity to be together.

"Come on," said Mary, "he'll be here soon. Let's wait downstairs. There shouldn't be any of the men around today, they have gone off to see a cock fight or something."

"Ohh," said Susan in sudden worry, "perhaps he won't come? He's changed his mind? Or maybe he will when he sees me!"

"Don't be silly, dear, he will be knocked sideways when he sees you. I bet you a pound to a penny he won't be able to speak for a few minutes! Then you will know he really likes you."

They went downstairs, Susan still fretting, and found Ricky waiting in the public area of the Inn, twisting his hat into a nervous wreck as he wondered how to tell her of his arrival. His mouth fell open and he froze, staring at Susan tripping down the stairs.

All her nervousness fled at the sight of him, and she skipped across the floor, taking his left arm in both of hers and swinging him round towards the door.

"Hello, Ricky, you look very smart. Is this Pathfinder uniform, I haven't seen it before?"

Ricky managed to close his mouth, and nodded, unable to speak as he looked at her. She was breath-taking, beautiful as an innocent fawn in the forest at dawn, and this confident young prince who had squired several ladies of quality, and bedded most of them, found himself bereft of words and confidence in the face of her radiance. With slow and unsteady steps, he moved towards the door, not taking his eyes off her face.

He walked straight into the door jamb.

Heroic self-control allowed Susan to control her laughter and go outside as he recovered his composure. He had brought a small carriage with two big wheels, and a rather splendid looking stallion arched his neck at her from between the shafts.

"Oh, Ricky, it's beautiful. I've never seen a carriage like this before." She said hello to the horse, rubbing his velvety nose, accepting Ricky's hand as he helped her up the mounting steps that he folded down for her.

"Wow, it's so high up here! You can see so far, right into people's houses." She was looking around as Ricky climbed up onto the box beside her and shook out the reins. He smiled, back in control again.

Mary watched them go off at a spanking trot, scattering some geese feeding in the road. Susan was chattering away, in the manner of a girl who is truly happy, while Ricky was nodding. Mary's eyes narrowed as she watched them go.

*

"Come in and join us, dear," said Mary to Susan as she skipped in through the inn's front door. Mary stood in the parlour door, holding it open. Smiling, Susan slipped in and halted at the sight of a wrinkled old lady with merry, black button eyes, shiny with mischievous intent. "This is Granny Sawyer, she's the best herb woman in Praesidium. Will you pour the tea, please? It's a lovely rosehip and rosemary mix that Granny brought."

Susan poured, self-conscious under the close inspection.

"Susan," Mary began, hesitant, and Susan was intrigued. Something was up! Mary was always confident and certain. "You clearly have feelings for Ricky, deep feelings."

"Oh, yes," Susan glowed. "He's just lovely, so handsome and so polite, he thinks about me and looks after me. He listens to me, is interested in what I say. He's just dreamy and perfect."

Granny Sawyer chortled, a lascivious, earthy sound, earning a stern glare from Mary and a startled glance from Susan.

"Oh, Susan, I am really very happy for you. Tell me, has he kissed you yet?"

Susan blushed prettily and examined her tea cup.

"Is that all you've done so far?" asked Mary with concern.

"All?" Susan looked at her in confusion.

"Ah," this time it was Mary who was embarrassed, to Granny Sawyer's delight. "I was concerned that he might want to go a bit further, and, ah, lay hands on you. Even take your clothes off."

"Oh, no, Ricky respects me far too much for that," said Susan with confident speed. "He wants to take me home to see his mother and get her permission to marry me in the spring. I'm going to be the next Duchess of Galicia! Ricky says he wants our first time to be perfect." She hummed a little melody in happy delight.

"Oh," said Mary, deflating, "well that's alright then. I was concerned that you might get a baby, you see, so I asked Granny Sawyer to make some special tea…" She trailed off at Susan's expression.

"Baby? I hadn't thought of that. It would be Ricky's baby. Just like him, with those lovely eyes… Oh yes, thank you Mary darling, what a brilliant idea. Yes, of course, I can't wait, we won't wait, oh thank you, darling!"

Susan jumped up and rushed out of the room leaving Mary gaping and Granny Sawyer laughing. The front door slammed as Susan rushed off to get impregnated as fast as possible.

Strollers

"It's not right," said Will, pushing his chair back from the table in anger and throwing down his quill to splat on the parchment. Kit stroked his beard and examined a knot on the table top, his eyes unseeing as he retraced the plot.

"Well," began Mary, "perhaps we should…"

"Enough," said Will. "We're working too hard at it. I'm going for a walk. Susan, join me." It was more a command than a request, and unusual.

"Me?" Susan said in astonishment from the edge of the table where she sat quiet and listened, not offering an opinion as the new romantic play turned into a turgid monstrosity under everyone's input. Will ignored her and made for the door, grabbing a cape on the way. Susan raised an eyebrow at Mary who nodded in slow and dubious consent, so she hurried after him, pulling on a cape and adjusting the bonnet.

Will waited for her in the yard, impatient. As soon as she appeared, he stumped off into the street and she ran to catch up, falling into step beside him.

"Tell me," he said after a moment's uncomfortable silence, "how you feel about Ricky."

"Ricky?" Susan said in some surprise, before she forgot everything at the chance to talk about her favourite subject and she proceeded to describe his actions and habits in excruciating detail, which became more and more involved as she realised Will was hanging onto her every word. The odd encouragement kept her going till they came to a tea parlour, where Will sat her down at a table. He managed to order tea without stopping her flow of devotion.

"Tell me," he prompted as the torrent slowed on the arrival of the tea, "how your feelings changed from before to after you made love for the first time."

"WHAT!" Susan cried, scandalised. "I'm a good girl."

"Yes, yes," said Will, "so explain how your feelings changed from before you rushed off, to after you came back with straw all down the back of your dress and a grin from ear to ear."

Susan glared at him, until her expression changed. "You want to know for the play, don't you? You are trying to understand how a girl in love is thinking?"

"Well of course, how else can we write the damn thing?"

Susan's demeanour changed, they put their heads together and discussed how people acted when in love. After half an hour, the tea cool in the pot, Will looked up and changed the subject.

"You see the woman on the long table, eating cakes daintily but without stopping? Tell me what she is thinking?"

Susan took a covert glance. "She is devastated. She sits here alone with a bright smile on her face, busy eating cakes to stop herself from thinking about something terrible."

Will nodded, thoughtful. "I agree. What is it? Love?"

"No," said Susan with consideration. "It's money. Her clothes are rich but old. Clean and well-tended, but repaired, not replaced. She is keeping up appearances, but has lost hope."

"Interesting. And the young blade by the door?"

"No job, not much money, hoping to snare a rich widow."

Will led her through half a dozen more people. "You are really very good at this," he said. "Are you bringing this into your acting? You should."

"Oh, you mean that I should act like these people?"

"Well, you are picking up on what they are really thinking. If you can see the tell-tale signs, you should be able to act them as well. What are you seeing that tells you about these people?"

"I'm not sure. Yes, I am. It's the way they hold their bodies, the way they breathe, but it is a combination of things. You can see through what they try to portray to the reality underneath."

"Exactly. That is the key to acting. Being able to show the combination. Most people fail because they only consider one characteristic."

"This is what you do all the time, isn't it Will? You are never there, you are always observing. When you touch me, you don't give an impression of wanting me, just seeing how I will react."

"You are not supposed to notice that. I wondered why you reacted differently to me than to others. Come on, let's go back and you can show off your skills on the way."

Will paid their bill and held the door for her. As they made their way into the street, a self-important young man strode with grand purpose down the middle, avoiding the puddles. Pulling away from Will, Susan rushed up to him.

"Oh please, sir, you have a kind face. Save me from this awful man. I have been kidnapped, dragged away from my family in Galicia, abused and imprisoned." Her voice was beautiful, perfect pitch, the epitome of a well-bred Galician lady. The young man stopped and stared at her in astonishment.

Will cursed and stepped forward, grabbing her arm. "Don't you mind 'er, yerr Lordship," he grated, "she's a lying bitch. Bloody slattern trying to get out o' doing an honest day's work on 'er back."

"Well," said the man, uncertain. A crowd started to form. Susan threw herself to her knees and clasped his hand.

"He beats me," she cried in piteous terror, raising her hand to her brow and smearing mud over it with a surreptitious motion. "Don't let him hurt me again!"

The young man went white, looked down at her and then at Will, who glared at him in a threatening manner. The young man took a deep breath and steeled himself.

"Now look here," he began.

"Shut it, mush," said Will, his voice fierce and threatening violence. The young blade recoiled. "I'll sort the little bitch."

"No!" Susan cried, turning to the burgeoning crowd, still on her knees. "Won't some kind gentleman save me from this devil in human guise?"

The crowd murmured, angry, and stepped forward as one, clearly prepared to lynch Will from the nearest doorway.

"Shit," said Will, "enough, Sue, you win!"

Susan laughed and jumped to her feet. "Thank you ladies and gentlemen! And you, kind sir, for your unwitting assistance! This is the famous Will Redcloak of the Orb and Sceptre Playhouse, with a short free demonstration of his prowess. Come and see him perform on Saturday, when he is playing the magnificent Northern King in his decline. Don't miss it, you'll be there, won't you sir?" She smiled at the young man, who nodded in relief.

"Ah, yes, certainly, of course I will. Great fun, delighted to be part of it." He babbled and escaped, no longer looking in the slightest bit self-important.

The crowd laughed and started to dissipate, a couple of kids throwing nuts at Will until they lost interest after fifty paces.

*

Ricky strode through the main doors of the Royal Pathfinders Officers Mess, resplendent in his midnight black uniform, and proud of the ethereal beauty of Susan floating along on his arm. He escorted her to the line waiting to be introduced to the guest of honour, the Honorary Colonel of the Regiment, King Richard. Susan smiled at the other ladies, nodding her head slightly to Colonel Devran, but did not speak.

The line moved quickly and in no time they were in front of King Richard, who looked at her in appreciation as they were introduced, ignoring Ricky.

"You are very lovely, my dear," said King Richard. "We are lucky that Praesidium is receiving the fairest Galician flowers to join our court." He smiled and started to turn to the next guest, then pulled back, frowning in suspicion.

"What did you say your name was? Susan? Susan Taylor?" He blinked, as memories came back. "Rose's little girl?" he whispered.

Susan nodded, smiling at him.

The king bellowed, flung his arms around her and swung her off her feet in a bear hug, to the shock of the sergeant major's wife who was next in the queue. It was apparent from her face that she expected the king to ravish Susan there and then.

"Susan," the king boomed, his voice becoming articulate again. "My Rose's little girl! She has come back to us. Gentlemen," he turned to the room and shouted down its length as he set her down. "You had better take care of whom you have brought with you, because this young lady is my official witch finder, the best one in the country. Ha!" He laughed and turned to speak to the Commander of the Royal Pathfinders and the official host of the Regimental Dinner. "Re-arrange the seating, Bobby. I want to talk to Susan, find out what she has been up to these last ten years."

"Certainly not, Dick, don't be an idiot," said the general, smiling at Susan as he rebuked the king. "You can talk to her before the meal and after. Her escort may be the Crown Prince of Galicia, but to us he is simply Cadet Galicia and sits at the bottom of the table, well away from you."

"Well," said the king, deflating. "We could always swap escorts, you don't mind if I borrow your girl for the meal, do you Ricky my lad?"

Ricky gulped, eyeing in some horror the Duchess of Grittall who was the king's escort that evening. Grittall was the mining part of the kingdom and the duchess appeared to have some dwarven blood, judging by her beard and capacity for beer. He quite understood the king's eagerness, so he nodded his head in obedience.

"Whatever you wish, sire."

The general sighed. "Get out of here, Galicia, and take your girlfriend with you. I'll sort out his majesty."

Reluctant, the king relinquished Susan after another brief embrace, his eyes shiny with unshed tears. Susan was crying, unashamed, the tears creating tracts through the light powder dusting her cheeks. The king watched her move away for a moment, before turning to the next guest, a hearty welcoming smile on his face. Throughout the room, heads craned towards Susan and the name of Queen Rose on many mouths ensured everyone knew who she was.

This was the first formal dinner that Ricky had attended at Praesidium, and few knew his name and rank. It delighted him that his partner was more famous, and he smiled as senior officers came to introduce themselves. He noticed many of them already knew Susan from ten years previous, whisking her off to meet their wives, so it was a hard task to keep up with her and not be left behind, made more difficult as other officers wished to know how he met her.

Once all the guests arrived, an aide appeared at Susan's elbow requesting her presence with the king, and she and Ricky made their way over to where the king stood in front of the bay windows, surrounded by senior officers. It was clear that some of these wished to discuss matters of major import with the king, and a couple glared at Susan, causing her head to go high.

The king reached out and took her hand as she arrived, examining her with care.

"Susan, please accept my heartfelt apologies. I should have come looking for you many years ago, and ensured your education and happiness."

Susan's eyes clouded again. She squeezed his hand. "We all

hurt, Daddy King." A few eyebrows raised at this endearment. "I know how you suffered." The king had responded to his queen's death by launching a furious campaign against the Uightlanders, in which he received a spear through the thigh which took several months to heal. "I always wanted to meet your daughter. Is she not here tonight?"

The king laughed. "No, the little minx broke into the armoury up at the border last fall. A young pathfinder caught her, thought she was an Uightlander brat and smacked her. She spent the night locked up and the fool of a commandant wanted to hang the pathfinder. Nobody else would have caught her." The king's pride in his tomboy daughter shone from his eyes.

"What was a pathfinder doing in camp?" asked Susan.

The general laughed, impressed that Susan would notice. "Young Russell was clumsy, took a spear through the thigh, copying his king. He was recuperating at the fort and sorting out the armoury for them till he could keep up with us again. Dick handled it well."

Susan raised an eyebrow, while Ricky admired a painting behind the king, happy to be out of the limelight.

The king smiled. "Made Russell her Master-at-Arms. She's off with him spending the winter in the wilds, learning to survive."

Susan was shocked. "But she's barely ten years old! That's awful."

"Need to be tough to survive in the Starr family. Don't worry, she is loving every moment of it, and anyway she is twelve now."

The general leaned forward slightly. "We keep a patrol observing them at all times. Good training for them as well. Make sure there are no undesirables in the area and at hand if somebody slips on ice and breaks a leg. I rather suspect young Asmara has already worked this out as I think she is deliberately creating problems for them. Russell looks to be tearing his hair out on occasion, but her weapon skills and field craft are becoming first rate."

Susan smiled wistfully, wondering if Asmara looked like her mother, while the king chuckled. Then his expression darkened.

"A secret report reached my ears, regarding Fabian. Were you the girl involved?"

Susan's face went blank, and she nodded. The king sighed.

"I am so sorry," he said and squeezed her hand again.

The general cleared his throat. "Of course neither I nor the king know what we are talking about. However, I would like to say that the Pathfinders are at your disposal, ma'am."

Susan curtsied, and her eyes sparkled with mischief. A thought had crossed her mind that she might become a better actress with a few more skills.

"Thank you, sir, that is most kind. There is something…"

"You are already a damn mascot," grunted the general, with some embarrassment as this display of emotion. "If we were some lord's plaything we would make you a Colonel of the Regiment."

"Yes, sir, but there is something more I would ask," she began.

"You are not getting young Galicia promoted, mind you," said the general.

"No, nothing like that. I would like to train with your master at arms, learn how to use a sword."

The king roared with laughter, the general smiled and Ricky showed alarm, while confusion covered male faces and horror the face of the ladies who were listening.

*

Ricky danced as if he possessed two left feet, his mind elsewhere, and Susan became more and more irritated. She kept quiet though, and simply held him as they danced. The king had announced the spring campaign would be against the Uightlanders, just the Pathfinders with volunteer levies from other regiments, clearing them from the northern mountains to ensure the wheat, bere and oat harvest for the year. What upset Ricky was the direct command from his colonel that he would not be participating, his training and fitness levels considered insufficient.

They returned to their seats and she declined to dance with Lt Tully, who had sported an erection the last time she danced the Lavolta with him, to her intense mortification. She accepted Captain Rogers who managed barely a circuit, before they were intercepted by the king. Captain Rogers was not used to being supplanted and bit off a snarl when he realised who was taking advantage.

King Richard brooked no modesty and used the first twirl as he lifted her high in the air to slam her in tight, where he held her firmly as they moved round the dance floor. Not that Susan was going to resist, she found she still loved the king, just as she had as a little girl. Not in the same way that she loved Ricky, but she gloried in his strong arms and nestled close as they swung around the floor. She felt him respond to her closeness and swell to impressive dimensions. Cushioning him against her stomach, she realised she would have been mortified if he hadn't responded to her and flushed, glancing at Ricky to see if he noticed. But Ricky was talking to his young friends, also banned from the campaign, so she lost herself in the music and the king's closeness.

The dance came to an end, and she stood smiling up at him, holding herself close enough to shield him from prying eyes while he relaxed, which he showed no sign of doing. She gave a little curtsy, careful not to rub.

"Thank you, your highness, that was delightful." Her eyes twinkled at him.

"Don't think you are getting away that easily," he replied. "That was only half a dance. We shall continue."

"Isn't that against protocol?"

"Protocol be damned. I am going to enjoy myself and as both our partners are busy drinking far more than they should, we are forced to entertain each other. Damn, what sort of a dance is this? Doesn't sound like a Volt, bit too fast for my liking."

"It's a salterello, as well you know. You are only complaining because you can't hold me, you naughty king." The Lavolta, or Volt, was a Galician dance and the only one in which dancers held their bodies close together. It involved the man throwing his partner into the air and catching her as she came down, then twirling together. All other dances were more stately affairs, many in sets of three or four partners.

With effortless ease, Susan slipped into the same style of well-remembered banter with which Rose had entranced the king, and he stared at her as they danced. Going through the more intricate steps, Susan noticed the faces of the non-dancing wives. She faltered for a moment as she realised she was the centre of attention, and more than one infinitesimal smirk showed other girls knew exactly what she had concealed during the Volt. A couple were annoyed, but more were pleased, not a few downright happy, to her surprise. She was not to know how long it had been for them to see the king so happy. Susan lifted up her head and danced with more vigour, laughing with the king.

The music came to an end and reluctantly the king allowed the general to lead her away for another dance. People were ready to leave, though they could not while the king was there. Ricky was still drinking with his friends, far too much in Susan's severe opinion, as the last dance was called, another Lavolta which was unusual but Susan suspected the king's hand in the selection, as he grasped her and brought her to the dance floor, throwing her high into the air and holding her close as she came down.

Susan suspected he would proposition her during the dance, and prepared her refusal, running through various scenarios as they danced. Her actress mind was fertile in coming up with scenarios, one involving dramatic gestures causing her to giggle. The king showed his suspicion, wondering which caress created the reaction. No proposition came, although on the final fling into the air he managed to hold her with one hand on a buttock and the other on a thigh, causing her to come down with much indecorum. So much twirling and throwing going on that she didn't think there was an indiscretion, but the rubbed descent caused her a great flush of warmth and desire. The lack of a proposition to turn down became infuriating, especially when he gallantly kissed her hand and returned her to Ricky without another word.

The king left with his small entourage including his escort. Susan curtsied deeply with the other ladies, and turned to find Ricky in deep discussion with his colonel. Something about the conversation drew her attention; they were clearly in disagreement. She drew the impression Ricky was holding out for something and the colonel finally agreed, appearing very dubious. Ricky returned in triumph to his friends, and told them he had won the colonel's agreement, they were going on campaign with the regiment.

The boys all jumped up shouting, another round was called for and they toasted the campaign. Draining their glasses, they were refilled and this time they all toasted Susan, somewhat to her bewilderment, but she was the only girl left. She tugged Ricky away from them, keen to go home and hoping the drink would not have affected him too much for she was still feeling decidedly warm from the dancing. She was not at all happy with Ricky going to the front when he was so untrained, but knew enough not to say a word.

Climbing into the trap with him, she hugged him tight, hoping for a kiss, and was astounded by a feeling of reserve, a stiffness in his body.

"What's the matter sweetheart?" She whispered while nibbling his ear. "Can we go home as fast as possible?"

"We're not going home," he muttered as he encouraged the horse and turned it in a new direction.

Susan thought for a moment, unable to think of what else they could be doing. She was irritated and wanted Ricky in her bed as fast as possible. She stuck a tongue in his ear and reached round the front of him.

"But wouldn't you prefer to go home now?"

Ricky shook his head in irritation to dislodge her tongue and pushed her hand away. She stared in amazement, feeling hurt and angry. Two rejections in less than an hour. She didn't know when she had felt so dreadful.

"We're going to the palace," said Ricky.

"The palace? But why?"

"Why do you think?"

Susan couldn't for the life of her think why they would be going to the palace. She couldn't think they would be allowed in without an invitation and Ricky might be Galician royalty but he wasn't in Praesidium, according to the official position.

"Oh," she said as realisation dawned. "You must have chatted with the king when I wasn't with you, and he wants to know more about your time here? After all, you are his cousin."

"No, you dummy," said Ricky, snapping the reins at the horse. "Your bloody flirting with the king has resulted in him requesting you for his bed tonight."

"WHAT!?! And you accepted? Why you damn…" She trailed off as a horrible thought dawned. "You traded me for the right to join the campaign didn't you? That's why all the boys were toasting me. Well, you can just forget it, buster. Turn this trap round and take me home. You can forget about spending the night as well."

Susan sat up straight and crossed her arms. Ricky sighed.

"It's your own damn fault for flirting with him. I just made the best of it. A request from the king cannot be declined. If you were my betrothed, we could perhaps plead your virginity. But he knows about Fabian and suspects me to boot. Anyway, that would have only kept you away from him until after our wedding."

Susan held onto the side of the trap, her mouth working but unable to speak. Trap, she thought with a bitter soundless laugh, I really am in a trap.

"What do you mean it can't be declined? I have never heard of such a thing."

"Royalty have first pick of the girls," said Ricky. "It is considered an honour to have your wife selected." From Ricky's visage he clearly didn't think it one.

Susan's eyes narrowed again. "You are royalty in Galicia. You've done this to other people's wives, haven't you?"

Ricky squirmed in his seat and didn't answer. Susan sat back in her seat and considered her options. She wondered how far she could run. The trap turned into the palace forecourt and before she knew it she was being handed down by a footman and escorted into the palace. She didn't turn round as Ricky drove away.

*

A wood fire roared in the grate and King Richard stepped back from poking it with fervour as Susan was escorted into the room. The footman melted away, the door closing behind him without a sound as Susan transfixed a very self-satisfied king with a glare. He strode towards her, the poker clattering as it missed its holder where he dropped it. She struggled to hang onto her coat as he eased it off her shoulders and hung it up.

"You might have asked ME."

"You were expecting me to and were all prepared to say no," he replied, moving in front of her and embracing her. Furious at being so easy to read, she burst into tears, beating away at his chest with both fists in a fury as she did so. Tender fingers lifted her chin and he kissed away the tears from each eye before settling gently onto her mouth. She held it tight shut while he teased at her lips with his tongue. Easing it forward through her lips, he found her teeth clenched. They opened with abrupt voracity to allow out a little moan and he slipped his tongue further inside, caressing hers as he did so and rubbing her back with slow, sensual strokes. Her body melted into his for a moment, then the teeth closed, trapping his tongue. He opened his eyes and found her glaring at him.

Only for a moment; the teeth relaxed and she kissed him with fierce and unrestrained eagerness, as he swept her off her feet and carried her to the bed.

When the king climaxed, he called her Rose, sending her even further into ecstasy. Both cried after this release, their tears mingling as they trickled down her breast and he held her very tight as they drifted off to sleep.

*

In dawn's early light, they renewed their lovemaking and she held him tight afterwards, not letting him go despite the weight.

"What happens now?" she asked in a small voice.

"I lock you in a small room where I can make love to you three times a day and never let anyone else see you," he replied.

She stroked his hair and inspected him in minute detail, remembering as a little girl sitting in the bed between him and the queen conducting a similar investigation. She giggled.

"Seriously," she said.

"What were you thinking about to make you laugh," he asked, knowing it hadn't been his poor joke.

"I was remembering being in bed with you and Queen Rose and inspecting your ear like this," she said, licking it.

"Ha! I remember that. I spanked you, as I recall. Rosie was angry with me."

"She knew I was in love with you then and enjoyed it when you touched me, whatever you did. She didn't want you encouraging me."

"Well, did I?"

"Oh yes. But stop changing the subject," she said nipping him sharply. "What happens now?"

He grinned at her concern, moved one leg outside of hers and rolled over onto his back, taking her with him.

"What happens now is whatever you want, my love. I could shower you with jewels and clothes and send you home. You can move into the palace and be in my bed every night."

"I don't want jewels and clothes. I am not a harlot. I can't move in here either, I have a life you know."

"Well I don't know. What do you do?" He asked with interest and she hesitated, not willing to tell him about being an actress. After a while she bent down and kissed him on the nose.

"I can't tell you. It's a secret and I will let you know in due course. We are working on something new."

"So what do you want to do? Go and marry Ricky and be Queen of Galicia?"

Susan's face fell. "Oh Ricky, what am I going to do?"

The king didn't speak, not unused to this reaction.

"Don't be jealous, it's not as if you haven't had half the women in the capital. Of course I love Ricky, and I love you too. In different ways. I can't explain it. My heart is big enough for both of you."

Training

Mary looked out of the window as a large coach pulled into the inn yard. A footman came round, placed a stool by the door and handed down a veiled lady, dressed in expensive and beautiful clothes who strode towards the door with purpose. Mary wondered what a lady was doing at the inn, concerned about Kit's philandering.

She walked to open the door, but it was flung open and the lady walked in and ran over to Mary, throwing her arms around her and starting to cry. Confused, Mary patted her back with uncertain hands.

"Oh Mary, it's so awful," said the lady between sobs.

"Susan?" said Mary. "What is going on? Here, sit down and we'll have a cup of tea. We have been very worried about you, no word, no message, not even a sign of Ricky to tell us what is happening. I sent Harry to find out but he hasn't come back."

She sat Susan down and called for the kitchen girl to make them some tea. Will appeared from nowhere, followed by Ben and they sat around the table. Susan took Mary's hand in a death grip and looked down at the table.

"The king was at the dinner," she spoke in a low tone, barely audible. "He remembered me and insisted on dancing with me, especially Lavolta."

"Oh my," said Ben. "You danced Lavolta with the king."

"Yes, twice."

"Twice," said Mary. "You certainly caught his attention then. And so he sent for you that night and Ricky couldn't refuse."

"Couldn't refuse? He damn well exchanged me for the right to go on the Spring Campaign when he was supposed to stay behind." Susan burst into a fresh flood of tears. "You mean that if I hadn't danced the Lavolta with him, he wouldn't have wanted me and Ricky would still be in training?"

"Well," said Mary, "I wouldn't quite say that. It is very difficult to refuse the king anything. Have you spoken to Ricky?"

"He's already gone. I asked at the Regimental Lines." It was plain from the woebegone look on her face that Susan blamed herself.

"Here, drink your tea," said Mary. She kicked Will under the table, where he was busy writing as he drank in the scene. Fortunately, Susan was oblivious. "Sweetheart, there is nothing you can do about it. Royalty don't live like us, and you are now elevated into their ranks, first with Ricky, yes, I know who he really is, and secondly with the king. You have a fast learning curve, my girl, and my word you are going to need it. Still, if it all goes wrong, you will always have a place with us."

Before she could stop him, Will leant forward. "Make sure you come and tell us all about life in the palaces. I will write a new play about a king, you must make sure I get it right."

This broke through Susan's thought pattern, which were on a roundabout of guilt and pity, causing a wan smile to appear. She giggled, leant forward and embraced him. "Oh Will, please don't change. You are so concerned with how other people are feeling that you forget to have any yourself."

*

The king moved apace to secure his new mistress. He decreed she was betrothed to Viscount Richard of Galicia and as his cousin he could not permit her to live outside the Palace, so he adopted her as his ward, moving her into a suite of rooms next to his, nice and convenient. Ricky and his friends were despatched to the frontier for intensive training in the cold prior to the campaign.

Susan received a formal letter from Lady Sol welcoming her to the family, and a friendly one from Alice telling her that the situation was understood and not to worry. This was a relief, for Susan was feeling rather overwhelmed. She went to the inn every day to work with the playwrights, having confessed to the king that she was involved in writing plays. He was delighted, helped and encouraged her.

One morning in her second week, Susan prepared to call for her carriage to go to the inn, when a footman appeared to announce a guest waiting for her in her reception room, the Galician Sitting Room. Susan inspected the guest through a spyhole concealed by a tapestry. She saw a large, blowsy woman, with an elaborate hair do and several strings of pearls. She sighed. The king had warned her of this lady's political acumen and influence.

"Lady Durrant, so kind of you to call," said Susan walking into the room, and pulling the curtains wider to let in more sunlight, knowing it made her skin more translucent. She tried to put a vacuous expression on her face, but saw the calculation flit across Lady Durrant's and knew she wasn't fooled for a moment.

"Please call me Caroline, dear," Lady Durrant replied. "I was just passing and thought I would drop by." Susan remembered the king saying she lived the other side of town, at least an hour away. "What a charming room."

"Thank you, I do like it. I wanted a less formal room where I could take tea with my friends. I can't stand the wood panels and heavy leather chairs the men adore."

"It's lovely," said Lady Durrant as she took in the large windows with cloth hanging beside them, obscuring the wooden shutters. "So comfortable," she raised her eyebrows as she sat gingerly on the proffered chair, seemingly too light to hold her substantial weight.

"I am experimenting and had the harness maker create this yesterday. It is based on a side saddle. I am calling this room my sitting room."

Lady Durrant was quiet for a moment, as she absorbed this information. She admired the understated elegance and wondered at this slip of a girl who had created this in little more than a week. Susan herself wore a light frock of grey wool, with a linen undershirt, belted with a simple, light gold chain. Her face glowed, and Lady Durrant couldn't tell if this was natural or artifice. Susan waited with a slight smile on her face.

Lady Durrant repressed a small shudder, her acute political antennae quivering. This girl was dangerous and needed to be brought into the fold. What a weapon she would be, ensconced so close to the King. She ruminated a little longer, unconcerned by the silence and to see if Susan would fill the void. She didn't.

"You have done wonders, child, in such a short space."

"I was honoured to have a great teacher, the very best," replied Susan.

"Indeed you did. So sad she was taken from us so young." Aha! Lady Durrant noted the miniscule narrowing of the eyes and filed away the sore point for future use. "All the more credit to you for learning so much, so young and remembering it."

Susan inclined her head and waited.

Lady Durrant changed her tactics. This was no country maid. She would be frank. Well, to an extent.

"Susan, it will be difficult for you at court." The changed tone captured Susan's attention. "You will need friends and you will be expected to take sides, as well you know. I am sure you are well briefed, so you know that the two main factions are mine and Lady Belvedere's. Oh, there are others to be sure, every family wants the best for themselves. As a Galician, you are independent. There are Galician families allied with both sides." This was partly true, but the strong ones were all with Lady Belvedere who was conservative religious which appealed to the Galicians. "While Lady Belvedere may appear a natural home for you, the reality is that she will be your ally on the surface, as Prince Richard's betrothed, while underneath she will scheme against you as she opposes mistresses."

Susan hadn't really considered taking sides, and her eyes narrowed as she looked at Lady Durrant without speaking.

"Accept her overtures, and feel free to deride me in public. In reality I will be your strong friend and give you advice in private. In truth, as long as you have the king's favour you are secure as nobody can touch you. But one day his eye will stray elsewhere and you must prepare for that day. Your future is not guaranteed until you are actually married to Prince Richard and you will see numerous obstacles to that."

"What sort of favours will you want from me?"

Lady Durrant laughed, delighted. "I want you to tell me what is happening, and to keep me informed as to who is likely to get certain positions. I will provide you with information in return, some of which may be useful in helping people to gain positions."

"How do I know that when the day comes that I am put aside, you will support me and not discard me like everybody else?"

"Land, dear child, land. The one commodity nobody can take away from you." Lady Durrant sat back and regarded Susan. She realised that this conversation was accelerating beyond expectations, but decided to strike now. "I shall present you with a small farm in Fearaigh that provides a respectable income as a token of my goodwill. It is far enough away that the transaction will not be noticed."

"Don't put my name on it. Just provide me with blank papers, please," said Susan, accepting the pact.

*

As Susan watched Lady Durrant from the window, climbing into her carriage and wheeling down the drive, her heart clenched around a massive, Ricky-sized hole. Fat tears dribbled down her cheeks and she wondered at this cold woman she seemed to be becoming, who was able to negotiate with the likes of Lady Durrant.

A hand rested on her shoulder, while another hand carefully wiped away her tears with a small cotton cloth.

"Bless you, Abigail," she whispered to her new maid. Her eyes narrowed as a thought passed through her mind. "Who pays you, I wonder, Lady Durrant or Lady Belvedere?"

Abigail smiled, not at all offended or fazed by the question. "They are too stupid to think that maids and servants might have ears. Count Rotherstone is the only one smart enough, but he only has a few of the men in his pay."

Susan let Abigail lead her to her dresser while this information percolated through her brain. As the still unfamiliar hair brushing began, she began to voice some of the questions.

"Count Rotherstone. I don't know much about him. Don't think I have ever met him."

"You won't, milady. He doesn't come to court. A God-botherer, that's what he is. He don't approve of all the goings-on here."

"So why does he have men in his pay, if he isn't interested in court and position?"

"I dunno, milady, but I could find out easy enough. Ol' Jenkins fancies me, he does. He'll tell me what you want to know."

"Good, do so please, Abigail."

Abigail was silent for a moment as she tugged the brush through a thick curl. "Of course I will need to look pretty to get his attention." Susan looked at her in the large mirror. Abigail was not meeting her eyes. Comprehension dawned and Susan smiled.

"I think you have just answered my other question, Abigail. I wondered why you brought the subject up. I will give you a crown for a new dress and you may borrow my special waxes for make-up."

"Thanks, milady." Abigail grinned her happiness and worked away at the blonde tresses.

"Are you friends with any maids in any other houses?" Susan smiled as she asked the question.

"Sure, my best friend Rona is the Abigail of Lady Sarl. She's a goer, she is! Tales I can tell."

"The Abigail? I thought that was your name?"

"Nah, I'm Treste, but all the rich folk call maids Abigail, then you don't have to remember our names. Don't worry about it, miss, you weren't to know." She smiled at Susan who had coloured. "We know your story, tailor's daughter and the prince who ruined you." She squeezed Susan's shoulder and went back to work. "Still, it's worked out pretty good for you in the end, hasn't it? In the stories you always wanted to be queen. I reckon you are in all but name, and the way the king looks at you, it won't be long."

Susan was speechless. Treste continued to brush her hair, a little smile on her face.

"Stories? People talk about me?"

"Oh yeah. Every pub you go into, there's a minstrel singing the tale of the Tailor's Daughter. Every one different and I'll wager everyone wrong." Treste leant forward slightly and whispered in Susan's ear. "Did you really sleep with six pathfinders to get them to kill the prince?"

"I certainly did nothing of the kind!"

"Thought not. That's only one story, mind, and most prefer the one of your innocence being ruined and the Old Gods being angry and taking revenge. You've caused quite a lot of folk to go back to the old ways, the church ain't happy with you."

"I had no idea," Susan whispered.

Treste watched her in the mirror. Susan realised she was a bit older than she thought. "You're a good mistress, and I want you to keep me. So here's some words you should think about. You have a lot of enemies, girl, who want you gone. Of course it is all the other girls and their mums who want to replace you in the king's bed, but the Church don't like you and neither do the Duchies."

"Why not?" Susan's eyes were big and luminous as she watched

Treste work her magic on her hair.

"Church don't like mistresses and because you don't go to church they think you are pushing the king towards the Old Gods. The Duchies don't like you because you like the Pathfinders so you will persuade the king to station Pathfinders in all their Duchies. Anyone who has influence doesn't like you because you have more influence than they do."

"Doesn't anyone like me?" Susan felt the tears brim again.

"Sure do! The common people love you, they love your story and talk about you a lot. Say, there is one story about you from a couple of months ago, pretending to be a kidnapped Galician Lady and then saying there was a play. They say you were a better actor than the man. Is that true?"

"Really? Well, I may have helped a bit... Do they really talk about it? Did it help the play?"

"Yup. You got loads of people coming to the play." Treste continued to talk as she moved on from Susan's hair to her face, while Susan thought deep and broached a new subject.

"Treste, do you think it would be helpful if I knew what the other houses were saying about me? Including Count Rotherstone?"

"Sure would. Would help you to do the right thing."

"Would you be able to get your friends to tell you?

Treste stopped working, the ceiling developing an intense fascination for her. "I can try. Might cost a bit of money."

*

Susan appraised Lady Sarl as Lady Belvedere introduced them. She appeared a year or two older than Susan, a curvaceous redhead with a creamy complexion and a wicked grin. She took Susan's arm in hers and smiled as she wheeled Susan away.

"Thanks Lady B, I'll take her now. Us young girls have our secrets, you know. Susan, you call me Irina. We need to be friends, we are the only young ladies at court."

Susan couldn't help but smile. She knew a great deal about Irina, thanks to Rona. She was married to the Duke of Sarl, more than twice her age. She spent most of her time partying in Praesidium rather than in the family seat and although she gave the appearance of the perfect wife, Rona smuggled a young carpenter from the town estate to her bedroom on regular occasions.

Irina kept up a constant stream of chatter, and Susan really found herself liking the girl.

"Go away, Grahame," she said to one young man who approached them. "Girl talk time." Once he was out of earshot, she continued. "He's a bit of a pest, but harmless, just trying his luck. Be more careful of the older men, in their thirties and forties. Think they are still adorable and tired of their wives. With a bit of luck, you will take some of the pressure off me, as they try and get into your pants. They never stop, I can tell you."

"Uh, I don't think that is happening," said Susan, who was aware that she was pretty but had no idea how beautiful and desirable she appeared to men, certainly nothing to compare with this red-haired goddess.

"Probably because they know the king has his arm round you. Dangerous to get in the way, not only is he quick to pull a sword but can send them to the frontier if he feels like it. Now, I've heard about your waxes and they look fabulous on you. You simply must share some with me. I have this seamstress who is just to die for, she knows just how to fit me and gets me the perfect colours. Do come round tomorrow when she is visiting and she can take your measurements."

*

Two weeks later the girls were fast friends, meeting most days. Irina replaced Susan's acting friends as her confidantes, for she found it more and more difficult to spend time with them. They were eating a light lunch in Susan's sitting room when a footman delivered a message to Susan. She scanned it and squealed with delight, getting Irina's attention.

"Oh, that darling General Roberts! He has come through!"

"General Roberts? The Pathfinder? What's he done? Getting Ricky sent back for the Spring Holiday, so you can get twice the rumply tingly dreamy time?"

"Irina! You are so bad. No, he's fixed a time for me with the Pathfinder Master-at-Arms. Tomorrow morning, early."

"The Master-at-Arms? What an earth for?"

"I'm getting sword training. I asked especially the night I met the king."

"Why in the world would you want to learn how to use a sword? You can get lots of young men who can do that for you."

"I just want to; I don't want to always rely on men for protection. I think it could be useful. And I want to know why they spend so much time doing it."

"Well, my girl, I think you are crazy but no way am I letting you go to the Pathfinder barracks on your own. I'm coming with you."

"You want to learn to use a sword as well?" Susan smiled.

"No way in the world. But those Pathfinders are so dreamy and you can never get near them, so it will be just you, me and about two hundred of the most perfect men in the country."

*

She screamed once, twice and again.

The blood covered her, little spatters all over her front as the man writhed, blood spurting from his mouth in a cloud every time he managed to take a breath for another hoarse scream of agony, the sword sticking high and proud from his back. One arm stretched out towards her, scrabbling at her feet, and she inched back.

"Well I hope you are satisfied now," said Lucinda, in tones of immense disapproval. "I told you this was a stupid place to sit. We are supposed to be incognito, but no, you had to have the most expensive seats in the house."

"Oh, but it is so worth it," said Marcia, a perfumed handkerchief dabbing ineffectual smears over a face wreathed in smiles. "I wasn't expecting him to die quite so quickly. Oh, my heart." She placed a hand over her massive palpitating bosom. Marcia Henderson's frame could generously be called large, and she added to the padding with a considerable, if discerning, appetite.

The actor, Ben, grinned at them as he started to roll away, stopping to pocket the coin Marcia threw him. They watched him slip off to the side and begin changing into new clothes for his next role, while Will declaimed his triumph at the front of the stage.

"We must go backstage afterwards," said Marcia, her eyes checking everywhere. "I do so want to see that delightful little Sam Delarosa, so handsome."

"You're a dirty old woman," said Lucinda. "He's barely fifteen, you should be ashamed of yourself."

"My motives are pure," said Marcia.

"In a pig's eye," said Lucinda. In her late twenties, the Countess of Westport bore a startling resemblance to her favourite animals, compounded by a tendency to neigh with laughter. The two ladies, up from Westport with their husbands, adored the theatre and currently occupied the best seats, up on the stage at the rear where the occasional hazel nut thrown from the pit could still reach.

They followed the play with intensity, only broken by Marcia peering into the wings, checking to see if Sam would appear. They applauded long and loud at the finale, before following the actors to the dressing rooms off to the side of the stage. Marcia engulfed Will in a bear hug, causing him to slop his ale.

"You were magnificent as ever, my darling," she said, eyes searching the room and landing on Mary. She released Will, who chugged his beer in haste before he lost any more, and advanced on Mary. "Darlings, a little token of my appreciation," she said, pressing a small purse into Mary's hand. "Now, what have you done with that delightful little boy, Sam? I was so anticipating seeing him again, and I am desolate at his absence."

Mary threw a glance at Will, who followed her, his eyes intent on taking in every mannerism for later repetition.

"Sam has moved on, my lady," said Mary, careful to keep any disapproval out of her voice.

"Oh no," said Marcia. "A tragedy! I have followed his career with interest, such a talent. I cannot believe you have let him go before he could flower into his true magnificence. Why, in time I believe he would have attained Will's starry heights."

"Nonsense," said Kit, giving a surprised Marcia a hug. "He overtook Will ages ago, but it will be at least a year before he gets near me." He bussed her on the cheek and released her, stepping back just out of reach as she restrained an automatic slap. "Come for the party, have we darling?"

Lucinda glided forward as her cousin struggled with the apparent joy of impropriety and desire to party with this raffish young actor, combating her awareness of scandal potential.

"Thank you, my good man, but we merely wish to convey our appreciation for your performance. In the play." She glared at an offending hand resting on Marcia's hip. "So where is young Sam now?"

Kit grinned and slipped his arm round Marcia who simpered in appreciation at this unusual attention. "Sam? Oh she's doing well for, ah, himself. Don't see much of him now. Now, can I get you lovely ladies something to drink? What is your name, my beauty?"

"Thank you, no, we must be going," said Lucinda, grabbing Marcia's hand and manhandling her out the door and forestalling her requests for gin.

The actors grinned and moved to a window where they could hear the conversation.

"Oh, Lucy, why do we have to go? He LIKED me."

"He's an actor, you never know what he really thinks or feels, but you can bet it was going to be expensive. I declare, I don't know what I would have done with you if you had managed to drink some of their gin."

"I know what I would have done with him," muttered Marcia as they moved out of range.

Mary closed the shutters and turned to the grinning actors. "Kit, you're an idiot. Well done on getting rid of her, and recovering from nearly letting the cat out of the bag. Why you had to let its head out in the first place, I have no idea."

"Too busy trying to work out what I was fondling," said Kit, eyeing Will who scribbled in a note book. "Who were they anyway? And why do they want to know about Susan?"

"Duchess of Westport and her cousin," said Mary, considering her gin. "Church spies, maybe? Digging for mud to ruin her? This is the first time anybody has tracked her back here."

"They're from the south, Fearaigh, so they won't be church. Too free with their money, besides," said Ben, biting a coin and winking.

"They're just court ladies looking for a different time," said Will, coming out of his notebook and refilling his ale. "They just remember her from last time, think she's a boy. Any word from Sue? Is she ok?"

"Not really" said Mary. "It would be nice to see more of her, but she's getting new friends now."

"People seem to like her," said Kit. "Everyone is talking about her in the inns and markets. She's getting right popular just for being pretty."

"Nice to hear of a girl doing well for herself, that's why. She's a breath of fresh air, no airs and graces."

*

The Master-at-Arms was not quite what Irina had in mind, with a dreadful scar where his right ear once lived and his eyes weren't quite level. It was not clear how many times his nose had been broken or what it had once looked like. Also, he didn't like girls.

"Let go of my arm, lady," he said, coming to an abrupt halt as Irina did her best to ingratiate herself, holding tight to his arm in order to negotiate a light patch of mud as they made their way to the exercise ground from the gate. Irina moued at him as he shook his arm and glared at her, totally ignoring her low cut dress and obvious charms. "You cannot swing a sword dressed like that."

"I wouldn't dream of it, dahling," she cooed. "I just came along to keep an eye on Miss Hrunna here." The Master-at-Arms raised his eyes to the heavens and stomped off. Hrunna was the ancient goddess of the hunt, renowned for giving the bow to the people of Fearaigh. The new religion had made her a saint and changed the story out of all recognition, but she was still martial.

"Riggs," bellowed the Master-at-Arms as he pushed open a door in a wooden wall, to reveal a small arena, sanded, with small workshops around the side. Irina's smile widened as Riggs came running up, a brawny young soldier with massive shoulders. "Show Miss Lah-de-dah here where she can watch the show in safety." He whirled on Susan with such languid speed that she sucked in a breath. "Now you. Give me your hand."

He grunted as he looked at it with disgust. "No chance of you holding a proper sword. Riggs! Bring me a rapier, training blade, and a glove, small. You will wear a glove until your hand toughens up. Try and hold a sword without it and the leather of the handle will tear your hand. Too soft. We make the leather of the swords from the skin of a big fish, it's rough and sharp, ideal to stop it turning in your hand but tough on officer cadets."

Susan said nothing as she pulled on the glove, beautiful and soft like a second skin. Her eyes widened. She had never felt anything so fine and wondered that these soldiers should have such fantastic gloves for training, before realising a moment later that these were the perfect tool. She grasped the sword in clumsy hands, shocked by the weight, and tried to stand the way she had seen the officers back in Galicia.

"No," grunted the Master-at-Arms. She didn't know his name, he still hadn't offered it and hadn't asked for hers. "I want you side on, balanced, with the weight centred over your right leg. Yes, that's good. Don't worry about the blade now, let's get your legs moving. It's like dancing, I'm sure you've spent plenty of time doing that. Now, I want a rhythm from you, so imagine there is music playing and dance for me."

To her astonishment, Susan found herself moving with lithe and elegant poise around the arena, the sword seeming a perfect extension to her body. The stamping attack came naturally and she revelled in it. He kept her going through various paces for a good ten minutes, till she was dripping with sweat.

"Right girl, take a break, get yourself a drink over there," he nodded to the horse trough. Susan walked over and dunked her head under the water, letting it cascade down her shirt as she stood up, revelling in the coolness. Her hair was tied back and down her back, out of the way. Scooping up some water with her hands, she drank deeply and came back. She was oblivious to the way the water stuck her sweaty blouse to her body, or the way her tight trousers enhanced her legs, and concentrated on the sword, not noticing the onlookers gathering.

"Right, sir," said the Master-at-Arms, deciding the best way out of his dilemma was to treat her as a young man. "Now you will cross swords with me. Don't worry, I have a wooden blade. Yours is good steel so you become accustomed to the weight. How's your arm? Tired? It will get worse but you are holding up well.

"We will start with defence. There are eight basic positions, four sets of two. I will show them to you and expect you to copy me as I go through them. Will go slow. In a fight, you will hardly ever get to use the top and bottom sets, just the middle ones. Most heathens have no defence and no answer for a scientific approach like this. They can't get through. Spakka a different matter with their axes, never go up against one with a sword. Same thing for Uightlanders and their spears."

He kept up a constant stream of education as he ran her through the basic defences, then showed her how they kept out the different lunges and slashes. Susan was exhausted but fascinated and delighting in the swordplay. She was a natural! She could feel it. In just an afternoon she had grasped the essence of swordplay and felt ready to take on the world. She wondered if she would be able to keep the rapier and the glove; she could just see herself wearing them to the next dance. She would have a dress specially made to allow her to dance wearing a sword. She would be a sensation.

"Sergeant Craig," came an authoritative voice and a whipcord thin man with greying hair stalked into the arena. "Why are you teaching this girl sword play?"

The Master-at-Arms snapped to attention and Susan stopped her hack at his side. "Orders, sir. General Roberts said to teach her."

"Well, you are a fool, man. Can't you see she cannot possibly develop the skill to use a rapier effectively? Look at her wrist, no muscle, no chance of becoming a blademaster. This isn't a game for this young woman, she has enemies and you pretending to train her will help her not at all. Dismissed. I will take over."

Susan gaped at him in shock, recognising him. She was pretty sure she had danced with him, but couldn't remember his name for the life of her. Oh yes, Colonel Donnell. She bit her lip hard to stop the tears, welling up in rebellion at being told she couldn't make a blademaster.

"Susan, you have some limited natural ability with a sword," he said, a note of kindness in his voice. "Enough to see off a footpad, but not sufficient for the trouble you will have coming."

"What trouble?" Susan whispered, her tears drying up.

"You have, through no fault of your own, risen to a position of influence in this country, considerable influence. You have already earned the dislike of two of the major political factions in the country and they will move against you, sooner or later. Not necessarily with violence, indeed they will no doubt send suitors first, followed by potions. But at some stage you will be offered violence. I am sure of this."

Susan stared at this strange man, so straight and confident, with his clipped accent and disturbing words. The audience had evaporated on his arrival. No sign of Irina either.

"Fortunately, you do have some allies, for the Pathfinders have adopted you, almost to a man." He glared at the departing back of the unfortunate Craig. "We are not a political faction that takes sides, but we consider you one of our own. So I am delighted that you have given us this opportunity to train you. Not just with weapons but that will be the excuse. Sergeant Craig will meet you each morning, and put you through some paces. We will need to develop some callouses on your sword hand, after all. Then I shall take over."

He evaluated her build and stance, before stalking to a rack and pulling out two poles, turning and throwing one at her in the fluid motion all these Pathfinders seemed to perfect. She caught it one handed without thinking.

"Good! I thought this would suit you. This is a quarterstaff, and in the hands of an expert it will defeat all but the very best blademasters. In fact, it is the most lethal close quarter weapon we have, one that few are even aware exists. You can carry one in plain sight and footpads will come running up to you for dispatch. I watched your movement earlier, and if ever a weapon was made for you, it is this one. See, with no instruction, you are holding it in the correct, most lethal manner."

Susan held the staff parallel across her body with both hands. Without thinking, she twisted it to deflect his darting, unheralded attack, her feet dancing across the sand to allow the stick to riposte at him, which he managed to divert at the last moment.

"In fact, I have used one before. I love them, hadn't realised they were considered a proper weapon." She was feeling good, all of a sudden, and liking this little man, feeling his empathy and concern.

"Well it most certainly is, and we shall make you a master in no time. Quarterstaff training will follow sword training each day and then I shall instruct you in my own skill." His eyes twinkled at her unasked question. "I am the king's chief political advisor, his spymaster if you will. You, my girl, are a tool that I shall forge into a perfect weapon."

"You assume a lot," Susan said, wary and resentful as her mood changed with his words.

"Indeed I do," he agreed with her in an infuriating manner. "I conceived some plans for recruiting you and this training is perfect synchronicity. Except I was away in Galicia, checking up on your background amongst other things. Your father did not retain the army contract, and his business continues much as it was. He has remarried, a woman who was once a prostitute, a Madam Heather. She is not a pleasant person. They clothe most of the night-walkers now."

Susan's eyes glittered. She hadn't realised how much she hated her father.

"Do you wish revenge on him?"

Susan considered this offer with care, wary of a trap. She took the impression that a word from her would condemn her father but didn't think it was that simple.

"The dish is cold," she said. "It will keep and at the right moment I shall know if I wish to do anything or if I have moved on far enough to be content for his own fate to en-wrap him. It sounds as if he is going in the right direction."

"Did you know he was not your father?" Colonel Donnell gave no evidence as to whether she had passed a test or not, but she was sure it had been one. Susan grunted as she only just evaded a jab and slid her staff along his to bloody his knuckles. She smiled at his smothered curse, which made him smile back.

"I suspected. Do you know who is?"

"It is common for aristocracy to marry off their pregnant mistresses to artisans and merchants. It is even possible that you are related to the king. I can certainly produce evidence that you are a missing princess of Galicia, should we deem that worthwhile."

Susan considered this, twirling and dancing with the staff, moving with unconscious precision as she thought this through. Colonel Donnell watched her, waiting to see her conclusions.

"You're planning to make me queen," she said in wonder.

"It is possible," he inclined his head a fraction, then pulled out of reach of the smacking end of her staff. "You are the first girl we have found capable of the position. The country demands a male heir and doesn't care who provides it. The king wants a woman who keeps his attention."

"What about the princess?"

"The country will never accept her as queen. She is brilliant and would make a fine ruler, perhaps the best we have ever had.

Fearaigh would take her, but everywhere else is too hidebound by custom and religion. It is also unlikely she will survive."

"What!" All Susan's maternal protective instincts came to the fore in a rush of blows that the colonel did well to stave off. "You are not planning to assassinate her?"

"Stop," said Colonel Donnell, stepping back and lowering his staff. "You will need a better hand than myself with the staff. I will have one for you tomorrow. No, the princess is too independent and she takes too many risks. We are trying to train her and get it out of her, but Rotherstone will always watch and have his vultures waiting. We cannot protect her from her own nature."

Susan walked over and racked her staff, turning once more to the water trough and again dousing her head. Shaking it dry, she turned and spoke again.

"I want regular reports on her progress and what she is up to. Make sure she has reliable friends. How am I going to manage coming here every day? I already have Lady Sarl as a constant companion, and she reports to Lady Belvedere."

Colonel Donnell grinned at the order, liking the way she responded to his explanations and questions, growing before his eyes. "We are well aware of Lady Sarl's, ah, predilections. She will be sure to want to come with you on every occasion and will spend not a moment of the hours here with you. You will notice she will question you on the way back, to create the report she will make to Lady Belvedere and the parliamentarians. "

Susan was confused for the first time. "Predilections? What's she up to? Has she not been watching? Where has she got to? Oh, I hope she is okay and hasn't got into trouble. I am sorry, I couldn't leave her behind."

The colonel coloured. "She is being... entertained. Corporal Riggs is trained as a companion."

Susan wasn't sure she understood what the colonel meant, and the ache in her arms and legs distracted her. "Colonel, I am not sure that coming every day is a good idea. My legs and arms are killing me, I need a day of rest between exercises and two rest days at the end of the week."

The colonel frowned. "That may be better for your exercise and weapons training, but we don't have much time and you have a great deal to learn."

"I don't care. I am not even sure I want to be queen any more, it's a lot more trouble than I ever thought. Three mornings a week and that's final."

"Very well. Susan, you are a special person, more than you know. I am impressed with your abilities. We will make something special of you, that I promise. Now, I think it is time to return – here comes Corporal Riggs with Lady Sarl."

Susan turned to see Irina coming through a door while holding on to Riggs' arm. A half smile across her face, she walked with care, taking short steps. She rolled her head from side to side, stretching her neck before catching Susan's eye. She smiled.

"Are you finished, darling? Eeew, you are all wet! Your shirt is just sticking to you, even your trousers are wet and is that dirt on your knee?"

Susan laughed. "I've been training, Irina."

"Well, there is no need to get into this sort of state. We must get you presentable before anybody sees you. Did you bring any spare clothes? I need a hairbrush. Don, please bring me some warm water – make sure it is a silver bowl, now."

"Don't bother, Corporal Riggs," said Susan. "Come, Irina, I have finished so we shall take the coach and I shall bathe when I get home."

Irina muttered, but was distracted as she staggered to be caught by Riggs. Susan pretended not to notice her careful walk and led the way to the carriage. She climbed up first and sat down as Riggs handed Irina up the step. She held onto his hand as she manoeuvred her dress through before pulling his head into the dark interior where she kissed him passionately.

"You are a veritable stallion, darling," she whispered, "and I cannot wait to be in your arms again."

Riggs smiled, and ran his hand up her dress and along a leg. "Till next time, love."

He closed the door and thumped the side to send the driver away.

Susan arched an eyebrow at Irina who smirked in pleasure. "He was wonderful, darling. I can't wait to see him again. His body is magnificent, so tight and hard. And his stamina! I thought he would never stop; he couldn't get enough of me. Oh, I'm sorry darling, I hope yours was as much fun? Who did you get?"

"Who did I get? The Master-at-Arms."

"He was awful, so rude and smelly. And his eyes," she shivered with disdain. "Did you have a number of soldiers from which to make a selection?"

"Irina, I have truly been learning to use a sword. A rapier, no less. See, I have kept this beautiful glove, so soft, to protect my hand. I am going to have a dress made that allows me to wear a rapier."

Irina regarded her in horror. "You actually did it. I don't believe it. I so thought you wanted to play with the men." A thought crossed her mind and her eyes widened further, her hand covering her mouth. For the first time, a look of steel came into her eyes and her brow creased, while her voice lost the playful affectation. "I thought we were the same, girls who love men. Sorry if I break your illusions."

"I have no illusions, darling. I knew what you are and I still love you. I am not shocked at all." She leaned across the seat and hugged Irina, who sat stiff for a moment before returning the hug. Susan gave a secret smile, delighted to see the real Irina surface.

Irina broke off, fiddled in her bag before speaking while keeping her face averted. "I'm married to an old man, Susan. He might have lots of money, but for the last year he hasn't touched me. Not that he ever did, much. Thought he was interested in boys at first. I was so lonely, so desperate to feel a man wanting me. I felt trapped in his great house with nobody to talk to. I married him on my sixteenth birthday. I thought I was successful; all my friends were jealous as I became the great lady of Sarl."

A tear crept unnoticed from the corner of her eye, tracking slowly down a cheek shorn of its usual powder. Her eyes were faraway. Susan moved not a muscle, fascinated to see where this would go and not wanting to break the spell.

"For two years I was a good girl, but he barely touched me. It didn't hurt, but it wasn't nice, he smelt of old sweaty clothes and I didn't know what I was missing. On my eighteenth birthday he threw a party for me. I didn't know or like most of the people, it was awful. But I knew how to be a good hostess and I knew the party wasn't for me, but to show off his power and ability to marry the prettiest girl in Sarl. I danced with all the old men till my feet hurt.

One by one, they went home leaving a handful of younger people, the sons and daughters. I didn't need to be the hostess anymore and allowed myself some wine at last."

Irina's voice changed and warmth crept through the ice, a slight smile spreading over her face. "I watched them flirting, kissing, and saw the boys' hands roam. I wondered what it would be like to feel those hands but I knew I couldn't. I had no friends. I saw them out, and turned back to the wine when the door closed on the last of them. Holding out my full glass was the son of one of our Barons. The only person left, he must have hidden when the others went. He didn't say a word as I took the glass and drained it. The orchestra was long gone, just a few candles guttering. The servants were to clear up in the morning. He took the empty glass, set it down and swept me into a dance, a Volt. With no music. He whispered in my ear, said what he wanted."

Irina turned back to face Susan and her usual great smile broke out. "Well, it was my birthday! We continued our secret affair till he went off to his seat when his father died, and he had to get married. Nobody knew, we were so careful. Sarl is a small place, I couldn't do anything there but I needed a man. Men. So I came to the capital." Her eyes narrowed. "Lady Belvedere introduced me to a handsome young man. The next day she came round and told me I had slept with a carpenter, a common carpenter, and the whole world would know."

"The conniving bitch," said Susan. To the Galicians, calling a woman a bitch meant a great deal more than a female dog. A scheming harlot and worse. "So she set you on me, to make a mistake and trap me as well."

"I'm sorry," she whispered. "Please drop me home. I understand you don't want to see me again."

"Nonsense, darling," said Susan dragging the older girl into a hug. "You are mine now, and we will plot your revenge on Lady Bitch. Oh, you are going to be so useful to me!"

"What?" Susan asked at the expression on Irina's face. "You think you have to be an old lady before you can do politics? Now, let's concoct the story you are going to tell her about today."

Spiders

Susan burst into the office trailing water and spun into her seat opposite Colonel Donnell, suppressing a little song.

"You are full of yourself this morning. What mischief have you been making?" Colonel Donnell regarded her with a suspicious eye.

"I've started my very own network," Susan announced with all the satisfaction of a cat discovering an unguarded cream jug in the pantry.

"A network," said the colonel.

"Yes! I now know what is happening in Lady Sarl's house, and I am working on Count Rotherstone." She sat back, a smug expression on her face, waiting for the accolades.

"Indeed," said the colonel, adjusting some papers on his desk. "And just how, pray, are you party to these wondrous secrets?"

"I recruited my maid, who is gathering information for me," said Susan, revelling in her cleverness. "She has a friend in Lady Sarl's employ, and Count Rotherstone's man in my household has the hots for her. She is going to recruit more servants for me, she says nobody thinks about the servants and talk openly in front of them."

"'Hots for her'," said the colonel with a peculiar expression on his face. "What a particular inelegant expression, one I do not believe I have ever had the privilege to hear from a lady at court."

Susan glared at this flagrant avoidance of her due congratulations and the colonel sighed.

"The first thing that anyone thinks about is placing a servant in somebody else's employ. The second thing is that sensible people start to take great care what they say in front of everybody, never mind servants, but in particular lovers. One of the best ways to confuse the enemy is to have a lover plant false information. The court is riddled with servants, every single one of whom is in the employ of at least one person, not a few are employed by a dozen lords and ladies, each of whom thinks they are paying for unique information. Why, I believe the major part of the Chamberlain's income comes from servants paying for their positions."

Silence welled through the room. The colonel gave the girl time, going through his papers and in due course a small voice came from across the table.

"Who employs my Abigail?"

"Your task for the week – find out. Tell me next time. Dig a little, scratch under the surface, don't be direct, use oblique words and listen, listen all the time, especially when you are not expected. No individual fact is to be treated as correct. Everything must be correlated with other reports, and we find the possibility of truth when we receive confirmation in a minimum of three separate reports from different sources."

For the next five minutes, the colonel studied reports from various agents before a voice of a different timbre broke the silence.

"You employ her, don't you?" Susan's voice rang with certainty. "Most of the servants, including the Chamberlain are ex-Pathfinders. Trustees. I recognise their movement, their silence. Jenkins is different. Does he not realise he stands out?"

Now the colonel showed his pleasure. "Excellent. Of course he doesn't. Rotherstone thinks he is so clever, but we chaperone him and channel the right information. Never kill a spy, he may be replaced by somebody you don't know."

"The girls aren't Pathfinders. How do you recruit them?"

"Treste, yes I know her real name, is the daughter of my first sergeant. She likes you." The colonel raised a curious eye. "For somebody who I rated as loyal to the crown, she is becoming reticent about you. You inspire loyalty, girl."

"She is asking me for money."

"Is she now. That is interesting. What for?"

"To pay her friends for information. Rona in Lady Sarl's retinue. Some others."

"Where do you plan to get the money for this?"

Now Susan's face broke into a sunny smile and the colonel laughed.

"How much do you need? Fifty crowns enough?"

"For this month, but I will need more soon. By the way, I can't keep calling you Colonel like this. What is your given name?"

"You're in the Army now, girl. You don't call your superior by his given name, just sir or his title."

"If I'm in the army, what is my rank?"

"Hmmn. I guess you are a cornet. Keep up this rate and you'll make major by the end of the year."

"Major, schmajor, I'll outrank you by the Spring. What's my rate of pay?"

*

The black carriage drew up in front of the grey stone house, disgorging a woman in a cape, the hood drawn high in a pointless disguise as the matched bays of Lady Belvedere would be recognised throughout the capital. The doors opened as she approached and she swept past the butler, ignoring him, and made for the study. She knocked on the door, scowling at the delay before a word allowed her entry.

Gloom filled the room, drapes obscuring three quarters of the small windows, casting light across the desk at which an indistinct figure sat, quill scratching as he underlined phrases in the reports he studied.

Lady Belvedere walked slowly past the shelves stocked with a fortune in rare books, all religious texts, and pulled out the bare wooden chair, wincing as her well-padded rear met the stark wood. The long nose stiffened across the desk and she froze, realising the lack of invitation to sit.

With agonising slowness, Count Rotherstone raised his head, the widow's peak catching the light against his pale domed forehead and the grey eyes transfixed her soul. For a long moment he held her eyes, before they fell and she fiddled with her bag. The count enjoyed the fear emanating from the woman and stretched the moment.

"So what brings you to my humble home this day? A desire to reinforce in everybody the knowledge that we commune?"

"I came in disguise. Nobody will know I came."

"Interesting. Of course, they would not recognise your famous horses."

Lady Belvedere found her thoughts running in several directions, and struggled on with her mission.

"The mines are short of operators. We are expanding, increasing production."

"By some strange miracle, for which we can thank the Lord for his gift of paper, reports appraised me of the situation earlier in the month."

Lady Belvedere inspected her shoes. "My factors are forecasting a good harvest, so we need to decide whether to amend the plantings in the Church fields."

"Good Lady Belvedere, please cease your prevarication. These matters do not require our meeting. Why have you really come? Did you wish to pray with me?"

"No!" Too sharp, she tried to bite back the words. "I mean, it is always our pleasure to pray with you, Your Eminence, but I wish to discuss something else."

"The correct title is 'My Lord'. I am a count, not a bishop. And have you received some title of which I am unaware, or brought an invisible person with you, that you refer to yourself in the plural?"

Lady Belvedere shut her eyes and prayed. Her breathing slowed and she centred, finding strength from a deep well in her soul.

"We must discuss Susan Taylor."

"Must? She is important? The king's little entertainment? Ah, perhaps my lady is jealous, has designs on the position herself?"

"My lord, the situation is serious. This is not a moment for levity. The minx is far too clever and her machinations affect the king's judgement, to our detriment."

"No, my lady, the situation is not serious. The child may be clever, she may entertain the king, but she is barely seventeen years of age and has not the experience to affect our purpose. No, let me finish. You fear the girl because she spends time, much time, outside of your view, and you create in your mind scenarios which do not exist. From other sources, I know her behaviour. For some unknown reason, she has persuaded the Pathfinders to teach her to use a staff, and is talented."

He paused and sipped a glass of water, considering the unhappy but determined face in front of him.

"Lady Belvedere, in one matter you are quite correct. The girl is clever, exceptional you could say. The correct course is to befriend her, to lead her into the Church and encourage her to bend this intellect to the devout. This you will do, or have your minions do so. Lady Sarl is entirely unsuitable, given her proclivities. Your error in judgement with this introduction is noted."

She seethed at this reprimand to the great joy of Count Rotherstone. He wished she would surprise him, exhibit disobedience. He could taste her pain, he would enjoy correcting her and leaned forward, eyes agleam and mouth open a fraction. His palpable disappointment at her continued silence tempted him to goad her further.

"Understand me, my lady. I shall speak plain, to ensure your full understanding. If you press the girl, or seek to undermine or indeed supplant her with one of your disgusting protégés from the Seminary, you will create an enemy, an enemy with sufficient intelligence and motivation to have the potential to become a threat."

Lady Belvedere sat still, eyes fixed on the desk, her deep and forced breathing indicating how close she came to losing control. Count Rotherstone smiled.

"Of course, she is indeed intelligent, smart enough to outshine your low animal cunning…" He bit off his words, regretting them in an instant. He frowned at his own behaviour, determining to spend an hour in the correction cell at prayer and in pain to atone for this lapse.

Lady Belvedere's eyes blazed with anger and resentment. She spoke in a sibilant whisper. "Thank you for the lesson, my lord. You are of course quite correct. If you will excuse me, I feel the need to spend some hours in the Cathedral to meditate and allow God to guide my steps in these difficult days."

She rose and left the room, back stiff and knuckles white. An idle thought flitted through the count and he concentrated on the floor, checking for drops of blood, his mouth pursed in disappointment at their lack. Her nails must be short and blunt after all, as the Holy Scripture instructs. He returned his attention to the papers, uncovering the missive from the foreign court and mulling over the possibilities. His thoughts flitted to the girl for a moment, and he shook his head. Irrelevant, the removal of the king made her immaterial. It did not matter what trouble the Belvedere woman dreamed up.

*

Susan pirouetted in front of the mirror, delighted with her

appearance. Her first formal dinner, so exciting. She wore a pale blue dress made from the finest wool from the southern marshes and trimmed with Galician lace. She emphasised her blue eyes with a necklace of sparkling sapphires, gleaming on her throat. Her hair fell in a glorious wavy mass over her shoulders and down to her waist, gleaming with strands of diamonds falling from the tiny tiara and woven into tiny braids of hair.

Her eyes shone, the new experiment with a touch of blue in the dark eye-liner effective, setting off the results of the belladonna in her eyes, making them huge and gleaming. Content with her beauty, she accepted her little bag from Treste and made her way down to join the king. She blinked, deciding never again to use the belladonna. She knew it as a poison, knew how to prepare it and didn't like the idea of using it on her eyes, no matter the fashion.

King Richard awaited her in his study, deep in conversation with Colonel Donnell, who stepped back on her approach. The king's mouth dropped open as he held her at arm's length, evaluating her dress with a delighted eye. She grinned in pleasure, which dimmed as she appreciated Colonel Donnell's expression.

"Don't do it, your majesty," he said. "She has terrific potential and you could throw it all away."

The king smiled down as Susan as he bent to kiss her. "Nonsense. I am simply letting them see how much she is appreciated. How much she means to me."

"What are you two talking about?" Susan asked, whisking some specks from King Richard's shoulders as she inspected his dress with a critical eye.

"Nothing to worry your pretty head," said the king, taking her arm and escorting her from the study. A herald stepped through the doors to the main hall as they arrived, blowing a short fanfare.

"His Majesty, King Richard, Lord of Harrhein," said a flunky in a white wig whom Susan didn't recognise, "and his consort, Lady Susan Taylor of Bresol." Susan missed a step, her breath catching and the room seemed huge, cavernous and still. The king's fingers tightened on her arm and he chuckled.

"I'm your ward," she hissed through part open lips.

"Not anymore," he said, smiling to the people left and right, revelling in their shock and enjoying his moment. All Susan could see were disapproving faces, some glaring at her, and she could feel waves of hate and disgust rolling over her, an endless ocean into which she drowned.

Unable to look at the sneering faces, she concentrated on the far wall, navigating by the king's arm. At last she reached her chair, allowing herself to be seated without awareness of her surroundings, trying to process the moment. How could the king be so insensitive? Silly question, what else could he be in such matters? A grim and effective warrior, brilliant general and astute in his choice of advisors, she realised he either ignored or didn't notice people's thoughts and emotions. She understood Colonel Donnell's disapproval, and a quick return to the present allowed a scan to locate General Roberts' worried face. At least one person who doesn't hate me, she thought.

The first course arrived as the king knocked back two goblets of wine in pleased succession, laughing at his nearby cronies' bawdy jests. With care and precision, Susan built up mental walls around herself, till she felt sufficient protection to peer over the ramparts. Eyes glittered with malevolent intensity behind wide insincere smiles whenever a lady caught her eye. She dropped her sight to her trencher and chewed the sawdust and ashes in front of her. The king, unaware of her torment, embarrassment and dread, pressed a glass into her hand and forced her to gulp a too-large amount of her favourite delicate white wine.

An ember glowed deep inside. How could he do this to her? Resentment fanned the ember which burst into flame. She raised her face and allowed a defiant expression onto her mask, her lips a thin tight line as she studied those present. Adversaries, enemies, one and all, she realised, who would destroy her. Quick and fast now, her time surely numbered.

She sat at the high table, to the left of the king, with jolly old Lord Sol on her left. She realised that he, and his wife, did not join in the mental condemnation of her. He must realise her discomfort in return, for he squeezed her leg beneath the table, in secret support, she understood at once. Grasping a servant's arm, he relieved the man of a plate and which he deposited in front of them, serving a small portion of fish to a fresh platter in front of her while sweeping away the old.

"Have some smoked eel, my dear," he said. "Good Galician eel, delicate and subtle once we remove the fat. Just like us, eh?" He roared with laughter, into which his wife joined, smiling at Susan who managed a small grateful smile back them.

"The depths of depravity to which people will sink never ceases to amaze me." The voice slimed into her consciousness, and she realised it came from the man opposite, not looking at her but speaking down the table to Lady Belvedere. The Bishop of Praesidium, she forgot his name, a fat individual who ate with a mechanical determination, as if it were his ordeal to consume vast quantities of distasteful food, an ordeal which he perforce must suffer at every opportunity.

She knew his words were intended for her and she bridled, realising this was the first salvo in an attack on her. An attack which would lead in inexorable procession to the king's removal. She glanced at the king. He hadn't noticed, deep in conversation with the man to his right, over the mortified front of an ignored lady. General Roberts, on the lower table to the right, allowed his concern to show.

"I visited the church in Cridely on the last Sabbath. As a benevolent gesture to the priests, I like to assist them in the sermons," the bishop continued, while Susan thought of the control and persecution he inflicted. "Do you know, barely ten people sat in the church, not a young person to be seen! No doubt out fornicating and practising witchcraft. I gave the priest a piece of my mind, I can tell you." The bishop warmed to his theme, about to raise the volume as he grasped the king's attention.

Inside Susan, something snapped. The wall banking the internal fires gave way, and the flames poured out, but the cold blue flames of reason rather than the white hot heat of passion.

"Of course not, Bishop," said Susan with a gentle smile, in her best melodic actress voice, pitched to penetrate the entire hall, which fell silent. "Cridely is celebrating a record harvest, a gift from God for their piety and devotion. The people are working in the fields, showing their love and respect for God by accepting his benevolent bounty, not wasting a moment. And just in time, for it was a test from God. He sent the rains the next day, I believe, which would have ruined the harvest." Susan blessed Treste, who had bored her to death that morning with this very story while brushing her hair. "It would have been a terrible thing to waste such a gift, don't you agree

Bishop?" His mouth worked and Susan continued before he could speak, as his mind was still on denouncing illegitimate congress. "I am sure God sent you there to witness their devotion and to punish those who did not accept his largesse."

A small part in one of Will's plays as an angel now served Susan well, her eyes wide and innocent, full of piety and love for God with her lower lip trembling as she spoke of God's gift. The bishop's mouth moved again, no sound emerging and it was not clear whether he was masticating or trying to speak. The entire room held their breath, captivated by the drama, all knowing it to be an attack on Susan by the bishop but most believing Susan's innocent charade, entrenched opinions being revised at pace.

The bishop's eyes glittered with malice and anger at this slip of a girl having the gall to correct him. He prepared to blast her with the wrath of God, the true God, not this smarmy, supplicating balderdash she espoused, but a God to inspire terror in the unbeliever. He opened his mouth and the king cut across him, much to Susan's surprise.

"Witchcraft, hey? Well, if you think there are any witches in Cridely, Susan's your girl. We'll pack her off to Cridely and she'll sort out the witches in no time at all. She has been the official Palace witch finder for more than ten years, and damme but we've had not a single witch in that time. She's good." The king's eyes gleamed in satisfaction and Susan re-evaluated her judgement. Is he testing me, how I respond, she wondered.

Lord Sol bellowed with laughter, cutting short the bishop's next attempt to speak. "Hah, I remember the time she accused Lady Mary of being a witch. My word, what a to do. Great fun. Mind you, I don't think she was wrong. Peculiar woman." He winced as his wife kicked him under the table before continuing. "Little minx conducted an in-depth investigation into everyone in the Palace at Bresol. The Bishop of Bresol judged everyone she accused and she accused him of being a witch when he found everyone not guilty."

The spell broke as everyone proceeded to tell their favourite witch story and Susan beamed with innocence at the discomforted bishop, when a question came up the table to her.

"And how is your father, my dear?"

"I've no idea," said Susan without thinking.

"Oh, I don't mean your real father," said Lady Belvedere, eyes agleam. "I meant the tailor who took in your mother." She paused as the table again fell silent.

Susan floundered inside. She harboured her own suspicions on her mother's past, revolving around inns, dancing, parties and lots of men. She thought the tailor married her mother to save her from shame, a fact Lady Belvedere must share and intend to reveal. Her mind went into overdrive as she searched for a solution and found one in a play Will wrote for her, never acted as they felt it too close to truth and they feared repercussions.

"How could you possibly know which of your mother's, ah, guests, was your father?" Lady Belvedere raised her voice, speaking with slow deliberation to ensure her voice carried to everyone. Beside her, Susan felt the king tense and inch away from her. A bastard as well as a whore's brat, he would not be allowed to keep her. Nor would Dicky.

"My mother was never unfaithful to my father," Susan spoke with heat, slipping into the wronged noble lady actress persona, her Court Galician accent coming to the fore. "He spread those lies because he was jealous, unfounded jealousy. He thought everyone wanted her because she was so beautiful and he couldn't stand the thought of her being unfaithful. She was driven from her home to escape his rage when he discovered her pregnancy, certain I was not his. A fiction created in his own mind, because my mother was polite and responded in gentle terms to all who spoke with her."

"Nonsense," said Lady Belvedere, her annoyance showing. "She was a common harlot as is well known in Bresol. I have evidence to prove it."

"Of course," said Susan. "My father was a rich and powerful man, who hunted us down intending to kill us both. We had to hide, and my mother concocted many stories to hide our escape. She was loved by the people, who helped her create that image, that disguise, so he would not find us. It saved my life, but the fiction is no longer necessary as he died some years ago."

"A ridiculous story," said Lady Belvedere, annoyed at her prey wriggling in the trap. "This is a small country and we would know of such a happening. So who was your supposed father?"

"My mother would not tell me," said Susan, raising her glass and sipping with elegance, her little finger crooked just so. "She assured me I could be proud of my bloodlines, but she died before telling me. But Queen Rose knew. She spent a long time talking with my mother, and once she hugged me and told me she knew who I was. I didn't understand at the time, and she never told me."

Before Lady Belvedere could speak, another woman cut across the conversation. "Pray tell, Lady Susan, who taught you your manners? Queen Rose?" She tracked Susan's hand, still holding the wine glass and other eyes followed.

"Why, yes, she did, though most came from my mother. Oh, sorry, yes, Queen Rose tried to stop me holding my glass like that, said it was inelegant." She closed her little finger down to the base of the glass, in the Praesidium style, no longer in the perfect High Galician Royal style. She blessed the hours of training with Mary Sidney to perfect a role in the Galician court.

A buzz went around the tables as people whispered to each other, and Lady Belvedere inflated like a bullfrog in outrage at this ridiculous attempt to escape her meticulous snare.

"Jack," said Lady Sol, erupting from her chair with tears pouring down her face. "You know who she is, don't you? I said she looked like her, it's plain as a pikestaff, she's Louise's daughter. Oh my baby, how you've suffered." She enveloped Susan in her arms while her husband signalled a servant to fetch the gin, and Susan wondered who the hell Louise might be.

*

The king and his ward chose to breakfast in the balcony room, a light airy room overlooking the gardens beloved by generations of royal women. Susan refused to sit at the far end of the table; instead delighting the gossip mongers by requiring her place to the king's right, where she could tempt him with morsels from her plate. He derided this as foul Gallic muck, yet submitted to her insistence with appetite.

This morning Susan cooed with pleasure and inhaled the aroma from her plate with eyes closed and a groan of pleasure, while the king shuddered.

"That is quite disgusting," said the king, applying a kerchief to his nose, eyes wide in mock horror. "Why do you have the putrefying remains of a polecat for breakfast?"

"Mmmmm, so delicious. Please tell cook the omelette is cooked to perfection, if a little cold." She smiled at the servant who ducked his head and retreated. She turned to the king, a wobbling morsel on her fork. "Here, darling, so good for you, the garlic cleans the blood and the oyster strengthens you." She eyed him, a quizzical arch to her left eyebrow, and dropped her voice to ensure no one else overheard. "I think you need a little more oomph, dear, as I have plans."

"Blast your eyes, I don't need any strengthening damn you." He recoiled from the threatening fork, too close to focus. "What is that vile smell?"

"That beautiful aroma which swirls around your mouth and excites your tongue is from the truffles, and I do believe cook is at long last putting in enough truffle to flavour the dish. Open wide, there's a good boy, isn't it delicious?"

The king swallowed, savouring the rich and complex flavours but unwilling to admit defeat. "Truffle? Truffle! Wait a minute, you are the wretched reason there are Pathfinders all over the hills. The damn barracks are empty because they are all out truffle hunting. I thought it was some sort of baby troll, and this a public service, clearing vermin for the farmers. Do you mean to tell me they are all seeking your favour?"

Susan's eyes widened before closing in ecstasy as she consumed her own mouthful, silent while the aroma percolated through to her brain. "I may have bemoaned the lack of truffle in the market; you barbarians have no idea what you are missing."

The servant returned, bearing a tray with a large platter covered by a silver dome. The king perked up, following his breakfast with close attention. Whisking away the dome, the servant revealed a large chunk of meat, leaking blood through charred sides. Pulling his knife from his belt, the king prodded the meat, selected a portion with care and sliced it away to place on his bread trencher. Susan wrinkled her nose, which twitched as a further odour reached her. Her brow wrinkled and her gaze lost focus.

The king, oblivious, mopped up a little more juice before raising the bread to his mouth. As his teeth closed, Susan struck him hard on the side of the face, knocking the bread and meat flying across the floor to the startled bemusement of the servant and the two guards. Unable to speak, the king watched his breakfast go flying after the bread as a second blow from Susan struck the table, and he held his swelling lip while watching the departing meat with the distraught expression of a deprived lover.

"Guards," cried Susan as she leapt to her feet and raced to the door, whisking up her staff on the way and using it to indicate the startled servant. "Arrest that man and follow me. Poison, assassination attempt. Richard, don't you dare eat a thing."

She was gone, her bare feet making little sound down the corridor, but her voice carried bright and clear, summoning more guards. She burst into the kitchen, the flying door knocking a servant into a pile of dishes which shattered at the impact. The cook leapt from her place of rest at the table, mug of tea toppling into a steaming puddle, to be rammed against her own stove by the end of Susan's staff. The rest of the kitchen staff, another three women, backed against the wall, one hiding in the pantry and another slipping over to fall under the sink.

"Viper," said Susan, ramming the end of her staff into the cook's mouth. A trickle of blood eased down her cheek. "Who paid you? Tell me and earn a swift death, delay and face the torturer."

The cook paled, her eyes swinging in all directions and she gasped over the screams of the other women as Susan removed the staff from her mouth. Men charged into the room, guards, followed by a bewildered king.

"Arrest them all," said Susan, before the cook could speak. The cook retained her undivided and unwelcome attention, a regard so scary to the cook that an acrid stream trickled down her skirts. She moaned and sank to the floor.

"What is happening, Susan?" The king wielded his sword, a great heavy armour crusher, considerable overkill on un-armoured servants.

"This bitch tried to kill you," said Susan, unmoved by the panicked eyes and shaking head. "She covered your meat in belladonna, before she cooked it to boot. Sorry for the haste, but it took me a moment to recognise the smell. Now, bitch, where did you get the poison, who were your accomplices and who paid you? Guards, get her accomplices over here, we'll burn them on their own stove. Filthy, murderous, sneaking poisoners."

The king stood amazed at her vehemence, while the guards moved at speed to drag out the servants and array them beside the cook who wailed and pissed herself again. A guard grasped her hand, twisting it up near the heat, his face contorted in anger. Nothing engenders the anger of a guard more than a poisoner.

"Noooo," screamed the cook. "It wasn't enough to kill him! I just put a little on to kill the smell. I'm not a poisoner." She burst into tears, eyes transfixed by her hand over the grate, already turning pink.

"Hold," said Susan. "Let her speak. What smell, woman? Is there another poison to boot? Did you think to disguise one with belladona, so I would use the wrong remedy?"

"No, no poison, it was the meat, the smell, hide it." The cook wept, the words hard to understand through her choking tears. Susan wrinkled her brow and glanced at the other servants. The under cook sweated, the smell of fear pouring off her but her eyes still steady. Susan whirled on her and she recoiled, pushed back by a guard.

"Explain."

The woman fell to her knees, horrified at drawing the Valkyrie's attention. "Mistress, the, the meat is bad, old. It smells. She sought to hide the smell."

"Bad meat," said the king, incredulity in his tone. "But the budget, the kitchen budget, it costs a fortune to run this kitchen."

The wheels in Susan's head turned at speed. Would belladonna kill the odour? She didn't know. "You dare to serve bad meat to your king? That is also poison, which kills in a more painful manner. Guard, fetch the chamberlain."

"Mistress," said the woman, burying her face in her hands. "It is all we have. We, we… ohh.."

She fell silent and Susan left her to stalk to the pantry and the meat safe, recoiling at the smell and the flies. Her face white, she came back, shaking her head at the king when he went to follow her. The king found the situation fascinating and was content to allow Susan to conduct proceedings. Amazing his little girl could do this, he thought, having resisted the impulse to behead the servants.

The servants must have read his thoughts as now all were

incoherent and moaning. The chamberlain arrived, his eyebrows twitching as he took in the scene.

"Go in the pantry and inspect the meat safe," said Susan, her voice clipped and precise in perfect imitation of an officer issuing orders. Chamberlain Douglas obeyed without thinking, returning with narrowed eyes.

"Well, Douglas? The cook and the suppliers are corrupt embezzlers, the money spent on rotten meat. Are you corrupt or incompetent?"

Douglas flinched, his mind unable to cope with the speed at which Susan drove him to conclusions and he stood to parade ground attention, eyes locked on the opposite wall. "Incompetent, ma'am. You have my resignation."

Susan stalked round him in a circle, quivering in fury, in faithful imitation of Company Sergeant Briggs. Her voice dropped to ice. "I accept your resignation. You are no longer chamberlain, as of this moment. But you will not escape me so easily. For you escape beheading by the king and your life nestles in the palm of my hand, for you are now Chamberlain Major, assistant to the Chamberlain and your task is to discover the extent of this corruption. Succeed and I may retain your life. Guards, you will place these servants under arrest to await my pleasure, and I need a squad with me. Douglas, come with me as well." She moved towards the door, interrupted by the king.

"Hey, what about my breakfast?"

"You still have an appetite? Go to the barracks, you will get proper food there. I will tell you when it is safe to eat here again."

Susan had been reacting without thinking, the adrenaline coursing through her veins. Now, as she led the way, the import of her actions struck her with palpable power and she faltered, wondering in horror how she could possibly have spoken in that manner or acted in such a fashion. She cringed inwardly at the memory of her threat to torture the cook, redoubling the anguish when she realised she would have burnt poor cookie's hand.

"Don't you start thinking now, Duchess," came a voice from alongside. She turned her head and her eyes widened.

"Who, no, what are you?"

"Thanks, love you too, Duchess." The speaker was a guard,

surely too small to be a Pathfinder, scruffy and dirty with eyes that darted, rather than scanned, beady and brimming with devilment. Susan's anger rose again, that this vile creature would dare to talk to her.

"That's better," he said, not even looking in her direction. "You did real good back there, sister, but these barstids will be different. They're used to people leaning on them, they are, and they're tough. You can't just threaten them. "

Susan couldn't bear to look at him any longer and returned her attention to the corridor, her anger displaced by his words. "Where do you imagine I am going, soldier?" She emphasised the soldier in tones dripping with ice. He chuckled.

"Youse wants to know where the money is at, or was. Only one place to check, that's the scribes and ciphers. T'others will cotton on in a moment." Susan glanced at the other guards, noting the king followed behind talking to the chamberlain, his face wreathed in smiles. All bore looks of bemusement, none with the certainty of the unpreposing creature beside her, who's accuracy startled her.

"When we gets there," said the soldier, lowering his voice. "You lets me go in first. I'll announce you as the 'Igh Priestess. The chancellor, see, he's scared of magic. Don't give a rats' arse about being thumped 'cos he's a tough bleeder, he is, 'specially for a scribe. When you come in, wave yer staff like it's a wand, then belt him over the head when he twitches. Fast as you are, he'll likely think you blasted him with magic, see, and we'll get him talking."

"Somehow, I doubt he would speak that quickly," said Susan, feeling herself drawn into the plan and pleased she still wore a morning robe.

"Don't matter, really. See, while his nibs is confused, me and my mates will grab the books and stop him chucking the special ones."

"Special ones?"

"The real ones, see, he'll have a false set to show the chamberlain. Clever barstid, this one is, Duchess."

"You know, him don't you."

"We've 'ad words, love, time or two."

"I see. How much do you owe him?"

The soldier laughed, loud and harsh, more a cackle. The sound drew the attention of the king, who exclaimed.

"Please tell me that is not a Pathfinder."

Ex-Chamberlain Douglas groaned. "Oh no. She is talking to Private Little. They have their heads together."

*

At the double doors, Susan paused, waiting for the King to catch up and debating how much of the plan would suffice to keep him back. As little as possible, for sure.

"Darling, leave it to us. Wait till we have it under control before you come into the room." She pulled a cloth over her head, as a makeshift hood, hunched her shoulders and bent her spine, transforming into an old woman in front of their eyes. The king swore, bitten off as Little got down on all fours and shook himself, for all the world like a dog. From somewhere he produced a fur which he slung over his shoulders. Two guards kicked open the doors and Little scampered into the room, throwing back his head and performing a very creditable imitation of a dog, barking, howling and growling.

Susan glided into the room, hard on his heels and spoke a harsh, guttural phrase that crackled into the room. Little screamed, starting as a howl and standing up as he did so. To the startled clerks labouring over their desks, a dog had transformed into a man at the command of an old witch, just as they looked up.

Little boomed out a speech, his normal gutter accent transformed. "All rise, all rise, and pay homage to the High Priestess, Mistress of the Forest and the Night. Tremble, mortals, before her might and fury."

The confused clerks hastened to stand, quivering at their desks, all except the man behind the largest desk, on a raised dais presiding over the room. He sat frozen, mouth gaping wide, as Susan glided towards him, her staff acting as a crutch while she mumbled incantations from a play written by Will.

As she reached him, his wide eyes began to narrow, and a question rose inside him. She forestalled him, standing tall and throwing dust and spiders gathered en route into his face, while shouting a new incantation. As he blinked his eyes, she struck him between the eyes with her staff, moving too fast to see.

The chancellor tumbled onto his back and lay still. Little called out, and the guards rushed in, while the witch turned into a young girl who glared at the confused and terrified clerks. "Move an inch and I will hang your rotting carcass from the castle battlements to feed the crows."

In a moment, the clerks were rounded up, reinforcement Pathfinders arriving to assist in removing twenty men.

The chancellor sat up, to see Susan sitting at his desk, reading his ledger. A girl, who could read and appeared to understand figures. This was true witchcraft. He shook his head, still confused, to find Susan regarding him with a gimlet eye.

"I kept my father's books since I was ten years old." She let that thought sink deep. "How sweet, you even tally your personal wealth. Why, Richard, would you believe he has stolen over a hundred thousand crowns. Very impressive. I don't think I need him, darling, I have everything I need right here in his ledgers. I even know where he hid the money. Little, send to the barracks for the quartermaster and his clerks."

The chancellor gaped, his mouth working without sound. The king smiled as he reached down and gripped a solid handful of his shirt and cravat.

*

Susan sat at the Chancel's desk for over an hour, head bent and mouth working, feathers missing from her quill where she chewed the end. The king had long since departed, along with his prey, while the quartermaster and his clerks helped her understand the ledgers. The new chamberlain major reported the presence of every servant, awaiting Susan's pleasure in the Great Hall. Susan let them stew, while observing Little with a surreptitious and amazed eye, as he flicked through ledgers and orbited Susan, eyes roving in constant search.

"You did well today, Corporal Little."

"It's Private, mum."

"I do not make those sort of mistakes, Corporal Little, but it will be Private Little if you dare to call me love again."

"Cor! Thanks, lo.. Duchess, that's right handsome of you. Umm, I don't suppose…"

"Yes, I would suppose. I have your gambling debts right here,

Corporal Little, along with those of a further thirty-seven Pathfinders. Why am I not surprised that your debt is the largest? Ninety-seven crowns? How many years' wages is that?"

"Yer, it's a stitch up, mum, sure it is," said Little, truculent with a trace of nerves.

"Naturally." She raised her head from the ledger and spent five minutes examining him in minute detail, oblivious to his scratching. He failed to become embarrassed, which interested her. "You will be on detached duty in future, Little, available for my orders."

"Do I have to wash?"

"My orders are unlikely to bring you close enough for that to matter to me, Little, and being unwashed may prove a positive advantage for some of the duties I have in mind. Now, bring this ledger for me and attend while I speak to the servants. Don't try and remove your debts, I have a copy."

Susan miss-stepped on entering the Great Hall, for she found herself unaware of the number of servants in the Palace. Her nerve fled as she took her seat at the high table, looking down at all the faces raised towards her. Expressions in the main interested, some angry, a few scared, many confused. She ran her eyes over them and groped for the words she had rehearsed, to realise her agile brain failed her. Little thumped the ledger down on the table in front of her, the noise echoing down the hall and dragging every eye to the massive book.

"Douglas," she said, "please send for the king." She poured herself a glass of water, checking the clarity.

"The king is still occupied, ma'am," said the chamberlain major, his face without expression.

"Very well." Lacking any other excuse to delay, she brought out a list. "If I call out your name, please come to the front and stand here," she said, indicating the open space just in front of the table. Ignoring the murmur of surprise and query, she brought out a list and read out the names, checking the presence of each person before continuing to the next. Each name represented the head of a department, sometimes with the chief assistant, each department responsible for some area of procurement. A heavy heart reminded Susan they represented every such department with the notable exception of the Guardhouse. She eased her shoulders and allowed the banked embers of her fury to smoulder and blaze again. No trouble speaking when her resentment ruled.

"These sorry creatures have abused their trusted positions in the Court to embezzle vast fortunes from the money of the Realm. The secret ledgers of the ex-chancellor," she tapped the ledger beside her, "reveal the precise extent of your malfeasance. This precise amount will be recovered from your estate and no more, the rest provided to your heirs."

The sommelier, a Galician who affected clothes only in the colours of his wines, collapsed, mouth moving in silent agony, while the others stared with a complete lack of comprehension.

"Guards, deliver them to the king and tell him these are all the embezzlers." She sipped some water as conversation broke out in a buzz amongst the remaining servants, while a stout woman wearing an apron stepped from the condemned to glare at Susan.

"You little Galician trollop! I've served the Starrs all me life, I have, and the king sat on my knee for his breakfast as a little lad. He's not going to hurt me, he isn't."

Susan returned the glare with interest. "You expect loyalty from the Crown, when you have betrayed us, feathered your own nest and sought position to enrich yourself. Your actions betray you and I am fascinated you think the king will forgive your trespass." The woman dropped her head, the enormity of the rapid events sweeping through her and her shoulders shook as the tears came. Another man pushed forward from the back of the accused, wearing a priest's robes lashed tightly across his spreading belly.

"You have no provenance over me, you witch, you unnatural Spawn of the Nether Regions. Your lies cannot affect me, for I belong to the Church and only God may judge me. For you to attempt to spread these lies about me, in a blatant attempt to drive the True Beliefs from the Court, no doubt to replace them with the illicit debauchery you savour, consorting with wild beasts and fey creatures. This will not be tolerated by the Church. The Archbishop himself will lead a legion of the faithful to ensure my release, cleanse the court of your foul stench and exact the vengeance of the Lord on my persecutors."

Susan kept a level gaze as he ran out of steam. "You may well be right. I admit I will be surprised if the archbishop does claim you, but he may do so if he redeems your theft. Of course, I am unclear whether he can find the sum of," Susan opened the ledger and checked her notes, "twenty-three thousand, two hundred and forty-three crowns. And such redemption will bear witness to the Church's compliance and involvement in the embezzlement. Sergeant, please ask His Majesty to refrain from exacting judgement on Father Benn before the archbishop pronounces his decision. I shall send him a letter forthwith."

Father Benn opened his mouth to begin another tirade, but Susan forestalled him.

"I am sure the archbishop will be delighted to know you claim the patronage of the Church and imply the worship of Our Lord comes with theft, corruption, embezzlement and pandering."

"My Lady!" A voice rang from the audience and another priest pushed through the throng. "The Church most certainly does not condone these practises. The archbishop has recently become concerned as to the activities of Confessor Benn."

"Thank you Father Gregory. I appreciate your words, and perhaps you would take my letter to His Holiness, for I shall still arraign him awaiting the written word of the archbishop. Perhaps you will replace him as the Royal Confessor?"

"I thank My Lady for the compliment. The decision belongs to the Archbishop. May I ask in what position the Royal Ward stands that enables her to write such a letter and make such an invitation?"

"I am the current Chamberlain of the Court." A whisper, sweeping up to a tumult, followed eyes tracking to where Douglas stood at the end of the table, eyes fixed on a painting, standing to military attention. "The previous chamberlain is of course condemned to death for his failure to prevent this corruption in the Court. However, his actions since the discovery places his life in my hands. His every action decides when I shall open my palm to deliver him to the Lord."

A New Court

"INGRATES!" bellowed the King, hacking at a lump of firewood with his practice sword, chips flying across the room. "I never trusted that blasted chancellor. Do you know what I did to him?"

"Yes, dear," said Susan, as she ran the brush through her hair, the first of a hundred strokes. The king had recounted the chancellor's grisly end on several occasions, and this was the twelfth time he had used the word ingrate, his new favourite after Susan had used it and been required to explain the meaning to him earlier in the evening.

Undaunted, the king launched into a new description, re-enacting each move. As the king gyrated around the fireplace, sending wooden heads flying, Susan allowed her brain to move in calculation as she considered tomorrow's requirements. New heads of department were critical – she was sure the Court would grind to a halt without them, but she didn't know if she trusted any of the current teams. And chancellor? Where would she find a new chancellor?

The king came up beside her, panting from his exertions.

"...and then I stuck the damn ingrate's head on a spike and fixed it on the wall over the palace entrance. Do you know, there was nowhere to put it? In the old days we always had spikes for these things. Had to call a mason to fix a new spike."

"Wait, Richard, you don't mean you have put a rotting head on a spike above my FRONT DOOR!"

"Need to ensure everyone knows not to steal from the king."

"Of course they know. Even barbarians put severed heads outside the front of their wretched cities, they don't put them on a beautiful building in the middle of the city, a building meant to inspire the populace to dreams of a better future and they certainly do not put them OUTSIDE THEIR WIVES' WINDOW." Susan smacked her brush down on the table and stamped over to see if she could see the grisly relic. She could.

"You aren't my wife," began the king.

"No, I am not, and not likely to be, nor your wretched unfortunate mistress if you do not have this disgusting thing removed in the next five minutes. Honestly, what will people be thinking?"

Muttering under his breath, the king opened the door and cursed at the guard, telling him to move the head.

Susan had returned to her hair and inspected Richard in her mirror. "Richard, who are we going to get as a replacement chancellor?"

"What? Oh, hadn't thought about it. I expect Grittel will do it."

"How much will he pay for the position?"

"Was just going to appoint him."

"Did you know the chancellor sold servants positions in the Palace? I think we need to be careful and very, very certain with this appointment, Richard. Every noble will want it, as long as you don't chop their head off, but I don't trust one of them to do the job."

"Of course not. Why I suggested Grittel. We haven't allowed a senior noble to be chancellor for a long time."

"We need a Champion, Richard, a Champion of Money. How do we select a Champion?"

"Hold a tourney, usual way. How the devil would you have a money tourney? Get them gambling? Church will love that."

The brush stopped half way down her hair. Susan's eyes unfocused and her lips moved. A thought stirred in the recesses of her head, but she couldn't quite complete the process.

"Can you leave it with me, darling? I think I may have an answer, but I want to ask some questions."

"Yes, why not?" The king was amused. "Now, I must consider who to make chamberlain. That's an even more thorny problem." The king sat on the bed, waiting for Susan to help him remove his boots.

"You have a chamberlain, me."

"What?"

"Stop saying that, Richard, it is unedifying. You hear me perfectly well." Susan straddled the king's leg and grasped his boot, bracing herself. The king placed his other foot on her rear and eased his foot free. As it came out, he began to grin, out of Susan's vision. This could be most entertaining.

"You cannot possibly be chamberlain. You are a woman." He swapped feet, placing his stockinged foot on her behind and wiggling the toes, trying to annoy her further. Anticipating the toes, Susan kept her buttocks firmly clenched while her back stiffened.

"Yes, a woman. This one discovered not just an attempt on her ungrateful king's life, but uncovered traitors trusted by these so-clever men. She recovered the stolen money, identified every last embezzler and acted decisively to protect the Kingdom."

"My aunt complains you do not spend enough time at the Ladies' Court as it is. You cannot be chamberlain as the duties would interfere with your time at court. I understand your tatting skills are more than limited." He pulled off the rest of his clothes and moved to purloin Susan's mirror, inspecting his naked physique.

"The Ladies' Court! I hate it, and I will not attend again. It is not useful for you, Richard. The whole point of a court is to discover through the women what the barons are up to, and nobody will confide anything genuine to me. They hate me. The barons gain far more from the court than we do."

King Richard reached to ease an itch in his groin, before second thoughts caught up. Any indication of discomfort would result in a bed bath, a most unsanitary practice, very un-Gallic. The king was not pleased at this heather custom, blaming the Pathfinders.

"You have two weeks," he said with a smile. "If the Palace works to my satisfaction, you get an extension."

"No," said Susan, revealing a bowl of water and a washcloth with a flourish. "To my satisfaction."

*

Colonel Donnell pulled out a chair and sat opposite Susan, a half smile on his face at this reversal in roles.

"Good morning, sir. Thank you for attending me this morning, I have some questions I hope you can answer. Tea?"

"Thank you, Cornet Taylor. Smart work yesterday. You may have difficulty keeping Little a corporal. I expect he will break enough regulations to lost his stripes within two weeks."

"Doesn't matter, sir. The important thing is his actions were rewarded. But my questions do not concern him. I need a champion, the best person in the Kingdom with money."

The colonel raised an eyebrow, but did not speak.

"This would be the ideal person to become our chancellor, to look after the money of the Kingdom. I was thinking this would be the wealthiest merchant in the Kingdom."

Colonel Donnell nodded, hooding his eyes as he thought. His spoke with slow precision, measuring each word. "The richest person in the Kingdom would be Grittell or Redpond, but I'm not sure they are the answer. They are wealthy because of the riches they extracted from the earth, their mines. I think we need somebody different, somebody who makes money in a variety of ways. I will have an answer for you this afternoon."

"Thank you. My second task is to replace the embezzlers, which means I need to find replacement head of departments, yet I do not trust the deputies."

"You wish to duplicate the Pathfinder's Promotion Panel, I presume? Very well, I shall send for some suitable officers and we shall convene a meeting at, shall we say an hour before noon? Excellent. Now, our first action will be to establish the exact role for each department. We may decide to merge or split departments. Will you be attending the meeting, ma'am? Excellent. Once the parameters are established for each position, we shall take steps to fill them and convene the panel again when we have designated people."

Colonel Donnell rose and left the room, his lips working and his eyes faraway. He almost collided with Little at the door, who offered a semblance of a salute.

"Hey, Duchess, coupla old trout want to talk to you. Couldn't get rid of this one. Ow!" The exclamation came as a stick thudded into his side and a woman barged into the room.

"Couple of old trout indeed. You must learn accuracy, young man, or you do not serve your mistress. I may be an old trout but Lucinda is neither old nor a trout. Horsey, maybe. Susan, darling, what a to-do this is."

This formidable lady, with a younger version in tow, swept into the room and pulled out the chair vacated by the colonel.

"I apologise, madam, my education is sadly lacking…"

"Sadly? Sadly? Not at all, load of nonsense that wretched, pointless tapestry. I managed to portray the King of Galicia's squire stark naked in one wall hanging. Nobody noticed until it was hanging in the church, caused quite a stir, I can tell you. I'm Marcia Henderson, and my cousin Lucinda."

Lucinda smiled and pulled out another chair.

"A pleasure to meet you," said Susan, with a longing glance at the reports and ledgers on her desk.

"Susan, we're not here to interfere, we've come to help," said Lucinda.

"Yes," said Marcia. "We are unsuited to the Royal Court. Those harridans train young ladies in useful duties like tapestry, singing, dancing and how to gossip. You, my dear, have an opportunity and we're going to make sure you take it."

"We are your new Ladies-in-Waiting," said Lucinda with a smile, "and in this court we are going to teach young girls useful skills, like writing, book-keeping, managing the household staff, everything you are doing right now."

A slow grin spread across Susan's face. She liked these two cousins.

"Not to mention how to thrash a thieving servant," said Marcia with undisguised glee. "I shall give classes on how to ensure your husband does not stray."

"I think Susan can give a better class, Marcia, ensuring he doesn't want to stray in the first place. Anyway, Susan, first order of business, what shall we call your court?"

Susan barked a laugh. "The crows in the Royal Court will no doubt call us all baggages and hussies. The Low Court might be suitable."

"The Ruling Court," said Lucinda. "We shall be teaching girls how to manage their husbands' estates when they marry. Don't listen to Marcia, she's a bad influence."

Marcia reached over and snagged a ledger, pulling it towards herself. "So what are we working on this morning?"

Alarm flared through Susan, who retrieved the ledger before she could open the cover. "First order of business is for you to tell me something about yourselves, and your family. Are you friends with Lady Durrant?"

"Tut tut, my dear, we shall have to teach you subtlety before you show your claws to Lady Belvedere. We're from Westport, can't abide the fuss at court. We are only in town because Johnny is selling some horses to the Pathfinders and we wanted to see the latest fashions and a play or two."

Susan raised a figurative eyebrow at the mention of plays, deciding with regret they must be Belvedere's creatures to have this information about her. A subtle game, nevertheless she would play the charade.

Lucinda leaned forward, a restraining hand on Marcia's arm. "Susan, you do not trust us. You are beset with enemies and you would be a fool not to think we were sent by somebody. And we are country idiots when it comes to the deceit and subterfuge offered by the likes of Belvedere and Durrant. But we do know how to manage an estate, for both of us do so in Fearaigh. We can be useful, and it will be fun helping to run the Kingdom. Don't put us in positions where we can take advantage. Explain what you want and we shall show you how to achieve it without exhausting yourself."

"We'll teach you how to delegate, girl, that's the first lesson."

*

Timmy read the letter again and pondered. A business rival proffered a substantial leather factory in Praesidium for sale, his main competitor. The man claimed he wished to concentrate his efforts elsewhere, and needed the money for expansion into timber. It was a good factory and the price, although high, was fair. He would control most of the leather in Praesidium if not the Kingdom. A good deal, no, an excellent deal, but something nagged at him. He didn't trust the man, and couldn't see any problems, or anywhere the man would win from the deal apart from cashing out.

A knock on the door and his head guard stuck his head into the room. "Lady to see you, boss."

"I'm busy," said Timmy in irritation. "I told you I was not to be disturbed."

"Think you should see this one, boss. Information and money. Not sure I could stop her, neither. She'd be in here if she weren't distracted by some cloth."

"I don't have time to sell silks to ladies. Get Sandra to talk to her."

"Oh, she won't want to buy your cloth, sir. She's ripping Sandra a new one for miss-grading the cloth and folding it wrong."

"Oh, hell, send the old harridan in, then, I'll get rid of her. No, I'll come down." Timmy started to put the letter away as he rose from his seat when the guard backed into the room, a cloaked figure stabbing him in the chest with a vicious finger.

"Get out of my way, you useless lunk, before I throw you down the stairs." The voice rang true, and despite the words held not a trace of anger. Just confidence. Timmy paused, half way to standing as the lady swept into the room and the guard fled. A bonnet hid the hair, while a small veil covered her face, revealing a pair of intense blue eyes which measured him with a care. Timmy received the distinct impression he was found wanting.

The lady marched across the room, boots clicking on the wood, wearing a sensible woollen dress and jacket underneath her cloak. She appeared no different from any burgher's wife barring the confidence with which she took a seat and nodded to him.

"You can sit. Not sure I am in the right place if that is what you do with cloth. You are supposed to be a good merchant."

Timmy sat down, nettled. "It is not our normal business; I took a chance on shipment from Coillearnacha. I am conf.."

"You should have done your research, only a fool would buy silk with a fold. Needs to be in rolls and the grades are wrong. You've been stiffed, Mr Brown. This will cost you a pretty penny and I doubt you are the man I seek."

Annoyed, Timmy pushed back without thinking. "I will not lose money on the deal, as these are recovered from brigands. I concede my people know little about cloth and nothing about silk, however I am employing a person who is arriving tomorrow to investigate the shipment. I am unsurprised if what you say is true. What can I do for you, madam?"

"So, you deal in stolen goods." The blue eyes froze rooting him to the spot and his mouth fell open in outrage. She rose from the chair. "I seem to have received poor information. Look to your morals, Mr Brown."

"No, madam, I deal in recovered goods. Goods recovered by the border patrols who trust me enough to get the best deal for the crown." Timmy stood with his guest, little pink spots appearing on his cheeks. She paused at this information, half turned away.

"Indeed. Do you provide the accounting to the chancellor?"

"What, Baron Livesy? No, madam, I do not. His predecessor, yes, who provided me with several charters of Royal Appointment but I chose not to deal with Baron Livesy. We account directly to the regimental quartermaster who calls us in."

She turned back to face him, the eyes clouded and unreadable. "Why did you not do business with Baron Livesy?"

"Let us just say I preferred not to do business with him. I do not gossip about other people, madam."

"You can gossip about Livesy all you like. I had him beheaded last night."

Timmy dropped back into his chair, mouth working and conscious of sweat rising on his back and brow. The woman regarded him through those flat, steel eyes before taking her own seat once more. She reached up and removed her bonnet, the veil coming with it and revealing a young and beautiful face while a cascade of blonde ringlets fell down to frame her. Timmy continued to be speechless while she waited, a half smile on her face and amusement in her eyes.

"Who, who the devil are you?"

"My name is Susan Taylor, I am the new Chamberlain of the Palace."

"Susan Taylor? Chamberlain? But, why, you are the King's M…" Timmy snapped his mouth shut as the eyes narrowed. "Of course, my lady, I apologise for not knowing. How may I assist the Palace today?"

"I seek a new chancellor," she said, eyes following every expression.

"Me?" said Timmy in horror. "I am not a noble."

Susan waved a gloved hand, for the first time taking her attention away from Timmy and flicking her eyes around the room. Timmy felt as if a long needle had been removed from his abdomen.

"That does pose a bit of a problem," said Susan getting up to examine a painting on the wall, a bucolic scene of harvest from a world about which she knew nothing.

Timmy sat quiet in his chair, forcing himself to ignore her even as his brain reeled at the shock of realising this was a girl and not a woman. Could she really be chamberlain? Impossible, but she was so sure.

"Bart," he called and his guard put a head round the door, checking Susan's position with a wary eye. He paused on her face for a moment before giving Timmy his full attention. "Bart, send a runner to the Palace and find out who is the current chamberlain."

"She is, boss," he said with a shrug. "Bit of a ruckus up there last night, city is atwitter."

"And the chancellor?"

Bart's eyes slid towards Susan, whose fascination with the painting increased. "Urr, 'e's dead, sir." Bart indicated Susan with his eyes, showing a great deal of white. "She caught him stealing, she did, an' chopped his head clean off herself, she did. Some people are saying she did the same to his essentials first, and made him eat them."

Susan's eyebrow raised all of a hair's breadth and the corner of her mouth twirked.

"Why was I not informed?"

"You've been a bit busy, sir. Tried to pass the word meself, and I've got some messages for you, which I reckon are to do with it."

Timmy waved a weak hand in dismissal and Bart started to leave before checking and turning to Susan. "With permission, yer Highness, err, sorry Duchess," he stammered before leaving at speed with her nod.

"What should I call you, madam?" Timmy's voice sank to a whisper.

Susan returned her attention to him. "People call me so many different things that I cannot keep up, and I have no idea what my title should be. Why not Susan? It is my given name."

"Yes, my lady, of course."

"You are not going to be much use to me if you are going to be spineless all the time."

Timmy sat a bit straighter and considered his options. "I'm not a noble," he whispered, noticing for the first time the walking stick she carried was in fact a quarterstaff. He remembered some gossip about the king's mistress scandalising society by learning how to use it with the Pathfinders. "I won't last the day before somebody runs me through."

"Do you really think I would permit that? I can make you a noble."

Timmy perked up a little, before deflating. "I can't use a sword. Somebody would challenge me."

"I notice you are concerned with your own safety, not with doing the job."

"Job's easy. Just a bit of book keeping and making the right decisions. Knowing who to trust to do good work. Ensuring supplies are top quality and rewarding merchants who give good service." He bit back his enthusiasm. Susan removed a sheaf of paper from her purse and proceeded to make some notes. He watched in fascination, a gentlewoman who could write.

"I'm not really a lady, Mr Brown. I am a tailor's daughter who ran his business for him and have the misfortune to own a pretty face. I am a merchant like yourself, but without your experience and success."

Timmy wasn't at all sure about that, careful not to look at the pretty face or make a comment. He noticed the strength in her arms, the little stretch of bare skin between her glove and sleeve revealed corded muscle as he had never seen in a woman.

"Did you really behead the chancellor personally?" He wasn't brave enough to ask about what was in the man's mouth.

"Street rumours about me abound, it would seem." Susan sat perfectly still, poised and alert. "I am starting a new fashion, wearing my sword to the next Palace Ball."

'*Oh, you clever thing,*' thought Timmy, impressed. '*You didn't answer my question, let me believe what I want with a little misdirection. You know, this could be fun.*'

"May I present you with some silk? To make the dress?"

"No, I require quality in my clothing."

"Oh, not the stuff downstairs. I was thinking of sea blue, rare and expensive, from the south of Coillearnacha. With perhaps some red velvet, to show through the slashes."

Susan laughed aloud, a clear bell pealing through the room, and causing the workers below to pause. "Why Mr Brown, I believe you do have some depths and guts after all. I shall call you Timmy, I think that is what your friends call you. So, will you be my chancellor, Timmy?"

"You claim friendship and in the next breath sign my death sentence?"

Susan stood up. "You are my chancellor, Timmy, but only you and I will know it. I shall appoint a baron, an old dodderer, to the post, who will do what I tell him. And you will advise me, teach me what I need to know. You will also choose the book keepers for me, and guarantee their performance. Come to the Palace tomorrow at ten o'clock sharp. I will find my baron by then."

She replaced her bonnet with care, ensuring not a wisp of blonde hair escaped.

"And my fee, Susan?"

"Ah, Timmy, so brave when it comes to money. Here is an instalment. Do not buy that leather factory. The neighbouring land has been bought by the Duke of Sarl for a townhouse and gardens. He will no doubt object to the smell of tanning nearby."

Timmy checked his desk and saw the offer still lying there, half put away. When he raised his head, Susan was gone.

*

Susan slipped in the side entrance to the Palace, getting to her rooms unnoticed and changing from her street disguise. Raised voices came from her sitting room and she pushed open the door in time to hear Lucinda inform Irina of her correct title, Lady Slutbucket apparently, with the two girls hissing at each other like enraged cats, backs bent, bottoms up and heads back. Marcia rolled on the settee, clasping a heavy cut crystal glass of her favourite gin, tears of laughter pouring down her cheeks.

Thankful for her acting ability, Susan managed to separate the girls with a straight face and eased Irina into her study where she sat at her desk.

"Are you quite insane?" Irina fumed as she paced up and down the room, extravagant gestures ignored by Susan, who found a report on her desk from Colonel Donnell. "This ridiculous court, a court for tradespeople. I, Irina, the Duchess of Sarl, am being sneered at, laughed at, because they think I am part of your lunacy. Watch the invitations dry up, the king embarrassed, dances where we don't know the steps and our clothes unfashionable. How could you do this to me, Susan? I trusted you, I am your friend and I followed you, now you do this to me. It is not to be tolerated. If the Duke of Sarl hears about this, he will insist on my immediate return."

"Lady Belvedere should be pleased."

"What?"

"Lady Belvedere, she should be pleased with the new court. I am surprised she hasn't come to see us."

"Why should she? Sensible woman, will have nothing to do with this charade."

"She's the Church's mouthpiece at Court. I think they anticipated I would be conducting naked orgies."

"Now that is a good idea," Irina interrupted in her enthusiasm. "I will make up the guest list and we can put to bed these ridiculous ideas. Why, we could put on some shows. I wonder if I could persuade Donny to participate?"

Susan rolled her eyes. "The Church likes people to work hard, not party. This court encourages hard work and puts women to effective use. They should like that." Irina snorted. Susan cast her a baleful look. "And the husbands will be delighted to know their wives are helping out and participating, rather than frolicking in the stables with the farriers."

"I've never touched a farrier," said Irina, discovering a small plate of dainty cakes on a side table. "A blacksmith, though, that's a different story. Have you seen the muscles on them?"

"Quite," said Susan, in a hurry to change the subject. "Now, this court is important to me, I am really enjoying myself and I want to make myself invaluable to the king. I need you Irina, so please don't be difficult. I promise we will still have fun, but only if you make friends with Lucinda. We need to bring her along with us."

"That stuck up baggage called me a trollope! How dare she, as if she has never played the two-backed beast, the snivelling little virgin."

Susan needed to stop and try to work out what Irina was trying to say, but gave up. "I think you are mixing up your words a bit, darling. She can't be a virgin; she is married to the Duke of Westport – she's actually your equal. "

"Never! I am beautiful, with a sensuous body made for love while she looks like a mangy, cross-bred horse with a spear shaft thrust rampant up its ass. The little bitch had the gall to tell me I was smelly. Me, the Duchess of Sarl, famous for its scents and perfumes. She's a bitch with a dried up little twat that no man would want."

"Yes, yes," said Susan, who had heard the word twat being used by soldiers and now had a far better understanding of its meaning.

"She's from Fearaigh, they think we are all smelly up here. They bathe every day. But enough of this nonsense, I have work to do and you are distracting me. I am training tomorrow afternoon, if you would like to a come with me, I'm sure that Riggs will be around."

Politics

'Well, that was a success,' reflected Susan, looking down on an exhausted King Richard, a satisfied smile across her face. Irina had been talking to her about different positions and, after getting over her shock at the idea, she determined to try the least adventurous. She had pushed him backwards onto the bed before climbing aboard. Now, careful not to dislodge herself, she adjusted to a more comfortable position before leaning forward and tickling his nose.

"Darling," she cooed. He grunted slightly, falling fast towards sleep.

"How much do you love me, darling?"

"Lot…" His eyes snapped open and narrowed in suspicion as he bit off his words. "What do you want now?"

She rocked gently on him, smiling at him. "Can I have some money, darling? Just a loan, I'll pay you back."

"Purse in the drawer. Keep it." He started to respond to her rocking, stroking her leg at the same time.

"I need a bit more than that, darling."

"What? There must be a hundred crowns in there. How much do you want?" The king had lost interest now and was playing with her nipple.

"I think twenty thousand should be enough."

There was a small explosion on the bed, King Richard bucked hard, throwing Susan sideways and off as he deflated, and turning to look down at her while she giggled.

"Twenty bloody thousand! What the hell do you want that for? Raise your own blasted army?"

"I'm going to buy some land. On Larkspur Point. Don't worry, I will sell it soon and pay you back. Would you like interest?"

"Interest? Damn the bloody usury. Larkspur Point is a useless marsh. Why would you or anyone want to buy land there?"

"Well, I do need you to send some Pathfinders down there. Surveyors."

"I see. This is some sort of sting you want to pull, and you expect me to not only finance it but help you rope in some sucker and not send you to jail. What is going on? You've never been interested in money before?"

Susan climbed out of bed and went to a table, selecting an apple from a bowl before bringing it back and biting into it. "The sucker is Lady Belvedere." She offered him a bite.

"You are quite mad. Do you realise how much political pull she has? She can call in favours right across the country. You keep on the right side of her, too dangerous."

"I'm on the wrong side anyway. So are you. She won't permit you to marry anybody, let alone me, and I think she plans to assassinate you before too long."

The king stared at her. "What do you know and how?"

"There is nothing definite, but the idea has come up in conversation, not dismissed."

"Who told you this?"

"I have a little bird, listening in."

"Who? Oh all right, keep your damn secrets, I need more information."

"She's all sugar and cream when we speak, but she has dinner parties with various groups where she encourages certain people and actions. Particularly the Church. Count Rotherstone is a frequent visitor."

"I know, damn it. Taking some money off her won't help. She'll just borrow some or sell some land."

"The money is just part of the plan. You don't need to know the rest – better you don't know any of it. But I am going to break the bitch and none of it will reflect badly on the throne, I promise."

*

Sweat poured down Susan's back as she dunked her head right into the horse trough, holding her breath for several heartbeats before emerging, glowing. She smiled at the soldier doing the same beside her, giving a little wriggle of pleasure as the water trickled down between her small breasts. Her muscles ached in that glorious, well used way and she felt fabulous.

"Thank you, David, you were brilliant today. I really enjoyed that workout. Sorry about your knuckles, you rushed me."

The soldier looked at his bleeding and smashed fingers with a rueful expression. "Tell you what, Duchess, when they recalled me from the frontier and told me I was training a girl, me first thought was the princess, the second I was fucking, ah, sorry 'bout that, ah, bloody angry. Thought the Pathfinders were having a down on me for being a staff specialist." He paused, running a hand in a loving caress up and down his staff, standing beside him as if it belonged. "You've made me twice the staffer I was." He smiled at her, eyes twinkling. "Not bad for a girl."

Susan's eyes went round in mock outrage and she swung her staff at his head, where he caught it, laughing, as the Master-at-Arms came up.

"Playtime over, you two. Cadet, briefing room, Brand, get the hell out of my training area." He stomped off. David Brand rolled his eyes and performed a perfect imitation of the Master-at-Arms as he made for the door. Stifling a giggle, Susan waved to the usual spectators as she went deeper into the barracks. A few soldiers blocked her way, smiling.

"Thanks Duchess, made a pony on you today."

"Looking prettier every day, Duchess." This was as risqué as the comments became, all the soldiers treating her as a mascot and senior officer.

"Good riposte you got there, girl, the way you dummy the backhand and break the knee with the front."

"I've started learning the staff too, thanks to you Duchess."

A gaggle of young men and an older corporal were at the tail end of the admirers. They shoved one of them forward, a pimpled boy who took off his cap and wrung it in his hands. Susan stopped and arched an eyebrow as they blocked her path.

"W-wuh-we're off to the front tomorrah," he said, breaking out in a sweat. "We wanted to all say thanks."

"Thanks?" Susan asked in genuine puzzlement. "What have I done?"

"We allus watch you train," said another.

The spokesman hung his head and scuffed his feet. "Jus' watchin' you makes us better soldiers, ma'am. We try to do the same in training, and when we're on the front, we're thinking of you." A crowd had formed around them by now, silent while he spoke, but as he finished there was a murmur of agreement and a nodding of heads.

Susan felt pressure at the back of her eyes. "Go along with you. I'm just making sure I can defend myself, for the days when you boys aren't around. And you'll be thinking of your families and girls back home."

"You're our girl, ma'am," said the spokesman with surprising bravado, while they all nodded.

"And we'll always be around," said the corporal, louder and fiercer than he perhaps intended, causing a cheer from all watching.

Susan burst into tears and embraced the shocked leader, kissing him on the nose, before moving on to the next one. "Take care, my brave boys, may your God look after you and the Spirits succour you in need." She made her way to each of the departing soldiers. The corporal, greatly daring, laid a hand on her waist in the nearest any came to returning her embrace. "Remember not to take risks. Work as a team and know that Harrhein needs you back alive, and I am waiting for you to come back whole and healthy."

Biting her lip, she threw her head up and walked fast toward the door to the administrative block, not seeing the faces behind her where men touched their faces where she kissed them. Colonel Donnell did not turn as she entered, but continued to take in the scene outside. Susan sat opposite his desk and composed herself.

"I wonder if I could recruit more girls like you to train with the men," he mused as he turned to her. "Now, Susan, today I want to cover the older families and their allegiance." He trailed off as Susan raised a hand.

"Did you know that Lady Belvedere operates a mine north of the Granthole, near the Coillearnacha border?"

"I am aware of her mining interests, yes..."

"Did you know she buys debtors from the state and puts them down the mines?"

"Well, …"

"People go missing and end up in her mines. They are all enemies of her and her allies, including the Church. In recent years she has become worse, disposing of people she doesn't like or who won't do what she wants."

"You are sure of your information?"

Susan smiled, happy he did not ask for her source. "Frankly, no, it is a new informant. I have tapped a well of resentment and it is flowing in."

"It fits with what I know. What is the name of her mine? She has covered her tracks and we are not aware of her actually owning one mine herself. I confess, most of our efforts are directed outside our borders."

"Lodestar."

"Very well. I will send a patrol to look into it."

"Sir, wouldn't it be better to time it?"

Colonel Donnell sat back and considered the girl, sitting back with a guileless expression on her face. "What do you have in mind?"

"In the spring, many farmers buy seed, but do not have the money to pay for it. They borrow the money. With the spring offensive, the army receives much in the way of supplies, but does not pay for it immediately, usually not till after their return."

"We should look into that, makes it more expensive."

"Lady Belvedere's stewards are heavily involved in these operations. They lend farmers seed in return for a guaranteed harvest and they supply the army. By the beginning of May, she will be fully stretched, like a drum skin."

Colonel Donnell began to smile. "Tell me what you have in mind."

*

Irina laughed, a joyous ringing sound that echoed through the ballroom as she spun Susan around. Their partners tried to keep up in the formation dance as they spun, left floundering as the girls invented more intricate steps while keeping the pattern. The music came to an end and Irina kissed her cheek, whispering in her ear.

"That'll keep the nervous ones at bay for a while. I'm fed up with the mobs."

"I know," said Susan, taking her arm. "No, thank you," she spoke politely to a young baron trying to tempt her back to the dance floor and ignoring Irina placing her heel into a forward viscount's instep. "We girls need a break and drink which we are quite capable of arranging ourselves and we wish to drink on the balcony, alone."

The Spring Dance, by tradition a month early so the officers could attend before the campaign, provided entertainment for all the nobility. Susan felt a pang for Ricky's absence, icebound on the frontier, as her gaze took in what seemed to be the entire nobility of the country.

"The Lavolta is not to be played tonight," groused Irina. "What nonsense. The Church can be so tiresome."

"It isn't the Church. The Privy Council warned Richard he could not dance it with me under any circumstances, and he banned it in case anybody else danced it with me!"

"They're really making life difficult for you. I don't know why they are so upset about you, did you refuse to sleep with some of them?"

"Irina! As if they would dare ask. No, but they think I am a bad influence on Richard. They're probably not wrong either, dreadful some of the things they want him to do. Also, the Palace suppliers are now the best, no chance for most of them to sell their rotten produce. The Pathfinders and the Royal Guards are following the same procedures we instituted in the Palace and the Crown is taking more money than we used to, money they think should be lining their coffers. And half of them do whatever Lady Bitch tells them."

"Hush. Here she comes now."

"Darlings! There you are! Why, I declare you two are the prettiest girls in the city and here you have hidden yourselves away. It is not to be countenanced." She strode up to them with her spare frame and gripped Susan's shoulder. "Nicky, you lucky boy, let me introduce you to Susan. Her fiancé is away on the front and so she is all alone. You must console her."

A tall, black haired boy with hooded eyes grasped Susan's hand and he brushed his lips across the back of her knuckles. A spark raced up her arm, tingling into her brain and her nipples tightened with an involuntary spasm. She gasped, covering it in an instant but not before Lady Belvedere spotted it. Her eyes gleamed as she switched her hand to Irina's arm and pulled.

"Come along, Irina. There is a boy I so want you to meet."

If Irina said anything as Lady Belvedere dragged her away, Susan missed it as she drowned in the boy's blue eyes. He sat beside her on the padded velvet lovers' seat vacated by Irina, keeping hold of her hand with his left while running his right over the back of her shoulders. She shuddered at his touch, finding herself longing for more. He smiled as her lip quivered.

"I dreamt of this moment, while I worshipped you from afar," he said and his voice played symphonies through her dreams as she relaxed in his arm. "You are the fairest jewel in our kingdom, the most perfect girl there has ever been. I adore your perfection." He released her hand and traced her brow, fire trailing behind his finger. He ran his hand with slow and languorous deliberation, outlining her right eye, down her nose and cupping her chin, while his thumb gently pressed her lips open. She moaned as he bent down and pressed his lips to hers, his insistent tongue pushing into her mouth and filling her up with fire. He breathed the fire into her mouth, it was all she could sense as it swirled up into her brain and rushed down to coalesce on her nipples.

In a moment her aching right nipple found release as his hand encircled her budding breast and the thumb flicked her nipple before trapping it between finger and thumb. She screamed into his mouth as unbearable pleasure flooded through her and her left nipple begged for release from its solitude.

A feeling of desolation swept over her as he pulled back, smiling as he pulled her dress down to expose her left breast and capturing it with his mouth. Susan gaped like a drowning fish, unable to make a sound now with the sensations and fires burning down her stomach and turning her belly to water, while her arousal seeped through.

"Come," he said, releasing her and standing up, "let us find somewhere more private."

She stood with him, grasping his hand and returning it to her breast where it belonged and she smiled, ready to go where he led. Conscious he wanted a bed and now desperate to feel him inside her. She moaned and ran her hand down his front to his trousers, ignoring his attempt to frustrate her but coming to an abrupt halt when she found only softness, not the rigid bar she expected.

Confused, she staggered after him as he started to pull her down the corridor, one hand pulling her dress back up, and resisting the inclination to rip it off. Nicky reached a door, having slipped past three and turned the handle.

"That's far enough, I reckon." A gravelly voice came out of the darkness and Nicky recoiled, before trying to push into the room. A spear dropped down in front of him and he turned to the soldier glaring at him, raising a hand. A sword touched his neck and another voice spoke.

"Cast that spell and you're dead, mate."

Susan shook her head, tying to brush away the cobwebs, bereft of Nicky's touch on her body.

"It's okay, boys, don't hurt him, he's my friend. We're just going for a little walk."

"He ain't your friend, Duchess and the only walk he's gonna do is to the bloody gallows!" The fury in the soldier's voice echoed in the dark, helping to wash away the cobwebs. Sudden fear burst from Nicky and she wanted to smooth it away, make him better.

"What is going on here?" Lady Belvedere's voice boomed. "The hussy! Look at the state of her dress! What is she trying to do with my poor Nicky? Only just arrived in the city and already prey to this conniving harlot."

"Disgusting," said the man beside her, dressed in a bishop's robes. "Who is the creature?"

"It is the king's low-born mistress, Your Grace," said Lady Belvedere, triumph in her eyes.

Susan just wanted them gone, so she could get into bed with Nicky. Her groin pulsed with need and she bit her lip.

"Now, my man," said Lady Belvedere to the nearest soldier, "you have the wrong miscreant there. Release my Nicky and bring this hussy out where everyone can see her."

The soldier grinned at her. "I ain't your man and I ain't one of your toy soldiers. I'm a Royal Pathfinder, extra duties for tonight. Betcha didn't expect that in your little schemes, didya, witch? As for your bloody fucking Nicky, 'e's gonna hang he is, and I'm gonna pull his fucking feet to make sure he's bloody dead."

Lady Belvedere went white, staggered back while the bishop looked shocked. "I say, you can't use that sort of language in front of a lady!"

"That's no fuckin' lady and the Duchess is too spelled up to hear a bloody word. And you can shut it, mush, or I'll arrest you as well as her."

Another soldier appeared behind them and grasped Lady

Belvedere's arm.

"Get your hands off me! Guards! Gentlemen! Help, I am being ravished!"

"That ain't happened in a long bloody time," muttered the soldier under his breath. "White, stop it. Put that away."

"But sarge, the Duchess is spelled and I was gonna fix it." The guard held a crystal in his hand.

"I know she is, you bloody idiot, but the king needs to see her spelled first."

On cue, a bevy of men arrived, the king amongst them and out of breath. Several of the men wore livery and bore candelabras which lighted the scene, revealing several more Royal Pathfinders in the shadows.

"Thank goodness you are here, your highness," began Lady Belvedere, "I can't believe what I found your mistress doing."

"Quiet, woman. Sergeant, report."

"Sir! The Duchess and Lady Sarl sat drinking at that seat when approached by this gentleman and Lady Belvedere." The way the soldier said gentleman was not a compliment. Lady Belvedere started at her name, appraising the soldier who actually knew her. "Lady Belvedere introduced the gentleman and left, taking Lady Sarl with her. It did not appear that Lady Sarl wished to go. Our crystals tingled and we knew he was using magic and he led her straight to this bedroom here, sir, where we apprehended him."

"That is not true! Oh, the infamy," cried Lady Belvedere with a note of unease in her voice.

Susan slumped to the floor, head in her hands, moaning softly. Her dress gaped and the king rushed forward, scooping her up.

"'Scuse me, sir," said the sergeant, stepping forward and pressing a crystal to her forehead. Susan shuddered and opened her eyes. She stared at King Richard in disbelief.

"Wha, what's, wha," she started before he interrupted her.

"Hush, baby, it's all right now." The king fixed the sergeant with a glare. "Why didn't you de-spell her earlier?"

"Needed you to see it yourself, sir, so you wouldn't object when we hang the bastards. All right lads, take 'em away."

There was a scuffle as Lady Belvedere resisted. Nicky could barely move, after a surreptitious thump on the back of the head.

"Take your hands of me, don't you know who I am?" The bishop was shaken and white as a soldier pulled him along.

"We hang this one too, sarge?"

"Nah, let him go. You, sir, need to watch what sort of people you consort with. I reckon this one just wanted you to witness her conniving. Best you stay clear of 'er. Run along now."

The bishop looked round for support and finding none he backed into the crowd of fascinated onlookers. A middle aged dowager grasped his arm and supported him, without taking her eyes of the scene.

Susan was crying, great hulking sobs racking her body. "A bath, please, I need a bath. He touched me. Oh, I feel so dirty. A bath, must have a bath."

"Hush, baby," said the king, standing up with her and glaring at the sergeant. "I think you left something out, sergeant."

"Her arm, she means, sir." The sergeant gave the king a frown. "We'll 'ang 'im straight away, sir, Pathfinder justice. In our barracks. She's one of our own, our mascot. The old biddy will keep till morning, mebbe she wants to tell us somethin'."

The old biddy started screeching. "No! It is a mistake! I barely know the man, he just arrived with letters from a friend up country. How was I to know he would do something like this… Ooooph!"

A hulking soldier lifted her up onto his shoulder, which sank into her belly and blew the wind out of her. Two soldiers followed him with a semi-conscious Nicky draped between them.

The sergeant snapped to attention as a spare man, General Roberts, whipcord thin, picked his way through the crowd. He nodded to the sergeant, but spoke to the king.

"Come on Dick. Let's get her out of here. Sergeant Baines has it well in hand. I'll oversee the court personally, Baines. Convene in an hour, two colonels on the bench with me. Colonel Donnell to be the summoner. No more than six witnesses and I want to hear from the bishop."

"We'll be ready, general."

Another interruption as Irina arrived, pushing past a restraining arm and barging the general out of the way. Ignoring the king, she tried to hug Susan who burst into fresh tears and managed to get an arm around her as well as the king, who staggered under the weight of two girls, and some feminine anatomy pushed into his face.

"Damn it, girl, get off!"

But Irina was crying as well and the general solved the conundrum by picking up Irina and the two men staggered down the corridor to the Royal bathrooms, while the sergeant's men kept back the enthusiastic volunteers wishing to help, including other officers.

*

Two hours later Susan, wrapped in warm furs, one hand holding Irina's in a vice-like grip and the other holding a tisane of warming herbs, watched through the steam as the king lost his temper.

"What the hell do you mean I can't hang the bitch? We caught her red-bloody handed setting up Susan, using magic of all things to get that slimy toad into bed with her. After hanging her we'll draw and quarter her and leave her head on the pike in front of the palace like we did in the old days. And it wasn't so bloody long ago! My grandfather warned me not to trust these blasted Gallic political spiders, told me I should execute the bloody lot of them."

"Times change, sire," said an old man patiently. He was the Leader of the Privy Council, and uncomfortable to be in Susan's rooms, but the king refused to leave her and the meeting was important to save the Kingdom. "The woman has a lot of leverage. She can bring down your throne, and she will if you execute her. Well, her people will. She must be released, released without charge."

"Never," roared the king. "I will see her hang in the morning. I will hunt down her family and…"

"Richard," said Susan. "That is enough. Lord Gower, please leave us now. Never fear, she will be released in the morning. You may tell your mistress you have succeeded, but tell her also that it is on my word, and I hold her life in my hands."

"She is not my mistress," began Lord Gower.

"Of course not," said Susan with a smile. "Good night, Lord Gower."

The general opened the door for him and after hesitating a moment, he left the room. The king fulminated from beside the fire and he rounded on Susan, who spoke before he could.

"The revenge is mine to take, darling. I will break her first, and then finish her."

The king subsided, shocked by the look of steel and hatred in his little girl's eye.

"How can we help, my dear?" asked the general.

"Colonel Donnell and I have it well in hand, sir. We shall strip all influence, wealth and position from her before the summer. Irina, darling, you are moving into my house. You will stay in the room beside mine, I won't have you subjected to her threats. General, there is a certain carpenter who needs employ in the Pathfinders."

"Since when did it become your house?" King Richard complained as the general nodded. "It's supposed to be a palace."

"Since the day you abducted me," said Susan with a flat stare. She struggled to her feet. "I need to sleep. I'm sorry, darling, but tonight I am going to sleep with Irina. I love you, but after that I don't want a man touching me tonight, even you. General, your men all have charms, to protect them from magic, I think. May I have one tomorrow? I do not wish to go through that again."

"Of course, I will speak to Colonel Donnell. Come on Dick, leave these poor girls."

With bad grace, the king followed his general from the room.

*

The door crashed open and both girls jumped up in bed as a figure lurched into the bedroom and fell on the floor. Irina squealed and grabbed Susan who held her back and they watched transfixed as the figure muttered and pulled himself up using the bedstead. The first rays of dawn crept through the cloth Susan hung in her windows, revealing dishevelled red hair, shot with grey.

"Buggrit," said the face as it appeared, smiled and fell forward.

"Richard?" Susan peered at him, while the door swung shut with a creak, loud in the dawn, and she wiped the sleep from her eyes. "Are you drunk?"

The girls moved away, repelled by a gust of brandy fumes emanating from the corpse on the bed. The king started to snore. Irina started to giggle and Susan turned to her.

"What?"

"All the stories we read as little girls, when we dreamed of marrying a handsome prince who would whisk us off to his palace on his dashing white charger? And look how we end up. Me with a duke too old to do anything and you as mistress to a drunk!"

"It's not funny, Irina," said Susan in annoyance. "You forgot to add being groped by every wretched courtier in the place and political assassins seducing you with magic." To her irritation, this served to redouble the girl's laughter.

"Oh sweet, always look on the bright side. Come on, let's get him ready for bed. Can't leave him like this."

"Why not? I told him to leave me alone tonight."

"And he couldn't. He was so upset he got drunk. Means he loves you. Come on. She pulled off his shoe. "Oooh, nasty. You should wash him more. Bring the water and flannels here, we'll do it now, can't have this smell in your bed."

"He's never been drunk before," said Susan in a small voice, bringing the water bowl over.

"Sometimes I forget how young you are," said Irina, pausing with a sock in her hand. "We need to get him out of these clothes or he will stink the place out, and we must get him to use the garderobe too."

"I don't think he is capable of that," said Susan in a tone of wonder as she worried at a shirt button before finding it was an ornament, not a fastening.

"Well, you don't want him pissing on your bed, so we'll have to help him."

Susan twitched, yanking off the button in the process. "Help him? I'm not doing that. What are you doing?"

Irina had removed the king's trousers and underwear, and was now inspecting his manhood with a critical eye. "Hmmph. Not very royal like this, is he? Come on, get a move on with his shirt." She dunked a flannel in the water, wrung it out and started wiping the king's body down with quick, efficient strokes. The king protested in his sleep, with weak shoving motions from his hands while Susan found herself a shade of deep red as she eased off his shirt. She realised this was the first time she had seen the king naked since the witch incident when she was a little girl, but was too embarrassed to reveal this to Irina. Copying her, she cleaned his torso, smiling for the first time as she washed his face and kept away his hand which tried to stop her.

Irina left the bed and opened the garderobe doors, pushing the clothes out of the way to reveal the hole going down the outside of the palace and wrinkling her nose at the smell. "Phew, you should get your maid to burn some juniper here every day. And she can empty your chamber pot elsewhere, not be so lazy as to use yours. Come on, let's get him up."

She strode to the bed and took the king's left arm, nodding to Susan to take the other. Both girls pulled and the king sat up, opened his eyes and looked at them with bleary interest. The girls wore their nightdresses, Irina's borrowed from Susan and a little too small. His eyes alit on the insufficient cloth covering her breasts and he responded as they pulled him standing. He staggered and Irina put her shoulder under his arm, while Susan put aside her uncertainty to follow suit. Irina led them slowly towards the garderobe, one hand supporting the king's back and the other trying to push his left hand off her breast.

"Do you need to be sick?" Irina asked, releasing her breast. The king thought about this and nodded. The girls eased him down so he knelt in front of the hole and he heaved twice before vomiting copious amount of liquid. Irina massaged his back with practised ease. "Good thing you didn't burn the juniper after all. Get him a drink of water, love, he will need it now."

She retained a damp cloth and wiped his face before allowing another regurgitation. The king accepted the glass from Susan and drank. Irina hauled him upright and held him in front of the hole. "Pee."

Nothing happened for a moment, while Susan found the fascination with the foreign process of male urination sufficient to overcome her embarrassment and she watched with avid interest.

"Can't," said the king. "Might miss."

Irina muttered under her breath before speaking out loud. "Susan, you must hold it. Point it for him."

Susan stared for a moment, realising that if she didn't, Irina would. Steeling herself, she grasped the dangling flesh and raised it to point at the hole. Immediately she felt a vibration and watched the water gushing out, down the hole and she could direct it where she wished. Absolute power. Fascinating. The king finished all too soon, just as she was getting the hang of washing away bits of dirt and Susan found herself reluctant to release him, but accepted the cloth from Irina to wipe him, ignoring the increasing girth.

The girls helped him back to the bed where he hung on to them both as he fell backwards laughing, Susan clamped to his side, while she saw Irina break free by rolling away. "What now?" she asked.

"Looks like you have a new pillow," she smiled. "Aren't you glad we washed him? I will go find my bed in my room." She slipped off the far side of the bed and came round to kiss Susan. "Good luck."

Richard erupted from the bed, causing both girls to squeal, grasped Irina and threw her into the bed beside Susan, before climbing between them with an arm round each to ensure no escape. "Need both," he muttered.

Both girls erupted in a fury of wriggling limbs as they tried to escape, but the king hung on tightly. He hauled Susan in and on top of him, to discover his enjoyment of the scene.

"Richard! I told you I wanted to be alone, without a man tonight. Have you forgotten what happened? Have some respect, please. Let me get over it. I just need a few days." She stopped struggling and wept on his chest. Richard responded by pulling her into position and pulling her nightdress out of the way. "Please, Richard."

"Don' worry. I make you forget. Best way. Best way to get over it. Me. Fix you." He nuzzled her hair while with his left hand he pulled Irina, who had stopped struggling in order to listen, closer. She managed to get a grip of his little finger and tried to pull it outwards.

"Richard, no, I said no, especially not with Irina in the room."

"More fun." He pulled Irina towards him and attempted to kiss her. Susan struck, her little fingers digging into his ribs and scratching violently. The king's back arched, throwing Susan into the air as he shrieked with laughter, releasing Irina. "No fair. Tickling, no fair!"

Irina stood at the bottom of the bed, hesitating as to whether to help or not. Susan was now trapped underneath Richard and met her eyes, the sparkle back in them.

"Go! Go find your room. I'll be okay."

Betrayal

The flimsy table groaned under the weight of food, situated in a bow window overlooking the gardens. A smitten manservant eagerly waited for another command as Irina checked stability and inched her chair closer. She dismissed him with a wave and spooned honey onto a small bowl of porridge.

A door opening caught her attention and Susan approached, also wrapped in a robe and yawning as she came up, sniffing in appreciation.

"You look better darling. And how is his naughtiness?"

"Snoring like a grampus, both ends." Susan put a hand over her mouth, shocked at her own words, quickly checking the servants had disappeared. Irina snickered.

"True love, so romantic. Salt on your porridge? I thought you were Galician not some hardy northerner."

"Eat sweet, lots of meat," said Susan, glancing at Irina's well-hidden figure.

"Hey! It's all in the right place. Bosoms and bottoms, that's what they want."

"Well, your bosoms certainly got Richard going last night. Wretched man wouldn't stop."

"I'm sorry, darling," said Irina, swallowing some porridge and looking pleased with herself. "I hope it was fun, and made up for all the unpleasantness?"

"Oh, yes," said Susan with a small smile. "I think some of the magic was still in me and I transferred it to Richard. Most satisfactory. Can anyone get hold of that stuff?"

Irina eyed her in amusement. "Not easily. The Church tries to keep a monopoly on it, trains anyone with any ability to become a bishop. That laddie will have been from the seminary. Of course there are a few who escape the net and work it out themselves. Most kill themselves as there isn't any other training, but the odd one gets through. Go to the right shop in the market and you can buy trinkets that work for a while. If the stallholder trusts you."

"I am so embarrassed though. What must you think of me, to see him treat me so." A tear trickled unnoticed down her cheek.

Irina did not answer at first. She weighed her options. She knew now that bedding the king would be a simple matter. But could she keep him? Susan was her patron, keeping her safe, but she was still a child, how long could it last? The moment the king tired of her, the wolves would gather. They already scratched at the gate. Would she be better off if Irina took the king? She could then protect Susan. For a moment, her imagination ran riot as she imagined being taken by the king, a sober king, rampant but malleable under her expert hands. She shuddered in delicious anticipation before pulling back from the brink. She could not survive the choppy political waters and she knew it. Perhaps Susan could. She sipped her tea and composed herself.

"He has placed himself in your power. What you do now dictates your relationship and control." She applied herself to spreading a liberal amount of butter on a slice of warm bread, fresh from the oven and nutty with half milled wheat.

Susan contemplated Irina, aware of the slight flush, the distension of the nostrils. She realised the girl was aroused and tried to make sense of it. She recalled the king grasping her breast and bitterly thought of the half-hearted resistance Irina had put up. Why, now she thought of it, she was certain Irina's nipple was erect. She ground her teeth as she realised she had a rival, nurtured in her very bosom.

"What do you suggest I do?" Inside, she thought that if Irina told her to withhold her body, she would upend the cream bowl all over her.

"Well, first you have to punish him." Irina paused and picked over the apples, selecting one with a hint of red blush. Susan's knuckles whitened on the cream bowl. "You will have to be angry with him." Irina bit into the apple and chewed slowly. Her eyes flicked over Susan's hands and she spoke with care. "With a man like King Richard, you must not refuse to sleep with him. He would just go elsewhere, and after last night I would be the first target. We don't want that, do we?" She looked into Susan's eyes as the cream bowl quivered, but survived.

"Certainly not, I would like us to continue to be friends. So, what do you suggest?" Inside, she was still fuming and the king chose this moment to push through the doors and come over to them, beaming a wide and hearty smile.

"Good morning ladies! And isn't it a lovely one. What an excellent place to breakfast. You are looking ravishing as always, my love." He bent down, hugged and kissed an unresponsive Susan, before he turned to Irina. "Wonderful to have not one but two beautiful ladies joining me for breakfast." He bent down to Irina, hugging her and planting a kiss on her cheek, about to test the waters with a squeeze of her breast when Susan hissed behind him and he froze, his hand spread in mid-air.

"Bastard."

"What?" He turned to her, worried she had spotted his hand.

"Bastard. Don't you remember what you did to me last night?" Her voice dropped low, ice cold and sibilant with anger and pain.

"Well, I thought I made you feel better..." his voice trailed off as Susan rose from her seat, and he back-pedalled as she advanced, prodding him in the chest to punctuate her words.

"You" – prod – "rotten" – prod – "bastard. That animal attacked me, I was distraught, in need of sympathy, love and affection. AND YOU GOT BLOODY DRUNK!" The windows rattled as she shouted at him, and he wilted. The manservant about to check on their needs backed away from the door, with a glance to the guard outside, who shuffled his feet wondering what to do. The guard tried to remember his instructions for irate mistresses and came up blank.

Inside the room, King Richard fared badly as Susan found a stick. It wasn't a staff, but used to push the windows open. She treated it like a weapon, and the king cried out as she smacked the hand held up in protection.

"And if that wasn't enough, you burst into the bedroom and jump into bed with me and my friend. A lady. Married to one of your dukes. You were smelly and dirty." She lunged with the stick like a sword and sank it into his belly. The king collapsed with a most satisfactory sound.

"Stop it," he cried. "I'm sorry, I was worried about you and wanted to check you were all right. Guard! Help!"

"Get out!" Susan screamed at the unfortunate guard who put his nose round the door at the king's call. He slammed the door behind him and the king whimpered at his rescuer's departure.

"So. You wanted to check I was all right. And you thought you would do that by feeling Lady Sarl's tits?"

"Ah," said King Richard, warding off another blow from the floor. Outside, a hurried consultation with the Sergeant of the Guard ended with a runner being despatched for the Officer of the Watch.

"You wanted to sleep with both of us," cried Susan, her righteous wrath fuelled by the success of her blows and the memories of the night. The king dodged a blow and exposed his bottom which Susan managed to strike with a very satisfactory smack, a noise that made the guards outside wince. Irina had retreated to the corner of the room, with her sleeve stuffed into her mouth to stop the laughter.

"I was in pain, emotional pain, after nearly being raped, and I needed you to be there for me, to support me in my need, to give me time to recover. Did you? Oh no, instead you barge into the bedroom, fondle my friend's bosoms in front of me, while holding me, and then, and then, and then you RAPED me, on the bed, when I PLEADED with you not to." Sobs started to rack Susan's body and her blows on the prostrate king eased sufficiently for him to knock her legs from under her, and she collapsed on top of him, sitting astride his chest and looking into his eyes.

Outside, the Officer of the Watch arrived in time to hear the tail end of the conversation. He viewed the door as if it might explode at any moment, while wishing he was manning a forward outpost with a Spakka invasion coming over the hill.

Finally, the king did something sensible, and instead of denying all charges, he wrapped his arms round her in a hug, pulling her close to where he could whisper in her ear.

"I'm so sorry, my darling, my love, I love you so much and never want to hurt you. I made a mistake, it won't happen again, I wanted to make you happy, it hurt so much to see you sad."

Susan sobbed into his chest, eyes tight shut, arms round his neck. When he paused, she smacked his head. "Keep talking."

He did. The king used one hand to push himself up from the floor, taking her with him. He kept up a stream of murmured endearments while accepting a hand from Irina to pull them both off the floor. With the reduced volume, the door opened for the Officer of the Watch to peer into the room, poised to retreat from danger. The king gestured sharply for him to go and the door shut.

King Richard swung Susan up into his arms and carried her from the room back to the bedroom while she continued to sob into his neck.

*

The King left the bedroom to be surrounded by people vying for his attention, whom he waved away while his valet dressed him. Susan could hear his personal steward complaining about missed appointments and a furious bishop.

Irina pushed the door open with a plate of sweet pastries in one hand and two mugs of tisane in the other. She closed the door with a foot before coming to the bed, eyes shining. Susan sat up, a multitude of pillows behind her.

"Looks like a good apology," said Irina, surveying the wreckage of the bed.

"Oh yes." Susan accepted a mug and selected a pastry.

"Did you tie him to the bed?" Irina asked, as she inspected a sheet twisted round a bedpost.

"What? Of course not. Why would I do such a thing? Gosh, I hadn't realised I was so hungry. Thanks, Irina."

"My pleasure, darling. So what did you get?"

Susan grinned in satisfaction. "Lots. A villa in Fearaigh, down on the sea, remote and lovely, with a famous horse breeding business attached. Good manager."

"Nice but boring. Where's the jewellery?"

"Box on my dresser."

Irina scooted off the bed and over to the dresser, opening the box and pulling out a magnificent heavy gold necklace with a rampant Elven dragon leaping out as a pendant. "Wonderful. My word, that'll get them looking at your tits." She put it on, arranging the dragon in her cleavage while pulling the robe scandalously low and pushing up her breasts with both hands. Susan choked on a roll. "Clothes?"

"New ball gown. Seamstress coming tomorrow. Satin, Elven satin."

"Nice. What else?"

"His balls on a plate if I catch him looking at your tits again. Even if he catches you naked in the bathroom."

Irina had returned the dragon to its box and now rolled on her back on the bed, laughing. "Poor dear. I shall have to tease him now."

"You will not. Especially as I have dispensation to wear a rapier with my gowns."

"He didn't give you permission? Wow, that's unique. The people will love that, their Warrior Queen. Not sure what the Church will think, they want you on your knees in the kitchen, praying in between popping out brats."

"I don't care what they think. They attacked me and I will make them pay."

"Don't fight the Church, darling, they are too big and powerful. Besides, it wasn't the Church but that hateful woman. What has happened to her?"

"Warned to leave Praesidium for the summer. No doubt she will now plot my downfall from her estates."

"But you have something in mind, I think? Wait, there's something else, isn't there? You are holding something back. Come on, this is the biggie, I can tell! What is it? Proposal of marriage? Are you to be queen?"

"No – it's actually better. He's given me power, political power."

"Umm, I don't get it. How is that better than being queen?"

"Queen is just an official mistress, really. You are now looking at the Chancellor for the Royal Estates."

"What? What does that mean?"

"Close your mouth, Irina, it isn't pretty to gape at me like a lizard. It means that I have to select grounds for development for government projects, like the new shipyards. I am to decide on the final grounds, buy the land and build the yards. That is just one project, and I have a huge budget to administer." Susan ate another pastry with sensuous pleasure, while Irina groped for words.

"You've been angling for this, haven't you? This is just like being bloody chamberlain. But you don't really do anything, you have everyone else doing things and the Duke of Brandton as chancellor. You don't know what to do."

"Don't be dense, Irina. Do you really think Brandton is capable of deciding what to have for breakfast, let alone the palace finances? Who do you think really runs the palace?"

"This is that stupid court of yours. I knew I should have stopped your from doing anything."

"The Ruling Court is brilliant. You may not have noticed, but we have more ladies in the Ruling Court than the Royal Court. Lady Marcia does a terrific job training them to run their estates and Lucinda is a tower of strength. They will help me with the new responsibility."

*

Temperatures climbed as spring gave way to fall and the girls saw less of each other as Susan became busy, though Irina made sure she came to many of her training sessions at the barracks and spent time with Riggs. Susan kept her up to date with her progress as she identified the land she wanted and sent surveyors in. She made Irina go back to Lady Belvedere, through an intermediary, to find out what mischief she was causing.

The news wasn't extensive, it seemed her stewards conducted most of her business while she stayed in her estates, driven there by the feelings of the public. Minstrels wrote derogatory songs about her and small boys would chase her carriage singing them when she ventured out.

Susan managed a visit to the theatre troupe at least once a month, and always booked gallery seats for the first night of each play, taking her growing group of friends. Lady Marcia became most skilled at hurling hazel nuts. The king could not attend as the Church disapproved of theatre and he steered a careful route to avoid offence. Susan attended mass each Sunday with King Richard in the cathedral, keeping a wary truce with the Archbishop with each careful to be polite to the other. She even invited him to supper once a month and discussed ways to improve the training of the Ladies of her Court. The Archbishop did indeed approve.

*

Will walked down Rand Street, turning into Royal Row with a view to watching the new porters at the coach station who were reputed to demonstrate wonderful and colourful invective when provoked. While he considered how best to provoke them, he became aware of a boy walking beside him, matching his steps. He put a hand on his purse, double checking for a cut or slit.

"Hello Will," said the boy, amused. "I bet you are on your way to check out the porters."

Will missed a step and darted another glance at the boy.

"Not today, you're not, because we are going to take tea in the Palladium. Honestly, Will, you taught me to act and to walk and you still don't know who I am?"

Will missed another step. "Susan? Is it really you? What are you doing here, in disguise?"

"Sebastian, remember? Sebastian Delarose and don't you forget. Come on, I'm parched and we need to talk." She led the way to the Palladium, chose a table separated from the rest and hidden in the back. She sat down with her back to the wall, as Will noted with some excitement.

"Quince and apple blossom tea, please," she said to the waitress, while looking at Will.

"Ah, the same will be fine."

"And two of your apple turnovers, please." Susan watched the girl walk away while Will observed her closely. She reached into the inner pocket of her jacket and pulled out a thick sheaf of papers, which she laid on the table. Will looked at them with grave suspicion.

"It's a play. I wrote it."

"You want us to put it on?" Will picked it up with enthusiasm now. "You will have to fund the props and costumes, of course."

"No, it mustn't be associated with you. I want you to read it, tweak it to make it usable without putting your stamp on it, and give it to the Twilight Players through an intermediary. They mustn't know it comes from you. I can arrange funding to make sure they play it. Needs to be anonymous."

"Those bastards. Why would I do anything to help them?"

"This isn't helping. Read it." Will stared at her for a moment, before pulling out the manuscript and starting to read. Susan kept quiet. The tea arrived and without thinking Will sipped from his cup as he read the play. He skimmed through it and after fifteen minutes he laid the papers down with care, as if they would burst into flame. Susan waved for more tea as he stared into space.

"Some of your writing is good enough. I can fix the rest." This was high praise and Susan relaxed, realising she had been as taut as a bowstring. "That woman you had a run in with, Lady Belcher or something, this is her, isn't it?"

Susan inclined her head, then said "Yes," when she realised he wasn't looking at her.

"It will destroy her, won't it? She'll come after the players?"

"Not on its own, it won't, but it will remove a large part of her support and make her vulnerable. I don't know that she will attack the Twilight boys, but she might. I don't think they are smart enough to realise."

"You are doing something else as well." This wasn't a question. "You wrote those songs people are singing about her. You've planned something huge and you want me to help. To put my neck on the line."

"This is part of a plan, yes, but I have worked it so there is no risk for you."

"Stow it, Susan. You knew I would want to do this. I'll re-write this bloody play so it will devastate her, and shake the bloody Church to its foundations. Sod anonymous, I'll put my name on it and we'll do it ourselves. This is real, girl, real stuff, doing good. Nasty piece of work that woman. I want in, all the way."

"She is indeed a nasty piece of work and she is very dangerous. She nearly destroyed me at the Spring Ball, would have if the Pathfinders didn't like me. She is powerful and clever but she is my enemy, not yours, and you mustn't put yourself and the others in danger. Mary cannot risk it, and if Kit gets into any more trouble they will hang him. Re-write it by all means, put your stamp on it, but don't put your name on it. Then if it goes wrong you can claim it was a student, but if it goes right you can claim it. After she destroys Twilight, which she will."

Will stared at her unblinking, before picking up the manuscript again and leafing through it. "How much truth is there in this? Did you make it up?"

"She trained as a Druid when she was young, and the Church don't know. As for the moonlight orgies, who knows but I thought it made a good story and impossible to disprove."

Will smiled for the first time. "About this time, the archbishop died. You're too young to remember. I do though. Big scandal, nobody knows quite what happened, but everybody remembers and has their own ideas. I'll work that in, she seduces him and brings him to a wood where he is sacrificed to the moon."

"Druids don't do sacrifice or worship the moon."

"Yeah, but churchgoers don't know that. Don't worry, they'll believe she did it. The Church then wipes out the coven in revenge and she escapes by pleading her relationship with the Archbishop, says he converted her and she was his disciple."

"I think she does say she was an archbishop's disciple. Did something like that really happen?"

"She does indeed, and who knows but it doesn't matter. By the time I've finished, the whole country will believe it. Damn it, Susan, this is so big, it will be the most popular play ever. The Church will protect us, thank us. We'll put it on, the Twilight mob just can't do it. No, you can't have it back." He folded the manuscript back into the envelope and hid it in his jerkin.

"I need to speak to Mary and Kit." He stood up, turning to leave without paying the bill or saying goodbye, immersed in the story and his lips moving as he composed.

Susan smiled and paid the bill.

*

King Richard strode along Kingsward from his court to the Palace, his guardsmen trailing, their eyes scanning the passers-by. He stopped at a fruit stall and selected a pear from the goodwife, who smiled at him, flirting happily. Round of body and red-cheeked, one of her daughters sat on the stall, thumb in her mouth and regarded the king with round eyes.

A guard stepped forward and gave the woman a silver and the king bit into the pear, turning to go.

"Yer 'Ighness, ang on a mo," said the woman, rummaging under a sack. "Fer the Duchess, keep 'er 'ealthy." She gave a broad wink. "When we gonna 'ave a little prince then, sire?" She proffered a bag of pears, clearly the pick of the crop.

The king threw back his head as a ripple of laughter came out and he leaned forward and touched her cheek. "Not for want of trying," he whispered with a returning wink, accepted the gift and went off, a greater spring in his step. The stewards were always trying to remove the common folk from the Sward, but he wouldn't let them and the folk knew it. The women could move freely here, and the merchants did not worry about being robbed. The only proviso the King made was that the vendors could only sell their own crops or goods and could not own a shop elsewhere.

Today's council meeting instilled more pressure on him, and he needed to think in peace. Lady Belvedere's machinations for the Church assailed him from all sides, cutting off funding he needed for the army. The Pathfinders were stretched thin on the northern frontier and Count Rotherstone ambushed the funding for his planned navy. He was sure Lady Belvedere worked for the Count, but his spies still failed to make a connection. He considered asking Susan, impressed as he was with her ability to find information. He hadn't pressed her on how she built her network, not being certain he wanted to know. Briefly, he wondered if she was faithful, the obvious way for a woman to get news. But no, she was too innocent in bed, he loved the way she responded to the simplest of caresses. So beautiful and he revelled in his possession. His only regret was her lack of upper structure, but there was still time and he intended to develop her, although her political knack was extraordinary. His mind moved on to her friend Lady Sarl, now there was a girl with plenty of frontage. He recalled holding her with pleasure, especially the instant response. Pity Susan was so wary and there was so little time.

He closed the court early today, needing to think, and Susan would be plotting with her stewards. He knew she had cooked up some massive scheme to ensnare Lady Belvedere, but was hazy on the fine points. Colonel Donnell had refused to enlighten him, just told him he was lucky to have Susan and it was a damn fine plan. Considering the twelve thousand crowns missing from the Royal coffers that he needed to cover, it had bloody well better be.

His head buzzed from the fumes of unwashed bodies in the courtroom, and the disgusting scents many used to cover their odour. The Sward wasn't much better. Although dumping night soil carried a serious penalty, people took advantage of the bushes and some of the vendors sold cured meats and cheeses which advertised themselves from afar.

Coming to a decision, he left the Sward and cut down a short passageway to a door in the wall, guarded by a soldier. He dismissed his guardsmen, sending them the long way round as he wanted to be alone. The door led into the palace gardens, planted by his grandmother and loved by his mother, by Queen Rose and now by Susan.

The fresh air with the scents of flowers and resin cleared his nose and head and he ambled, taking time to touch gnarled bark and feel for the life of the tree. Anyone seeing him would accuse him of being a druid, he thought with a laugh. He couldn't feel anything, but liked touching the trees. He knelt by a clear pond where the stream swelled, and smiled as big gold fish, the only ones in Praesidium, a present from the Elf Queen, sucked his fingers.

Standing, he brushed leaves from his trousers and made his way to the Glade, his favourite part of the gardens with an ancient maple, the trunk smooth and glossy, bent into the perfect position for lying back against to look at the sky and think.

His pace quickened in anticipation, he rounded a tree and bumped into a body, which grabbed his arm and pulled. Shocked, he resisted, reaching for his sword before realising it was a girl, trying to avoid falling. He just caught her as she fell and righted her, red hair in a mess obscuring her face.

"Oh, I'm sorry, your highness, I didn't know you would use the gardens." Irina pushed her hair back and showed her face. "I will leave; I am so sorry to disturb you." She didn't move, just smiled at him. "Thank you for catching me."

"My pleasure," he replied, answering the smile. "Why are you in the gardens anyway?"

"Oh, I came to see Susan, but she is so busy with her stewards and had no time for me. She asked me to wait till half past four when she will be free. I thought I would take a turn through the gardens rather than wait in the library."

King Richard smiled again. "Well, then you can entertain me as I walk. Come, let me show you the glade." He held out his arm and she slipped her hand onto his. He turned and walked down the mossy path towards the glade. "So, we don't seem to see so much of you at the moment, what have you been up to?"

"Lord Sarl required my presence for the Spring Festival and I only returned to Praesidium last week." Irina arched her back ever so slightly, pushing her breasts into prominence and checked the effect on the king from under her lashes. She smiled and inhaled a deep, full breath, wobbling on completion. "I've missed it, I don't think I managed to dance once in Sarl. But the journey was awful. You really must improve the roads, sire, they are so bumpy and the inns simply dreadful. The smell of the horses permeates the rooms." She wrinkled her nose at him and shuddered, bouncing in dramatic and riveting fashion.

The king laughed. "You know perfectly well the upkeep of the road is Lord Sarl's responsibility. Now, here is the glade, what do you think?"

They turned into a small open space, short turf surrounded by wild flowers with a bank of bluebells on one side complimented by the pink of ragged robin on the other. Irina gasped in wonder, as if she had never seen it before, and skipped into the centre, twirling with her head to the sky and raising her bosom to greater heights. She plucked a big, blousy tulip from where it nestled at the base of the maple, adorned in the beautiful, pale green new growth leaf and turned, leaning back against the trunk, placing the tulip across her mouth, the stalk gripped firmly in her little white teeth.

The king stepped towards her and she watched him come, eyes sparkling with invitation. His eyes dropped at last to her bosom, widening as he realised how much she exposed. He closed the last few feet and stood, not quite touching her, close enough to feel her warmth, eyes glued to her breasts as he fought for control.

Irina raised her arms in a slow and languorous movement to the sky, before shrugging her dress loose and exposing her bosom. The king groaned as she pulled him down to meet them.

In the palace above a curtain twitched, from the only window overlooking the glade. Inside, Susan stood, frozen as Irina loosened the king's clothing and pulled up her skirts. "I had to know," she whispered to herself. For two months the image of her lover caressing Irina's bosom rose at every opportunity to obscure her vision, stopping her from concentrating. She needed to know they would not take an opportunity, so engineered this meeting. So simple to do, she knew them so well. Pretend business for Irina, arrange a heavy morning and light afternoon for the king. He would always go to the glade when he wanted to think.

She tried to move away, to go down to the garden and confront the pair. But her eyes would not leave the scene unfolding beneath her and her mouth fell open as she watched Irina gyrate, driving the king to speeds and frantic movements beyond her imagination.

"I can't compete," she whispered to herself, a tear escaping down her cheek, her world crumbling. It was a wonder the tree did not break at the crescendo, and Irina caught the king as he collapsed. She turned him round to lean against the tree while dropping to her knees and administering to him with her mouth. Susan gaped in horror, as she watched the king rise again under her skilled tongue before turning her to the grass on all fours and riding her like an animal, a horse or a dog, she thought to herself, not a human being.

This thought sustained her as she repaired the damage to her face and created a mask, her battle mask, she thought, as she sat herself in the library and allowed Treste to serve her tea. '*I am human, not an animal, and my brain is my weapon.*'

The king walked in, escorting Irina as if nothing had happened. She could see no guilt from either of them, though Irina radiated satisfaction. Different from the satiation after she was with Riggs, thought Susan.

"Look who I found in the gardens," said the king as he hugged her and planted a kiss on her cheek.

"I hope you rescued her from Prince," said Susan, inhaling Irina's scent from his hair.

"Prince?" Irina asked. Susan felt exhilarated when she did not flinch as Irina's lips touched her cheek, after seeing where they had been moments before.

"Gardener's cat," said the king, helping himself to a biscuit. "Very dangerous. So what has you so busy today, my darling?"

"We are making the final decisions on where to place the shipyards. I considered both sets and decided on Oyster Bay instead."

"Why not Larkspur Point?"

"Not possible. Marine survey showed there is a sandbank there that channels the tide and would flood where we build. Oyster Bay is the only possibility. We'll start buying the land next month. Prices will drop once crops are in and there is no more seed."

"Can I see the plans?" King Richard smiled when Susan placed them in his hands. Irina peered over his shoulder, starting to rest her breasts on him in possessive style before thinking better. "First time you've let me see them."

"They are finished now. All done. We won't change, all is fixed bar the building and land purchase."

"What is the budget? Are you on course?"

"We are not sure quite how much we will have to pay for the land, so I have prepared figures for the worst case, should one of the farmers get an inkling and put the price up." She pulled another paper from the carrier beside her and let him see it. Irina leaned over to have a look, and Susan pulled it away.

"Sorry, darling, a bit secret, I'm sure you understand." She put the papers away in the carrier, stood up and placed it in a drawer on the desk, locking the drawer. "Now, I am desperate for some entertainment. Something different. Why don't we all dress up as drovers and go drinking in the taverns on Barter Road?"

"You're as bad as my daughter," the king complained while Irina blanched. "We have an unofficial dinner tonight."

Susan's eyes gleamed. "Did Rotherstone accept? I can't wait to see what he looks like. I imagine tall and pale skinned, with swept back short black hair, a lantern jaw and skinny cadaverous looks."

"Not far off. No chance of him coming. I don't know what you've done, but he pulled back after you arrived. Not nearly as troublesome and annoying. I'm wondering if he is going to offer a truce."

"No, he's just using a catspaw," said Susan, inwardly cursing herself for revealing too much, and just biting down on Lady Belvedere's name.

"You have someone in his employ?" King Richard showed interest while Irina helped herself to another biscuit.

"Just guessing. Irina, will you stay for supper? I need somebody to entertain the Bishop of Westport."

"As long as I can borrow a nice dress and freshen up first."

"I still have some things of yours in my room. No trouble."

Champion

"I swear you've broken my bloody arm."

"Don't swear in front of the Duchess, Brand."

"Ah, sod it, hurts like buggery. Stop laughing Duchess, you're going to need a new sparring partner and I don't reckon anyone here will give you a go. I'm stuffed for at least a month."

"You should know better than try to block with your arm, Mr Staff Champion of the Regiment."

"She's too damn fast. I bet you didn't even see it, Riggs, at least I tried to stop her. And I reckon she is now."

Sergeant Murphy jumped up on a bale and called out in his stentorian voice. "Regiment, SHUN! Turn to face the new Champion, the Duchess, Staff Champion of the Pathfinders. By my order, preseeennnnnttt ARMS!"

All the soldiers in the training ground stamped their feet at the same time, those with weapons holding them aloft in a parody of the Guards. Pathfinders were not so good at drill.

"Idiots," said Susan, smiling and throwing her staff at the sergeant. She dunked her head in the horse trough and surfaced to find herself surrounded by men wanting to shake her hand. "Come on boys, I'm late for my strategy meeting. Brand delayed us with his acting."

"Acting? I'm dying, so I am," said Brand in outrage and proved it by falling over. Another soldier inspected him, before kicking him hard in the ribs.

"Yup, he's dead. Nothing to worry about, Duchess, you carry on."

Still chuckling, she walked in and sat in front of the desk, appreciating the hot tea anticipating her arrival.

"She's started buying," said Colonel Donnell, his head in a report.

"What is she paying?"

"More than I expected. A lot more. Still leaves her with a 100% profit when we move in. Can't understand why she is unable to buy it lower. That land is worthless. I'm surprised it even has owners." Susan sipped her tea serenely. The colonel looked at her, suspicion growing on his face. "What have you done?"

"She will buy it all before the end of the week. She is on a deadline, as she thinks we start buying next week."

Distracted as intended, the colonel read his figures again. "She knows that? You got to her, didn't you? I couldn't figure out a way. And I screened your committee personally, she never even tried to get a spy in."

"She placed the spy elsewhere. The spy thought I didn't know. I reeled her in, made her secure." Susan's face contorted. "I even let her sleep with the king, she thinks I don't know. And she's better than me. In bed. I can't do what she does. He's going to kick me out and take her instead, I know it." She buried her face in her hands and the tears overflowed, dripping down.

Colonel Donnell saw Susan break for the first time and rose to comfort her. Half way round the desk, he stopped, thinking, before returning to his seat. He let her cry for five full minutes before she stopped and raised her head to look at him.

"Better?" He asked, without expression.

"I'm sorry," she said. "I don't know what came over me. I am usually stronger."

"Susan, you are one of the smartest people I know. Your mind works fast and sure, finding complex, elegant solutions to problems most people don't even recognise. You are still just seventeen, your training has barely started, how can you expect to have the same experience as a woman several years older than you? A woman who has enjoyed, I might add, considerably more partners than you probably know about. No, let me continue. The king is a man and susceptible to flattery and an enticing bosom. Yet he is no fool, and in you he knows he has a rare jewel. He will not discard you for Lady Sarl, that I promise."

"You knew."

"I did not. I suspected it would happen, knowing the woman."

"You could have warned me."

"To what end? You would not have believed me and now you have created your own solution."

"I watched them. They were in the garden and I was in the window overlooking the glade. I set it up because I needed to know." Her gaze went out the window, following the flight of a sparrow that chirped in anger from its landing spot on a rail outside. "I didn't know a woman could, would, do those things. I couldn't imagine moving your body like that, or that a man would like it. She did not just pick these things up, did she? She didn't work them out herself? She was taught, wasn't she? Who by?"

"The Seminary takes in girls as well as boys, and finds each their calling. They married her to Sarl to strengthen the ties of the Church in his dukedom. They recalled her to help Lady Belvedere when she needed a woman of quality to befriend you."

Susan was quiet for a moment before raising her head. "I have no friends, do I? You are not my friend, are you?"

"I cannot be your friend, no. Because my duty is to my king and country, and you are a tool that I must temper and train. That training is painful at times, and you will suffer. A true friend would not let you go through that. I will drive you through and make you a better person."

She studied his eyes for a long moment before sighing, long and hard. "Maybe that makes you a truer friend. I know the training I need now. I just don't want it." She wept now, letting her tears fall unchecked. "Don't let it be Riggs, I couldn't stand that. Find me a nice trainer, please Colonel."

Colonel Donnell stood and turned to hide his emotion. His fists clenched so hard he felt blood welling in his palms. "You are eighteen next month. Let us at least wait till then. I believe the king has plans."

"It is supposed to be a surprise. I am busy checking his plans and amending them to make them suitable. I shall be delighted, of course and suitably thankful." She arose and made for the door.

"Susan," said the Colonel. "You wanted this." She held the door open, her face towards him, eyes huge, luminous and tragic, denying his words. "From when you were a little girl, you wanted to be queen. Queen Rose graduated from the Seminary. She was a damn good queen. You will be better."

*

"Who the hell are you?" King Richard's voice boomed in the small room causing the balding man to jump out of his chair, from where he sat with his head against Susan's as they went over figures on paper.

"Sire! I am Sir Timothy Brown, merchant by your charter."

"What are you doing with my wi-, ah, ward?" The king's eyes glowed in anger.

"He's teaching me about futures, darling, grain futures. Fascinating stuff. Come and have a look."

"Damme, don't you know what bloody time it is? It's gone five, its already getting bloody dark outside."

"So it is," said Susan, peering at the window. "I am so sorry, Timmy, I have kept you late again. Can we continue tomorrow at three? That won't inconvenience you? Excellent. I shall show his highness the charter and we should be set tomorrow."

Sir Timothy Brown nodded in agreement, swept his papers in to a sack and scuttled from the room.

"Charter? What bloody charter? I want some tea and your company, damn it, not some tomfoolery with paper and futures. And who is that bloody man? I don't like him." The king felt in need of being the centre of Susan's world. His own recent indiscretion with Irina welled up feelings of guilt, which he assuaged in time honoured fashion by being jealous of anyone with Susan.

"That bloody man is the finest financial mind in Praesidium, perhaps the richest man in the city, my tutor in money and our partner. He makes most of the money you use to pay the army."

"Partner? Oh, never mind, tell me over tea. Any more of your friends going to jump out of the woodwork or can I have you to myself for once?"

"I thought you liked it when Irina came round?" Susan spoke with as innocent a tone as she could muster and smiled inside at the look of guilt flashing over the king's face before he changed the subject.

"I told the cook I wanted a high tea. Means we can have an early night. I want you to myself for once." He leered at her and she pretended incomprehension.

"Oh, but I'm not at all sleepy. Of course it is a good idea to lie down after a heavy meal, we can't take any exercise for a good two hours after eating a high tea. Shall we stroll down Kingsward beforehand?"

He gave an inarticulate roar and picked her up, carrying her to the bedroom while she giggled in satisfaction and called to the servant, as he came in the door, to serve the high tea in an hour.

*

"So tell me about futures," said the king as he tucked into some pork. "Damn, doesn't taste like boar, what the hell is it? Tasty, mind."

"Raised on your farm in the Forest of Antarch. Black saddle pig. Fed on acorns and chestnuts for flavour. The ham is excellent too. Futures are how the Church make money from farming." The king grunted and ate some more pork, chewing methodically while he waited. Susan took a moment to gather her thoughts.

"Farmers and buyers agree when the seed is planted what to pay for the crop when it is harvested. Neither can change the price. The buyer will sometimes pay a percentage to the farmer at planting time. That is what the Church do, to get a better price later."

The king furrowed his brow. "This is not making money. It is just agreeing a deal in the future."

"Mmmmh. But it takes risk away for the farmer. He knows what he will get and allows him to plant more, get more fields under cultivation, while the bakers knows they have enough wheat to expand and set up another bakery, for example. People like certainty, and they will pay for it." Susan helped herself to another portion, noting her increased appetite and wondering if she was pregnant at last. She made a mental note to speak to the herb woman Mary knew.

"The Church isn't very nice. They pay a premium now and get the wheat cheap at harvest, selling it to bakers who haven't managed to get enough. By storing as much as possible, they hope to force the price up. Other merchants are doing the same, result is that they are making more money out of the wheat than the farmer or the baker and people pay more."

The king placed his knife and fork down with deliberate care. His face devoid of expression, he spoke. "That is outrageous. I shall ban it."

"You can't," said Susan. "You don't have enough power. The Church will block you in parliament and twist your intentions. Every pulpit in the country will tell the devout how you are stopping the Church from putting bread on their tables."

"Damn you," said the king. "Come on, out with it. What are you doing?"

"We are setting up a bank."

"What," said the king with remarkable patience, "is the edge of river doing in this conversation?"

"In this case it is the edge of a dirty great pile of money. Here's the charter, I need you to sign it tonight. You have the authority, don't need parliament, I checked." She placed a large ornate scroll on the table, impressive seals and ribbons dripping from it. The king regarded it with grave suspicion.

"I'm not signing this until I understand." The king looked worried now, it was a long scroll and the earlier adjournment served to whet his appetite for more Susan. This gave every indication of postponing the next course.

"A bank is a place that makes money. Every king should have one. People can store their money in the bank so it is safe and they can borrow money from the bank." The king pricked up his ears at this, as kings never have enough money and are always seeking new ways to raise taxes and borrow from their nobles.

"No," said Susan, a narrowed eye focusing on the king. "You can't. I specifically wrote into the charter that you are exempt from being able to borrow money from the bank. This is a Royal Bank for the People. Farmers can borrow and so can bakers, but not kings."

"So this bank will mean the farmers don't need to go to the Church? And sell wheat futures? The Church won't like that."

"The Church isn't going to realise until it is too late. They have already sold this year's futures and by next year the bank will be too popular."

"If there is so much money in one place, won't some wide boy walk in and make off with it? Probably a priest."

"I did a deal with Bobby."

"Bobby? General Roberts? That lecherous old sot! You've been meeting him without my knowledge? What sort of deal?"

"He's my commanding officer, don't forget. I am a member of the Pathfinders too. I am entitled to talk to him."

"Only if you call him sir or general, not bloody Bobby."

She reached out with unexpected speed and pulled his nose. "You're sweet when you're jealous. Anyway, he turned me over to his quartermaster with a seal of approval, and now the Pathfinders will all have their wages paid through the bank. Anybody who steals from it will have Pathfinders after them and Pathfinder justice."

Richard sought another option, beginning to feel pushed. He decided to refuse to sign, after all, he was king. As he opened his mouth to refuse, Susan cut across him.

"Of course, although you can't have a loan, you can and will tax the bank. Not in the first year, as we are getting it established, but in subsequent years it will pay a special bank tax, as will other banks when the Church decides to open its own."

A thought struck him. "Where is the money for this bank coming from anyway? Your wretched merchant? Did you sleep with him as well as bloody Bobby to get enough money?" As soon as he said it, he regretted it. Susan's face pinched down, reminding him of a warhorse before it reared and struck.

"Actually, I gave him fifty thousand crowns of my own money. A bit less than fifteen thousand of that is yours."

"Fifty fucking thousand? Where in hell did you get that sort of money?"

"Don't be crude, Richard. I sold some stuff. Some land actually."

"Land? What bloody land? When did you buy it?"

"I spent the last three months buying up Oyster Bay through a number of friends. Last week Lady Belvedere bought the lot at fifty percent of the price she thinks we are going to pay for it next week. Comes to a little over fifty thousand. I kept the change."

"She thinks she is going to make fifty thousand in a week?"

"Yes, I'm most impressed actually. She had to scrape together all her spare cash and call in all the loans she could. Why, she even borrowed some money from me at a horrible rate. She doesn't know it is me, of course."

"But how did she know about it?"

"Irina, of course."

"Irina? But you locked the plans in the drawer. And Irina hates Lady Belvedere."

"Irina knows where I keep the key. She belongs to Lady Belvedere, always has."

Susan helped herself to a portion of bread and butter pudding and started to spoon it into her mouth, closing her eyes in pleasure at the texture of the coarse bread softened in sweet custard.

"This is my favourite room, you know Richard." He eyed her with wary concern, not used to this steel woman grown from his little girl. "I love working here, the view of the gardens is beautiful and I find it restful." Susan took another spoonful of pudding.

"Go to the window, Richard, and tell me what you see."

Sensing doom, Richard approached the window wondering what he would see in the swift gathering dusk. "Ah, trees. The stream. Gardens."

"Just right of centre, about fifty feet away, do you see that lovely young maple in the glade? Such a lovely view of it from here, don't you think? Sit down, Richard. Sign here." She pushed a quill into his hand. He scrawled his name. "And here."

"Good boy. Such a clever decision, this is going to make you a lot of money. It's all right, Richard. It wasn't your fault. She was trained at the Seminary, you know."

"What are you going to do to her?"

"You care? Why? Do you want her again? You can, you know. I don't mind. I will wait till you tire of her. After all, I don't have those skills, do I Richard? I wasn't trained at the Seminary, not like Irina and Queen Rose."

"I don't want her again; it was a mistake the first time. I'm sorry, all right? It won't happen again."

"Stop babbling, you are the king, remember. Of course it will happen again, anytime I let you out of my sight when some Seminary harlot is thrown at you, or the big eyed daughter of a duke." She paused and returned to the food, serving Richard a portion of pudding, pouring extra cream over the top. "Would you like me to have those skills, Richard?"

King Richard closed his eyes, praying for the shouting to start. These quietly spoken words with realms of meaning turned him inside out. He knew whatever he said would make it worse. Maybe silence would work.

"Richard? Would you like me to have those skills?"

He smiled bravely at her, opening his eyes and trying to look honest and open, failing. He opened his mouth to say yes, and perhaps some herbs to make her bosoms bigger, but his inner self smacked him figuratively on the head before inspiration struck.

"Darling, I love you. Whatever makes you happy is fine by me."

She inspected him with minute care, and convinced him she had read his mind. "I couldn't possibly go to the Seminary. I would need special tuition. It might be fun hiring somebody, don't you think?"

He brightened. Irina was the obvious answer and that sounded like a lot of fun. He knew that he and Irina could train her together, with superb results. He started to tell her, getting enthusiastic as he put a train of thought together, when his inner self smacked him again, causing him to snap his mouth shut.

"I made some enquiries and there is a trainer from Coillearnacha, an Elf, who is very highly regarded."

The king thought about an Elf trainer and smiled. Not much in the way of breasts, but beautiful, lithe and limber. This could be excellent.

"My one concern is that he is supposed to be very large, and that might stretch me badly. Do you think I would become too loose?"

At last the pit she dug for him was revealed, and it was a yawning chasm, with sharp stakes at the bottom. King Richard knew he was already impaled.

"No! I don't want you trained. The only skills you should have are ones I give you." Susan smiled and changed the subject.

"On Saturday, we are going to see a play. Yes, I know, you don't see them, but this one will have massive political repercussions and you are coming. Your presence will serve to reinforce the message. You are sitting with the Archbishop of Praesidium who is sharing our box. You will commiserate with him and offer him all your support and assistance after the play. I will even have your toy there."

"The archbishop will never come."

"He's coming with a party of five. I spoke with him yesterday and he confirmed today."

Susan picked up the charter and locked it in her desk, placing the key on a chain round her neck, with a wink to the king.

"Now, all this bringing things to a head has made me quite excited. Shall we adjourn?" Her eyes sparkled at the king, who wasn't at all sure he was still in the mood. As he trailed her out of the room, a thought struck him.

"So who owns this bank anyway? Me?"

She smiled, exposing brilliant white teeth which she ran over her tongue, emphasizing their sharpness. Just like a lioness, he thought, never having seen the mythical creature.

"I do."

First Blood

The theatre in Harrhein was popular with the masses, and ignored by the gentry though the young rakes adored it, massing with the riff-raff, getting into fights and romancing the women. A performance took place in the yard of an inn, on a large stage where the wealthy patrons sat, with the actors, while the masses thronged as close as they could, in the pit as they called it. A large hogshead to one side provide relief for full bladders and added an overpowering stench to the proceedings.

Susan paid for the stage to be erected in front of the Rose, rather than in the small courtyard. A black flag flew over the yard, to let people know the play would be historical. White meant comedy, and red romance. Pathfinders closed off the street, keeping the crowd under control and overseeing people paying their penny to enter, kids free. Today no seats were available on the stage, instead the roofs and top floors of surrounding houses thronged with guests, while the Royal Party occupied the balcony of the Rose, out of smelling range from the hogshead.

Assembling at the palace, the archbishop brought an old man with him, whom he introduced to Susan as his predecessor, murmuring in her ear that he had lived through the events and would have insight. The Venerable Reinand did not seem capable of possessing any insight, with his wisps of white hair and blank gaze while he followed the archbishop, holding on to the hand of a young man, clearly his minder. The rest of the party consisted of a severe faced nun, radiating disapproval at Susan and ignoring her, and a tall sepulchral figure emanating magic, introduced as Bessin.

Given the attitudes, Susan retreated to stand by General Roberts and Irina, where Colonel Donnell joined them. Lord Bardton was a welcome addition with his much younger wife, who despite an extra fifteen years on Susan never failed to make her feel warm and valued. Marcia and Lucinda kept miraculously quiet in the background, accompanied by their husbands. She waited for the conversation to die down before nodding to General Roberts to lead them away. The king had accompanied the archbishop to the door when the Venerable Reinand woke up.

"Sister Veronica! I wondered where you were. I haven't seen you in ages. Look at you, just as beautiful as ever. Naughty girl, you've been hiding from me."

To Susan's alarm, he made a beeline for her, enveloping her in shaky arms which turned into bands of steel as they settled around her. He bussed her on both cheeks, before taking a death's grip on her right hand.

"Go away, Nicholas," he said to the young man. "I don't need you now I have Sister Veronica back."

"I am afraid this is not Sister Veronica, Your Eminence," said the archbishop with such care and consideration that Susan's regard for the man went up.

"Of course it is. Look at her aura, man, did you ever see one so pure? Couldn't be anyone else." The Venerable Reinand mumbled his words so it was hard to make them out.

"This is not Sister Veronica," hissed the nun, glaring at Susan as she spoke. "This is a fallen woman, not even a member of the church."

"Fuck off, you old hag," said the Venerable Reinand, speaking clearly and strongly for the first time and causing the nun to recoil in shock. "I don't know what idiot let you in the Refectory, but your aura is black as sin. Come, Veronica, time to go. Where are we going, anyway?"

"We are going to see an historical re-enactment, Your Eminence," said Susan, taking control and stepping forward with the old man on her arm and leading the way at his pace.

"Your Eminence? Your Eminence? What nonsense, you always call me Brian. Or Bashful Brian hurr, hurr." The level of lewdness the Venerable Reinand managed to put into his 'hurr, hurr' reached unheard of levels, causing the nun to retreat still further and the archbishop to shake his head in resignation.

"Come along then, my Bright Brian, let us lead the way." Susan smiled now, revelling in the discomfort of the nun. She noticed Irina biting her cheeks, the king annoyed and the soldiers laughing with no attempt to hide their pleasure.

"Like we used to, eh Ronnie? My Ravishing Ronnie, my, we did good works did we not?" He switched hands, taking her hand in his left and with unerring precision landed his right on her left buttock, squeezing hard and probing with his index finger, while emitting a satisfied "hurr, hurr." Susan leapt into the air with a squeal, coming down to grab the offending hand and keep it secure.

"Brian! Bad Brian, you mustn't do that."

"This is intolerable," muttered the king to the archbishop. "Will you sort this out?"

"I 'eard that," said Brian, "and you can shove -"

"Come along, Brian, we don't want to be late," said Susan, cutting him off and moving faster. "I've got this," she mouthed to the king and winked to the archbishop.

Arriving at the Rose, she escorted him upstairs and put him in a front row seat. "I have to check on a couple of things, now Brian. I shall get Nicholas to bring you a drink and I will be back in a short time to sit beside you during the performance."

"Tell 'im to bring me a stout, a nice dark one. Can't stand bloody ale," he confided to the king. "Bubbles go up me nose. Here, there's a lot of people down there." He stared over the balcony at the crowd, entranced at the royal party having difficulties with an old man. "Do they want me to say a few words?" He waved in experimentation, and when the crowd cheered and waved back he bounced to his feet, supporting himself on the balcony.

*

Susan caught the Archbishop on the stairs. "What's an aura?"

He hesitated for a moment. "It is one of the mysteries of the Church. Occasionally we have a man who can see the light around each person. The Venerable Reinand is such a man, a Saint, despite his humble birth. Please, this changes much in our relationship. Will you visit me in my offices?"

"Events are in process, Your Eminence. I cannot stop them now."

"Girl, I am not worried about mundane happenings here in this world. I wish to talk about your pure spirit."

Susan shifted her weight and prevaricated. "Who is Sister Veronica?"

"Saint Veronica ascended to Heaven more than twenty years ago, greatly revered to her passing day. The Venerable Reinand has not been the same since, until tonight. You have woken him from his slumber."

"I am not going to be his keeper."

"Of course. But it would be a kindness if you could visit him on occasion?"

"Perhaps we can arrange something for next week."

"After Mass tomorrow, I shall escort you from the Cathedral." He considered her for a moment before turning to the balcony. Susan walked down to where Mary received her with a warm embrace.

"You've the magic touch, love. Gentry no less. We've never had such an audience, and they're all atwitter. Somebody leaked some of the plot. Churchmen all over the place and you with the archbishop."

"I just worry it might rebound on you, Mary. Has Will really gone to town on the story?"

"He has, but don't you worry your pretty head. It's all truth, God's truth. The story must be told and these evil people rooted out of our Church."

Susan stared. "I am so sorry, Mary, I never realised you were religious."

"Don't be silly, duck. I'm quoting from the score! Oh, what have you arranged now?"

A strong voice boomed from the balcony. "GOD WALKS AMONG US TONIGHT. HE TAKES OUR BODIES AS HE SEES FIT, TO BETTER PASS HIS MESSAGE ON. SEE, MY CHILDREN, IT IS MANY YEARS SINCE I COULD SPEAK TO YOU, BUT THE BURNING LIGHT OF TRUTH RESTORES MY STRENGTH."

"Ohhh," cried Susan, turning to rush up the stairs and shouting over her shoulder. "I seem to be the only one who can keep him in order."

"Great job!" Mary called after her.

The Venerable Reinand no longer needed the railing. He stood tall, his lank hair now flowing backwards and the audience drank in his words, convinced he was part of the show.

"CORRUPTION!" He bellowed. "ITS STINK IS THE STENCH OF THE DEVIL, OF LUCIFER INCARNATE, AND IT IS RIPE AND ROTTEN THROUGH THIS TOWN. WE MUST ROOT IT OUT, BRING DOWN THESE MINIONS OF HELL… Get your hands of me, you cur, you spawn of Satan, you hound from the nether reaches of hell!" The audience roared in approval as he turned to Nicholas who endeavoured to pull him down.

Poor Nicholas shrank away, trying to ensure he was invisible to the mob, while the nameless nun buried her face in her hands and the archbishop hesitated. A waiter held a tray of drinks while he watched the Venerable Reinand orate and never noticed Susan liberating a mug of stout.

The chairs prevented her from coming behind him and she approached along the front of the balcony, catching the attention of the crowd, and Reinand.

"BEHOLD THE FLAME OF GOD," bawled the Venerable Reinand. "SHE IS PURE, SHE IS BEAUTIFUL, SHE WILL CLEANSE THE CITY and I say she has brought me a beer, a stout too, my favourite. Isn't she wonderful, my Ronnie." He grasped the mug, took a draught, put his arm round Susan and waved his mug to the crowd.

"It's the Duchess," cried a voice. "C'mon lads, three cheers for the Duchess! Hip hip, HURRAH!"

It seemed as if everybody joined in, even the actors coming on stage and applauding her. Susan knew a cue and stepped up beside the Venerable Reinand, held his left hand tightly to avoid indiscretions and waved to the crowd. The noise level increased, she blew kisses and held her finger to her lips. Slowly the crowd quietened, and she sucked in air to call out, "LADIES AND GENTLEMEN, IT IS TIME, TIME FOR THE PLAY! PLEASE WELCOME WILL REDCLOAK AND THE ORB AND SCEPTRE PLAYERS!"

Plays in Harrhein were rowdy affairs, the actors used to constant streams of abuse and missiles, usually nut shells or on occasion the whole nut if Lady Marcia was in a fractious mood. Actors playing women were a favourite target. Tonight was no exception, Will speaking the opening lines through a torrent of hazelnuts. His wide smile demonstrating how much he loved this. Susan knew he measured his performance by the whole nuts rather than shells.

The audience knew it was history, expecting juicy revelations about King Richard's ancestors. Bookies called out odds on various scenarios, the odds changing as Will spoke. He set the scene in dramatic tones and silence fell across the street as he started to mention names. Susan knew none of them, but the Venerable Reinand woke and his fingers sank into her leg with the strength of his emotion, his eyes riveted on Will. She began levering at his fingers when her other leg went into spasm as King Richard gripped it.

Freeing both her legs and replacing the hands in safer areas on their own persons, Susan measured the audience. The mob in the pit barely threw anything, and she could now make out groups as people pulled away from obvious Church goers. Ancient history was fun and exciting, but revealing stories from barely twenty years ago, stories about central figures in Harrhein history, that was something never done.

The audience in consequence fell silent, and the acting suffered, none used to performing in a vacuum. Only Will rose above it, but his character the archbishop was sacrificed by the witch all too soon. He was the only one to see through her as she integrated herself into the Church, pushing her own people forward to positions of power. Discussing her love life with her confidant brought murmurs of shock and horror, rather than the usual amusement, and Susan wondered if Will went too far with his descriptions of revelry abusing altars. The final scene showed the witch arranging her own marriage, and the last line named her new husband as Lord Belvedere.

The nun jumped out of her chair, eyes staring, and leant over the balcony. "No! Lies, lies and more lies. Lady Belvedere is a saint." She rounded on Susan, grey hair falling from her wimple. "Harlot! This is your doing, your foul taint is on this charade. Well know this, harlot, the forces of the Lord will strip this theatre, we will denounce you from every pulpit, the players will be crucified and you will be stripped naked, your hair shorn and paraded through every town in the land." Her voice trailed away as the Venerable Reinand rose, waving a hand at her.

"No Sister Mary, this is no charade." Gone was the powerful orator, gone the little old man. Instead he stood tall and stark, power in his body and sadness in his visage. Tears poured down his cheeks, visible to the audience. "My children, please forgive me. I knew this truth, yea and much more, yet I stayed silent and retreated to my God. I let the viper flourish and did nothing, for not only did she slay my archbishop but my dear Sister Veronica as well."

Everyone started talking at once and Susan saw Sister Mary turn round to the priest Bessin sitting in the back row. "Fool! Call yourself a magician. Why did you do nothing? Your job was to change this charade!"

Bessin sat still, and now his eyes flicked sideways. "Circumstances prevented my participation," he said, his voice a deep grating bass.

Colonel Donnell sat beside him, and now Susan saw his naked blade, resting on Bessin's thigh with the point pressing on his groin.

Bessin gently gripped the blade with thumb and forefinger, lifting it as he spoke. "Perhaps you could remove the threat now, colonel. I believe it is a little late for me to influence anyone."

General Roberts whispered in Susan's ear. "You did a good job, little spider, but you forgot to expect the counter. Bessin is a gifted illusionist and could have changed what people saw and heard. You will learn, and the other lesson is the Pathfinders will always have your back."

The king and the archbishop had been deep in conversation for some minutes, and now both rose together and stood at the front of the balcony, the king with his arm raised for silence. The Pathfinder guards dashed their spears to the ground as they stood to attention and the crowd fell silent.

"Good people of Praesidium," said the king. "I have offered the Archbishop and the Church all my resources to assist them in these troubled times. I assure you that Lady Belvedere will be tried, but she must be allowed to answer her accusers. I thank the Orb and Sceptre players for a most interesting evening, and congratulate them on their novel method of bringing this wrong to our attention. However, this is the last time this play may be performed. There will be no repeat performance, is that understood?" Will nodded from the stage.

"In return you have my charter – you are now the Royal Orb and Sceptre Players. Thank you, Ladies and Gentlemen, and good night."

He turned to Susan with a weary expression. "This was not wise. You have released a dangerous enemy, a serpent. She will strike at you and I don't know I can protect you."

The archbishop nodded beside him. "The king is correct. The woman is dangerous. I knew none of these accusations made tonight, but I believe they are fundamentally correct. The Venerable Reinand is never wrong, when he can be persuaded to venture an opinion. But she is wealthy, more than you can imagine and can bury this story in no time."

"She won't stand trial," said Susan cracking open a hazel nut. "She is gone." Susan ate the nut, enjoying the moment. "I asked Sir Timothy Brown to attend tonight as my guest. Timmy, would you please explain why Lady Belvedere has no money."

The little man ducked his head, and spoke with a strong confident voice that belied his nervous appearance. "Lady Belvedere currently spent her available cash on worthless land at Oyster Bay, for an unknown reason. She borrowed to finance the land for which she paid considerably too much and has notes due on Monday. She is not expected to have the money to meet those notes according to her steward who was in my office this morning, trying to borrow more." He checked a paper.

"Her main assets are wheat futures, and here lies another problem as her factors fundamentally miscalculated the market and she overpaid." Seeing the lack of comprehension in his audience, he expounded. "Ah, for some reason his factors thought there would be a small harvest so they guaranteed to the wheat at harvest for a price which is much higher than will be the case. Several of the contracts are open ended as well, meaning they have to buy whatever the farmer provides, meaning the farmer can buy the wheat from his fellows and sell it to her at a profit. She has to buy it and has no market. Merchants were alerted to her changed status yesterday and if she fails to pay on Monday, you can expect people to foreclose on her properties. If my forecast of her situation is right, and I am never wrong, she will lose all her property including her mansion and town house within the next thirty days."

"Thank you, Sir Timothy," said Susan as the little man nodded, shut his book and stepped backwards. "Colonel Donnell, I believe you found out something interesting yesterday."

"Indeed. Sire, one of our patrols near Lodestar became aware of a fall in the mine and went to help. The operators objected and in the ensuing argument were removed. On speaking with the miners, it became clear that they were not volunteers nor were they being paid. Indeed, sir, many are political enemies of hers and quite a few

Churchmen as well. Subject to your confirmation, the Pathfinders confiscated the Lodestar and its sister operations for the crown as a punishment for conducting business with slavery."

"Thank you, colonel. I think it highly unlikely that Lady Belvedere will stand trial. She has been in negotiations with an Uightlander chieftain for three months and earlier this week she agreed to meet him and view his emerald mine. She believes she can increase production. She left in secret two days ago."

Susan accepted a glass of wine from a waiter as he came up the stairs with a full tray. She sipped from the glass while her audience watched her, transfixed at these revelations. She winked at Colonel Donnell.

"Unfortunately for her I am the Uightlander chieftain, Corporal Little made an excellent go-between. But she will be met by a real highland laird who agreed to take her off my hands. You owe me a new necklace, Richard, as I had to use my lovely emeralds as bait."

Susan sipped her wine in the silence. "Ricky and Grey Fox are shadowing her in case of counters. He wasn't very pleased when he heard about the magician and his love spell."

Ashes

Treste poured the herbal tea in to a delicate service decorated with rose buds and a slight pink hue through the china. She arranged the plate of honey cakes a little closer.

"Duchess, I think this is a mistake."

Susan regarded her in some surprise. Treste seldom ventured an opinion.

"You should keep her close, keep her your friend. She'll make mischief otherwise and be in bed with the king quick as a wink. You mark my words." She left, bearing an empty tray, leaving Susan considering the fireplace.

"Darling! Sorry I'm late, Megan took simply ages getting my hair right. Oh, honey cakes, my favourite." Irina gave Susan a quick hug before taking a honey cake and eating it in three bites while Susan poured her tisane.

"I have a present for you, Irina."

Irina smiled, while inside she tensed. She was well aware of Susan's cooler attitude and wondered if the king had let something slip. Lady Belvedere's departure and Susan's triumph were unexpected and she knew she needed to repair damaged relations.

"Have you met or heard of Granny Sawyer? She's the best herb woman in the country. Has a knack for getting people just right. She can find what is wrong with people and heal them." Susan pushed her chair back and stood, walking to the window.

"I love this view," she sighed. "I spend a lot of time looking out of my window. There is this beautiful little glade just down there with a maple tree. The trunk is at an angle, it just makes you want to go down and lean against it." She walked back to her chair and sat down, sipping her tea. She admired Irina's poise, just a flare of the nostrils to show she understood.

"Where was I? Oh, yes, Granny Sawyer and my present. I invited your husband to Praesidium last week and we had a long chat. He has spent several days with Granny and I am pleased to report he is fully cured. Granny has put him on a special diet so the problem won't re-occur."

"What is wrong with him?" Irina's face held a genuine blank expression, this was not expected.

"Was wrong with him. He's cured. He was impotent, and embarrassed that you should know. He is fine now and keen to make up for lost time."

"Lost time?"

"Yes, he wants five boys, doesn't mind how many girls. Granny has made up some teas and a special diet regime to make you more fertile." Susan settled back to enjoy her revenge, and decided to make one more dig. "Never try and take what is mine, Irina."

Irina reached down and took another honey cake. "I had better build up some strength then," she smiled. She ate the cake, savouring the taste and smiling while Susan seethed at the lack of reaction. Irina finished the cake, smiled at her again and delicately wiped her mouth with a minuscule napkin.

"Darling, your trouble is that you are a cold-hearted bitch, always thinking, plotting and planning and never allowing yourself to be passionate. I could have been your best friend and taught you so much." She sipped her tea.

"You fucked my husband while I watched," Susan bit off each word in her anger.

"Sharing is caring. And he is not your husband. You are a mistress, nothing more, with no rights and no future. You are supposedly engaged to a junior officer who could be killed at any moment – most of them are. When that happens, you will have to leave the palace and the king will not be allowed to marry you. The scandal would be impossible."

"Get out," said Susan in a flat tone. "Your husband is waiting for you in his coach, to take you home to your marriage bed."

"Oh good girl, a bit of passion and anger. Let the ice melt." Irina stood up and smiled at Susan, a great big luscious grin from a happy face. "I'm off to make babies. Should be fun. Some of them will have big noses and red hair, just like their royal father. Guess what, kid, he is going to sleep with me a lot more than you over the coming years. And you know why?" She put her hands under her breasts and pushed them up as she swayed to the door. "I've got it and he wants it."

She slammed the door just in time as the tea cup smashed against it and Susan screamed in anger.

*

Richard came back from court in an irritable mood, throwing his valet bodily from the room when he started to correct the king's dress. Susan kept quiet and served him tea, a new blend from Granny Sawyer to soothe and quieten. She thought it worked, though the king's diatribe against a villainous baron who claimed his demesne too small for the royal tithe continued for the best part of half an hour.

After hearing more than she wished about the Baron's shortcomings, she patted his hand. "I'm sure it is simple to sort out. I shall look into it tomorrow. Have you thought further about the archbishop's request?"

She did not notice the king glare at her and was taken aback when his chair clattered to the floor as he stood. "I hadn't, but now you mention it, the answer is no."

"Where are you going, darling?"

"I'm going to see John's new boar-hound and try out this croquet game he is so excited about. Don't wait supper."

"But I thought we were going to learn together…" Susan spoke to the closing door. She sat quite still for a moment, before shrugging and moving to the library. There were some bank reports she wanted to go over.

Treste served her supper at her desk, and before she knew it she was yawning and went to bed. The sound of the door banging open awoke her and she peered through slits as the king stripped beside the bed before ripping back the bed-covers. Susan shrieked as the cold woke her and the king laughed. He moved onto the bed, covering her and some instinct choked back her protests. At least he was warm.

King Richard pushed her legs apart with his knee and rolled between them, his weight making her gasp. His fingers found her parting, at first she assumed to arouse her and she began to ask him to take care when the air rushed out of her as he took her in a rough and forceful manner, with no concern for her arousal.

It hurt.

She gasped and beat on his shoulders, unable to speak as he

pounded into her, trying to wriggle away from him. The king moaned in pleasure.

"Oh, yes, baby. So good. So tight."

Susan froze. He was enjoying this. He was enjoying hurting her. She realised that the pain had passed, the friction gone but it still wasn't nice.

She wondered what to do, and thought that if she lay still without moving, he would realise she wasn't participating and would stop. She concentrated on the dark canopy of the bed before realising her hands were still on his shoulders. She removed them and put them alongside. The king kept going.

After what seemed an eternity, just as she felt she would drop off to sleep, the king speeded up, hammering into her with ferocity. She gasped and returned her hands to his shoulders just as he started to jerk, raising his head with his mouth in a rictus of agony. Alarmed, she tensed and the king moaned. She felt him pulse inside her and she realised this was enjoyment, not pain.

He collapsed on top of her, his weight phenomenal and she struggled to breathe, pushing at his shoulders till he rolled off and lay on his back.

Sucking in a great draught of air, Susan felt fury rise up inside her. She tried to compose her thoughts and grasped for words to express her outrage, when the king's hand flopped on to her breast and squeezed, a further indignity.

"You were brilliant, girl, just wonderful. You're the best." His words slurred and as she absorbed them he started to snore.

Susan lay back and concentrated on the canopy. There was a hole in the corner where a mouse had gnawed at it, taking threads for its bed. She must tell Treste to sort it out.

Sleep would not come. She thought about life, and what she had achieved. She smiled as she started to count. In a scant two weeks it would be her eighteenth birthday and she was the most powerful woman in the kingdom. Scratch that, she thought. The most powerful person, and getting stronger daily. The bank gave her so much influence and power, she could do anything with it. She would build this country into a powerful force, a place where people lived happy, safe lives and nobody, not even princes nor kings, could abuse young girls.

The anger flowed back into her, replacing the satisfaction. Did he not realise what she had done for him? Eradicated his most formidable enemy, forged a lasting alliance with the Church, forced Rotherstone into his hole, provided funds to keep the Pathfinders intact and professional. Set up a new power base that would squash opposition with the power of finance. For a moment she revelled in the power the bank gave her.

And what thanks did she get? To be ignored, left to dine alone, then forced, no, raped in her own bed and have to lie next to this fat old man who snored loudly and reeked of brandy.

With savage intent, she slammed her elbow into his side, feeling the lower rib bend under the impact.

The king grunted, and stopped snoring. He rolled on his side, murmured in his sleep and a hand reached out, grasped her and pulled her into his embrace, digging painfully into her arm. His leg went over her and the next snore sent a wave of halitosis into her face from inches away. To her horror, she felt his member stir at her proximity.

She tried to wriggle free, but this only excited his member more and he hugged her, so tight she struggled to breathe. No, she thought, you will not rape me again, and pinched him in the tender skin under his arm. With a little cry, he rolled back and she was free. Jumping out of bed, she glared at him before leaving him to snore and going to the guest room, where Irina used to sleep.

*

The king woke late the next day, in a jovial mood. He found Susan as she left her breakfast and slapped her bottom.

"Morning, beloved. Missed you when I woke up. Now, what's for breakfast?"

Susan sputtered as he inspected the food laid out, before bellowing down the corridor. "Kippers! I want kippers today, and a mug of ale, not this blasted grass cuttings."

She marched into the garden.

He returned at lunchtime, not to eat but to speak to her. She sat at her desk and regarded him with flat and level eyes.

"Susan, sweet, I am afraid I must cancel your birthday party. I am sorry, I know how much you were looking forward to it." In truth, Susan had forgotten about it and viewed it as an interruption in her work, running the kingdom.

"I leave this afternoon, not sure how long I shall be gone."

"Leave?"

"The blasted Spakka are coming in force, along the northern marches. Made an alliance with the Uightlanders. I have to raise the armies and meet them." He turned and headed for his weapons room. Susan closed her books, replaced her quill, making sure she stoppered the ink, before following him. She found him swinging his axe.

"Damn thing needs a new handle. Will have to take Beatrice instead." He threw it in the corner where it clattered on a pile of discarded weapons, and pulled up a slightly smaller axe with a wicked crescent blade.

"You are not serious? You, expecting to fight? Yourself?"

"Of course I am. I am a fighting Starr, we lead by example."

"Richard, you haven't exercised in months. You will be a liability; soldiers will need to protect you."

The king frowned at her. "Liability? Damn your eyes, woman, I'm the best axeman we have and I'll bring you a dozen Spakka heads, taken personally, to prove it. Now, you will be fine here while I am gone, give you a chance to catch up on your needlework, I know."

"Needlework? Needlework! Is that all you think I'm good for?"

"Oh, you are fun in bed too, darling, that was great last night!" He beamed at her while she choked in outrage.

"What about Lady Belvedere? And the bank?"

"Yes, we were lucky the Pathfinders found her mine. Some good lads hidden in there. Still, I think the Church were on to her, they would have sorted her." Susan stood silent in disbelief while the king inspected swords. He pulled one out and swung it.

"The bank was a good idea, though. Means I don't need to raise a tax to pay for this army."

"What?"

"Yes, I stopped by on the way back. Do you know there was over fifty thousand crowns in it? Wonderful!"

"That was the money I took from Lady Belvedere, and the bank needs it to start operations. It will make money, but it cannot lend you all that money right now."

"Lend?" The King laughed. "Doesn't need to. Your wretched pen-pusher tried to give me the run around, so I revoked the charter, closed it down and took the money."

"Richard! No, please tell me you are joking? Richard, you can't revoke that charter. You must give me the money back, I will –urk!"

Richard's left hand shot out and grabbed her throat, lifting her with no strain from the ground so she dangled in his grasp, unable to speak.

"Listen you little tart. I am the King, you never, ever tell me what to do. You have done nothing, created nothing. You are a tailor's daughter that I lifted from the gutter and put in my bed. You do what I say, when I say, and your job is to please me in bed. As long as you do that, everything is fine. Right now, I am not enjoying you badgering me all the time. I don't want to hear another word from you, understood?" He shook her and her eyes bulged. She couldn't breathe, but managed to nod, waving her feet in feeble desperation for the ground.

He waited a moment longer before dropping her in a heap on the ground. She lay there, gasping. He thrust the sword in his right hand back into its scabbard and pulled forth another.

"Rosie, I've missed you, my love." He kissed the blade. "You I shall take with me." Picking up the weapons of choice, he turned to the door. "I ride within the hour. Make sure you are at the door to see me off. You are to look beautiful and sad, and you must cry when I go."

Susan nodded.

"As an incentive to make sure you look particularly beautiful, know that it will take two weeks to muster the levies before we can march. I must be at the muster point checking on the suitability of the troops. I thought of taking you with me, to entertain me in the evenings, but realised I don't need you. I chose Sarl as the muster point."

*

The light blue dress flowed down Susan's body, flattering her swelling hips and enhancing the brilliant azure of her eyes. Her red wax lay smeared across her face, proclaiming Richard's farewell kiss to the world and tears ran freely down her face as she waved her handkerchief.

The king leapt on his horse with the agility of a man half his age and he led the small troop from the courtyard and down the Kingsward at the canter. The cheers of the populace reached Susan as her tears ceased to flow. A good thing I am an actress, she thought, remembering Mary, Will and the players with a pang.

She strode with purpose to the library to find Sir Timothy Brown sitting opposite her chair. He rose as she entered, shoulders slumped and eyes downcast.

"How bad is it, Timmy?"

"I'm ruined, milady."

"Specifics, Timmy."

"All the money, he just took it. Asked for the charter, and tore it up. Called you a conniving witch and said he was sick of being led by the nose."

"Notes? Land titles? Futures? He would not understand those."

"Yes, I still have those, but we had barely started. We would have turned that money into hundreds of thousand before the year is out."

"What is done is done. We must make the dress from the cloth we have. How much are they worth?"

"I haven't counted it. What's the point? He will just come and take it again."

"Come on Timmy, this isn't like you. You have had reversals before, we must overcome. Now, how can we ensure this does not happen again? The Royal Bank is finished?"

"He revoked the charter. Tore it up. Into pieces, in front of me. Our future." Timmy began to cry.

Susan prepared to snap, before taking a deep breath. Taking her own feelings out on Timmy would not help. She needed him strong. She walked round the desk and cradled his head against her breast, stroking his hair till the sobs subsided. His arms went round her and held her tightly, as a last few racked his body. The last sob died away, and she waited, holding him and squeezing his neck in a gentle rhythm. His right hand dropped to her buttock as his face turned into her breast and his breathing changed as he nuzzled at her. She stopped stroking him, released her arms and he shot bolt upright, embarrassment writ large on his face.

"I'm so sorry, milady," he began, but Susan forestalled him.

"It's quite all right, Timmy, I understand. Now, if you are feeling better, let us continue. Can we save the bank?"

"Not a chance," he said after a little shake to get his emotional balance.

"I don't want to give up all our plans," she said. "Can we start afresh?"

"We don't have a lot of capital, so while we can start, it will take a long time and it will not make enough money to support me or my family."

"Could we run it as a side interest? How long before it becomes strong?"

"We could, but I can make more money elsewhere. It will take a few years, depending on whether you can bring in contracts like the Pathfinders. That would speed it up. But as long as you are involved, the king will help himself."

Susan still stood beside him, one hand brushing his shoulder. Now she walked back to her side of the desk, conscious of his eyes on her hips. This was forward from Timmy. She felt a flare of anger, but crushed it. She needed Timmy.

"What is the value of the assets remaining?"

"I'm not certain…"

"Don't prevaricate, Timmy. I don't need to know to the last crown. To the nearest thousand will do."

"Six. Ten if the futures pan out. I'm sorry, Susan."

"Who holds Lady Belvedere's futures?"

"Lady Belvedere's? Her grain futures? Why, a few merchants if they haven't thrown them away."

"Buy them. You should get them for a pittance, a half dozen pennies in the pound. But do it today."

"That's crazy. It will be a good harvest, why throw away the last of your money?"

"There is a Spakka army coming round the coast and approaching Hardenwall. The king musters the armies at Sarl. That is a lot of grain land which will be lost."

"Yes!" Timmy started to show enthusiasm. "Fearaigh, I will only buy those futures."

"In what name?"

"Name?"

"You can't do it in the bank's name, Richard would just take the proceeds. What name will own the futures?"

"It will have to be my name." Timmy didn't look at her, so she knew this was a bad idea.

"No, Timmy. If it is in your or my name, people will be suspicious and track it back. The king will still take it. We need a new bank, really."

"There isn't enough money for a bank, it would need to be a company with a wide ranging charter. We will need other investors, a range of them will stop the king from emptying the coffers. I can find them."

"I may be able to find a few as well. The Duchess of Westport for one, and Barndton for another."

"No, leave it to me. Better they do not know my source of information, some of them may sell you out. Now, what is in it for me?"

"I beg your pardon?"

"I can set up this company, and put your money to work. In secret. I can make you money, but what do I get out of it?"

"You will make money as well, isn't that the idea?"

"Not enough, not enough for the risk." His eyes glittered.

"I think you will find it is quite a lot, and not much risk anyway. What else do you want?"

"You."

The little man rose from his chair and came round the desk. He no longer appeared quite so small as he reached down to her chin and caressed her face with a feather touch. Susan sat motionless.

"You need me, Susan, my Susie, you need me. Without me, all your money is gone, poof! All your hard work wasted. I can keep it for you, keep it safe. All I ask is a little love." He pressed his lips to hers while her mind raced. His hand fell on her bosom, squeezing gently through the fabric and she raised a hand to pull it away. The other hand pushed him back and he looked down at her in triumph.

"Do you think so little of me, that you would take advantage of me in that way?" Her eyes raised and piteous, they filled with tears huge and irresistible, she thought.

"Oh yes," he said, kissing her again with greater intent. One hand held her face as he eased his tongue through her lips and rubbed it along her teeth, the other hand massaging the small of her back. It was not unpleasant and his breath was sweet, especially after the king. She thought fast. She did need Timmy. Could she do this?

Susan allowed her teeth to part a tiny amount and his tongue plunged deep into her mouth, forcing them apart. His right hand dropped from her face and he pulled her up out of the chair, turning her body against his and using his left hand to grind her against him, feeling his readiness. His right hand returned to her breast, now easing the strap of her dress from her shoulder to allow access and caressing her nipple with unexpected care. She heard herself moan into his mouth as it sprang erect and she pulled back, breaking the kiss to stare at him in wonder.

He smiled, stroked her hair. "My Susie," he whispered as he dropped his head to her breast. His tongue performed long slow caresses and she closed her eyes, losing herself in sensation before the sound of feet in the hallway brought her to her senses. She pushed him upright, waving to his seat and adjusted her dress, sitting down in a hurry and feeling a warm glow with dampness between her legs.

Timmy watched the door as a rabbit watches a fox, but the feet went past and down the corridor. Susan composed herself and found his attention back on her, a proprietary smile on his face.

"This is not seemly or suitable here in the palace," she began.

"Oh, I agree. One of the papers we hold is the deeds to a building just off the Kingsward. We will convert it to premises suitable for our new venture. Shall we inspect it?"

To seal the deal, she thought, wondering if she was ready, if she could find an alternative, if she wanted an alternative. Timmy was actually quite cute. On impulse, she leaned over the desk and stroked his face, running a thumb along his nose.

"Perhaps next week we could have a look," she said.

Timmy shook his head. "I was thinking right now; we want to get a move on buying up those futures."

"You don't need the building to buy them, Timmy. I have engagements this afternoon."

"Break them. This is more important." He leaned forward and

whispered. "I am afire for you, I cannot wait any longer."

His words struck home to her, lancing through her mind and sending shudders down her shoulders. She panted, nobody had spoken to her like this before. She closed her eyes, willing her body to quiet. Of course he rose and came round beside her, rubbing her shoulders and putting a hand down her dress to her mutinous breasts. She held the arm belonging to the fondling hand, not trying to remove it but rather stop it from escaping. She tried to remember how long since she was caressed, so different from the king taking his rights and assuming her readiness.

"The news is out. By tomorrow the farmers and merchants will realise the implications. You must buy them today, quickly. Borrow what you need, but today. You have enough time. I will meet you tomorrow, and if you have bought them, we will set up the company and I will give you what you want."

She felt his hand stop moving and bit her lip in frustration, desperate for it to continue. She wanted more, and something roiled deep in her belly. She opened her mouth to change her mind, to go with him now, to let him inside her and the thought caught at her throat, stopping her from speaking.

"You are right," he said, with blatant reluctance. He kissed her hard and she returned it with enthusiasm, running her hands up the inside of his shirt and loving his sharp intake of breath. He broke off and headed for the door, walking in a strained gait.

"Where?" She managed to gasp as her body screamed at the denial.

"Bowyer's Alley." He turned part of the way to speak to her, the strain visible on his face. "House with a green door. It is barred. Come round the side, the right side, to the back entrance. 10 o'clock."

Susan closed her eyes and willed her body back to normal, wondering at how she responded to the man. Never had King Richard or even Ricky caused this sort of reaction, and while she liked Timmy, she never thought him attractive, never considered him as a bedroom partner. She wondered if this resulted from the hurt from Richard.

She replayed Richard's words again through her head, her body cooled and her lips thinned. Heat rose through her body again, but this time from anger. Marching to her room, she threw open the door to her wardrobe to inspect the dresses, mindful that the more valuable, and heavier, clothes hung in the garderobe.

When Treste came in, she found Susan with a pile of clothes on the bed and a small stack on the dresser.

"Ah, there you are. Can you get me a bag or a sack, please Treste. And help yourself to any of these dresses on the bed."

Treste considered the pile for a moment before leaving. She returned shortly with a clean sack with a wooden handle sewn in the top.

"Having a clear out, miss?"

"No, dear, I am leaving. Tonight. I am sorry, but it is over. There is money already arranged for your people, and I am sorry, there is no more."

"You're giving up."

"No, I've been thrown out. Replaced. I am not wanted anymore." She tried to keep her tone light but spoiled it by tearing a dress from its hanger.

"He's not that stupid," said Treste as she started to replace the clothes in the wardrobe. "He won't have thrown you out on your ear."

"He might just as well. He told me he never wanted to hear another word from me."

"Lots of men say things like that when they're angry. You get used to it," said Treste as she put Susan's best underclothes back in a drawer.

"He meant it. I am nothing to him, just a tailor's daughter he pulled out of the gutter. All he wants is me to warm his bed. Yet he's gone off to Sarl." Susan's eyes misted and she stood with her head bent.

"Ah, so that's the problem. Not to worry, let him get his fill of that one. Those tits will bore him after a while, especially as they are sagging already. She can't hold his interest when he isn't bulling her. Not like you can."

"Treste, he doesn't want me, not as a wife or companion. Just as a bloody harlot, and I don't want that."

"There's people relying on you, miss, people who believe in you. You want to let them all down?"

Susan snorted. "They'll make money from somewhere else. You've still got a job here, after I've gone."

"It's not just your girls, miss, it's the people. Ain't you seen how they react when you go down the street?"

"They call me duchess and laugh at me, like they always have. Because when I was a little girl I said I wanted to be queen. So bloody funny."

"They ain't laughin' at you miss. An' they ain't callin' you duchess, neither," said Treste, her street accent coming out stronger. "They're callin' you the fuckin' queen, is wot they're doin' naw, they is, they think yer gonna save us, that yer care for us, even the fuckin' Church loves ya, and what yer bloody doin? Yer fuckin' off and leavin' us yer are, yah cold-hearted fuckin' bitch, to think I fuckin' believed in ya." Dashing at her eyes with the backs of her hands, Treste ran from the room leaving Susan dumbfounded.

"Why does everyone think I'm cold hearted? Why do they think I don't care?"

She sat on the bed and stared out of the window for a full five minutes, before getting up and stuffing the sack with a selection of clothes. She dressed quickly in stout cotton trousers, a dark blue shirt and a woollen sweater before covering the common clothes with a long fox fur coat. She slipped a heavy money belt round her waist, gold crowns sewn into the canvas and fastened her coat.

The sack weighed almost as much as a small child, and she thanked the exercise in the barracks as she lifted it. This reminded her to take her staff and after a brief experimentation, found a way to fasten the sack to her staff using another belt.

Nobody saw her come down the stairs and she slipped into the garden, making her way along the path to the gate, stopping only to smack the maple tree with her staff. She left a most satisfactory gouge, just where it would be uncomfortable to lean against, and moved on in better spirit.

The guard nodded to her, considering her with more lechery than curiosity. She saw the blue uniform of the Royal Guards and knew the Pathfinders had all gone. The thought saddened her, made her feel lonely.

Missing

King Richard luxuriated in his bath, enjoying the bubbles, and lay back in the half tub to allow Irina to scrub his chest. Through half-closed eyes he watched her heavy breasts swinging, just touching the water now as she checked to see if he was ready for another bout. Not much chance there, he thought, after the exercise she had put him through to need a bath. He was aware she was speaking, but had long tuned her words out, giving the odd meaningless grunt when a change in timbre alerted him to a question.

The door crashed open, causing Irina to squeal and grab for a towel while the king opened an eye. In stalked a bit of a girl, followed by a soldier who reddened at the sight of the naked Irina and retreated at speed.

The girl helped herself to an apple from a bowl and bit into it while inspecting Irina's frantic attempts at modesty.

"Hello Dad," she said. "You owe me five sovereigns."

"Why do I owe you five sovereigns and why are you here instead of back in Praesidium as ordered?"

"Always trying to weasel out. I bet you Irina would have you in bed before the summer, remember?"

"Something of the sort does seem to come to mind. You avoided the other question."

"Come on Dad, you know I wasn't going to obey that. You need your best scouts. I'll be off in the morning, just wanted to re-provision and I'll have that bath if you've finished with it. Whoops, hang on. You didn't do her in the bath, did you?"

"Do I look like a duck? And just where do you think you are going in the morning?"

"Hardenwall. Siege is holding, but they are flattening the fields and burning the farms." She selected another apple, inspecting it with a critical eye. She bit into it, looking at Lady Sarl. "Irina, get lost. I need to speak to Dad in private."

Irina started to speak, thought be of it and pulled on an expensive brocade dressing gown. "Yes, Princess," she said as she left the room.

"You've been bloody stupid this time, Dad."

He stepped out of the tub, rubbing himself down with a towel and Princess Asmara stripped off her leather and wool tunic, climbed into the vacated tub and completely submerged. She erupted spouting water, and lay back with a happy sigh. "It's nice to see you, though, Dad."

While he basked in this unexpected token, she located his glass of wine beside the tub and took a healthy swig before he could rescue it.

"How was the winter?"

She grinned in delight. "Thanks so much, Dad, it was awesome, the best. I am really strong now, I can march twenty five leagues a day in rough country, carrying my own pack and I can hold my own against the soldiers with a rapier. Hey, I can beat most of them, but a few are better. Can't go against an axe yet, well not a Spakka axemen, they are too fast."

"I don't believe it, you have discovered limits and boundaries."

"Temporary ones. I call them targets, things to achieve. Grey Fox is training me too."

"Grey Fox? He doesn't train recruits."

"He's training Ricky. Bobby put him and a few others onto watching over me. I spotted them in the first month, and it took me two months to track them to their camp. I was going to wake Grey Fox up by sitting on him, but he was awake watching me creep up. Andy was asleep back in camp, this was the middle of the night and Foxy said if I was going to come out into the snow to hassle them, they might as well all sleep in the cabin."

King Richard grinned, imagining the scene. "So how have I been stupid?"

"You know I have a few spies keeping me up to date?" The king didn't, but nodded anyway.

"Well, I received a present yesterday, a complete bloody network. Damn good one too. Given to me on a tray. With a message. It said, 'Look after him. This will help. He's too stupid to manage on his own.' Damn good network, finally given me a pipe into Rotherstone."

Asmara climbed out of the cooling bath, noting her father's blank expression.

"You pinched Ricky's fiancé." Startled by the change of subject, the king nodded.

"Ricky's still upset about it. But it was the best move you ever did. Smart girl."

The king rocked back on his heels, this was unexpected. Asmara never approved of his mistresses.

"What are you planning to do with her?"

"Well..."

"Are you going to marry her? Make her queen?"

"Well, I'm thinking about it. I wanted to see what you thought of her."

"Did you tell her?"

"Of course not, wouldn't do to get her excited before time."

"Dad, half the bloody country calls her Queen Susan, she's more popular than you'll ever be and she is clever enough to sort out that mess with the Church. It is well past time. Yes, yes, of course I know, do you really think I would let you pack me off without keeping up to date with what is going on? With Susan around, I could relax, knowing you were in good hands."

The king didn't know what to say to this, and looked at his hands.

"What did you say to her, Dad?"

Asmara wrapped a towel round herself. She located Irina's wine glass, refilled it and sipped without her father noticing.

"Dad? She's upset, what did you say? Did you congratulate her and reward her for sorting out the Church? Getting rid of that awful Belvedere woman? I was with the screening force, by the way, and watched when she met up with the Uightlander. He was quite pleased with her for some reason. Maybe she wasn't as hairy as his own women, but he took her into his tent and she screamed the place down. He laughed the whole time. Clever girl, that Susan. What did you say to her Dad? Did you thank her?"

"Not exactly…"

"Does she now you are up here having it off with Irina?"

"Uh, well, …"

"Oh, Dad, so not good. Come on, tell me what happened."

"It wasn't my fault, all right? She tested me, used Lady Sarl. I fell for it, well, with those tits what do you expect? And she could see us doing it. I didn't know, neither did Irina. And just because of that, and it was only the once, she packed Irina off back to Sarl somehow."

"Dad, Irina was Lady Belvedere's spy in the palace. Susan knew and used her to give Lady B the wrong information, which is how she was caught. I would have executed her. Stupid cow and her precious udders. I haven't got the full story of how she managed to send her back to Sarl, sounds great the little I heard. Now, what did you say to Susan? Dad?"

"I told her to stop badgering me."

"And what else?"

"I, uh, I closed down this merchant's thing she set up, used the money to finance this campaign. Saved us from having to tax the people."

"Oh Dad. So not a good idea. You should have married her, you know. Too late now. You are not telling me the half of it, I know, and you should be bloody ashamed."

"What do you mean, too late? I'm just teaching her a bit of a lesson. I'll make it up when I get back."

"She's gone, Dad. Done a runner. Whatever you said upset her so much she has disappeared. That was her network I received, a present from my nearly mum."

The king started to dress, pulling on his under trousers backwards in his haste. "I will ride through the night. Talk some sense into her." Asmara took advantage of his distraction by pouring herself more wine.

"You're not listening, Dad. She's gone. Vanished. Disappeared. Just a fox-fur coat lying in the street. The door barely shut behind you, same day. A girl that smart, you won't find her. And if you turn up in Praesidium right now, you'll get lynched. People aren't happy. They want their Duchess back. Everyone is looking for her and nobody can find her."

The king paused, looking at the wall, unseeing. "The insufferable, righteous, bloody beautiful, little bitch. I love her, Asmara. What am I going to do?"

"Come with me. We ride in dawn's early light. Get that fat off your belly, take you up in the hills to run with Foxy. Bit of exercise will sort you out. My spies are after her – hers too, and they really want to find her. Want her back in charge. We'll find her, and by that time you will be in shape. Maybe she won't mind talking to you then. Poor thing, inflicting this great belly on her." The king growled at her, for he did not think he was overweight, if perhaps a little unfit. The comment took his mind off Susan.

"Lord Sarl is a good enough administrator – he will get the troops sorted and be thankful to have the milk cow back. I'll get you up in the hills with Bobby and the boys and you can have a look at the Spakka yourself. There's a lot of them, Dad. We're in for a bit of fun for sure."

With this sombre announcement, Asmara went to the door, opened it and called. "Andy? Can you sort me out a new tunic please? Don't want to put this one back on, it's filthy. What? Oh, damn you. I'll see you in the morning, yeah, we still leave on time." She paused, her head out of the door. "Yes, come back, get me something to eat, would you?" She came back into the room, leaving the door open and picked up her discarded clothes with distaste. Irina followed her, now dressed in an evening gown, her hair tied back and with less cleavage than usual.

Asmara picked up her tunic and sniffed it. "Your quartermaster is useless, Dad. No spare bloody tunics my size, I have to wear this thing again."

"I'll provide you with some warm underclothes," said Irina, keen to be of different service.

"She's gone, Irina," said the king, a catch in his voice.

"What? Who? Where? You don't mean…"

"Susan. The day I left. Walked out the door, no sign of her."

"Oh my Lord. The poor girl. Richard what did you do to her?"

The king hung his head and both girls spotted it, rounding on him.

"Richard? You did something nasty, didn't you?"

"I had a bit to drink the night before."

"Oh, you didn't make love to her while you were drunk? She won't have liked that."

The king shot a glance at his daughter, mortification suffusing the skin under his beard with red. "She didn't."

"Well, if you noticed when you were drunk, she must have really screamed and put up a fight while you raped her." Irina showed her

205

anger as she browbeat the king, while Asmara kept silent, regarding this new Irina with delight.

"Of course I didn't rape her, she's my mistress," snapped the king in irritation.

"Oh, so you think that because she is your mistress you can't rape her? Or do you think you are entitled to any woman just because you are the king? Whether they want it or not?"

"Look, I didn't rape her, I just was a bit quick, that's all. And in the morning she wasn't there, slept somewhere else. Probably because of my snoring." Irina had both hands over her mouth, eyes wide. The king squirmed in his chair before going over to pour himself more wine. He avoided his daughter's eye. He took a strong draught of wine.

"She made me so angry, I couldn't help myself. She acted as if I was unnecessary while she ran the Kingdom. As if she knew everything, and I was to do what she said. Just a little chit of a girl. She told me I was too old to lead the armies, should stay behind and plan the war. Told me I was wrong to close her bank."

He shuffled his feet and concentrated on the fire. Asmara came over and took his hand. Both girls waited, let the silence fill the room.

"I lost my temper." The king's voice dropped to a tiny whisper and his eyes lost their focus as he replayed the memory. "God help me, I love her yet I lifted her up by the throat, and told her not to talk anymore, all she was good for was in my bed and I made her what she was, took her out of the gutter. She was to stop meddling and warm my bed. What have I done?" The king collapsed into a chair and tears rolled down his cheeks.

"And then you told her you were coming to me, to Sarl, didn't you?" The king nodded with his eyes closed. With the unexpected speed of a striking snake, Irina slapped the king hard across the face, green eyes blazing. "Bastard," she spat. "That poor child. And now she is all alone, she has no one to whom she can turn."

Shocked out of his misery, the king stood and loomed over her, his hands curled into fists. She did not flinch, glaring at him.

"Why do you care?" Asmara relieved a worried servant of a tray of food and he scuttled away. She closed the door and pushed between the two to put the tray on a table. Tearing a leg off the chicken, she plunged small white teeth into the flesh as she measured Irina. "You were her enemy, her betrayer."

"Betrayer, yes, but never her enemy. I wanted to teach her, to show her how to have emotions and be a normal person, how to love. She has been hurt so much in her short life, she hides herself and hides her heart in a great block of ice. And I betrayed her twice, the poor lamb."

The king subsided into the chair, running his hands over his face, which twisted as he thought. "Why am I worrying about this girl when I need to be saving my Kingdom? I have to put her to one side, concentrate on the Spakka."

"That's right, you do," said the princess as she licked chicken grease from her fingers. In the time since Irina struck the king, she had devoured nearly half the fowl. She washed her hands in the bathwater, considering Irina. "If we send you back to Praesidium, can you find her?"

The king raised his head and Irina thought about Susan, where she would go and what she would do.

"No," she said with reluctance, "but she might find me. She would be angry to see me in town, but also want to speak to me. I am still her friend, her only friend. The only place I can think she would go is the Pathfinder barracks, but is there anyone left?"

"Colonel Donnell," cried the king. "He will know where she is. He's billeted here in Sarl, let us go and see him now." The princess dropped her robe and started to pull on the underclothes provided by Irina, unconcerned by the effect of her nudity on the servant arriving with more wine.

The king, still in his bathrobe, strode to the door and told the guard to locate Colonel Donnell. He repeated where the Pathfinders billeted and Irina nodded.

"I know the way." She led off, with Princess Asmara still buttoning up her tunic.

If Colonel Donnell was surprised to see the king in his bathrobe along with this unusual retinue, he did not show it. Neither did General Roberts who showed the efficiency of Pathfinder communications by arriving on the king's heels.

"Gone?" said Colonel Donnell, echoed by his commanding officer. "What do you mean she has gone? I was relying on her to take over internal security."

"She's run away," said the king, hoping to gloss over the details. "Any idea where she might go?"

"But why?" Colonel Donnell asked in puzzlement. "She has so much going for her, and so much work to do. Are you sure she is not just tied up working in the bank?"

"Definitely not. She has left the palace and is not at the bank. Nobody knows where she is, she left everything behind and all we can find is her fox-fur coat. Now, where would she go?"

"Sounds like she has been kidnapped," said Colonel Donnell. "I thought we rooted out all of Lady Belvedere's organisation, must have been something left. I'll get the Pathfinders out looking for her."

The general nodded in agreement. "Everyone will want to help."

"You will not," said the princess. "You are needed covering the Spakka and telling us their movements. Besides, Daddy dear is not telling you the whole story. He's been horrible to her and she has run away from him. She is not in the bank because he closed it down and took all the money."

"You closed the bank? But that is our money," said the general.

"Why would you be horrible to her?" The colonel asked in a plaintive tone at the same time. "She did so much for you."

"Damn the blasted bank," said the king in frustrated tones. "Your money is safe in my strong room. It's all a misunderstanding, I wasn't horrible at all."

"No," said Asmara. "You weren't horrible, you just thanked her for her hard work by banning her from doing anything but warming your bed, stopping her from talking and showed what you thought of her by nailing her best friend."

"SHUT UP!" The king glared at her.

"I thought that was a good précis. Now, boys, given that the last thing she will want to do is be found and dragged back in chains, where is she going to hide?"

"In the regiment," said the fifty year old general, not at all pleased at being called a boy by a thirteen year old girl. "She knows we will do anything for her. Any one of us will hide her if she asks and she knows it. Marcus," he snapped to his aide trying to be unobtrusive by the door. "I want every new recruit, those we brought along but joined up in the last two weeks, on parade in the yard in five minutes. Jump to it. She'll be the best one, I bet."

Colonel Donnell shook his head. "Too obvious, too easy to be found. Too many people would know she was a girl from every time she took a piss. She'll be in Praesidium. Probably as a boy. Won't go back to Galicia, too many bad memories."

"She might think that and go to Galicia for that very reason," interjected the princess to earn Donnell's respect. "I'll put out the word to find a blond boy, not a girl."

"She won't be blonde. She'll cut her hair and make it black, and be doing something like a blacksmith's apprentice."

The king closed his eyes at the thought of his beautiful Susan with no hair but the thought fascinated Asmara.

"How will she make it black? Who would think of such a thing? Will she get a wig?"

"She's a tailor's daughter, remember. She knows all about dying cloth. Think of the make-up she uses, made it all herself. She will wash her hair in something and turn it black." He looked at Irina, ruminating. "I am pretty sure she won't be a redhead."

Asmara's thoughts turned away, this was wonderful information she would use. Her red hair often gave her away, and the idea of changing colour had not occurred to her.

"You are missing the obvious," said Irina. "The Church. They have no love for the king, but Susan can do no wrong. She removed Lady Belvedere, freeing many of us, myself included. And the Venerable Reinand declares her a saint, pure of heart. All she had to do was go to the archbishop and right now she could be hidden away in any nunnery in the country. And you will never know."

Silence pooled in the room as they digested her words, broken by the sound of soldiers assembling outside, the shouts of sergeants terrorising the recruits. King Richard went to the door, to see a dozen nervous men assembled under the wrathful eye of an excessive number of corporals and sergeants. His slumped shoulders proclaimed the impossibility of any of them being a slight, fugitive, young lady.

"Dismiss the men," the general said to Marcus and followed his king back into the mess.

"There are two other immediate possibilities, sir," said Colonel

Donnell, "perhaps three. There is the theatre group where she has friends, the Royal Orb and Sceptre players, and the retired colonel who rescued her from Galicia. What is his name?"

"Devran," said the general. "Good man. Lost an eye four years ago. Can't judge distance enough to survive on the front line. Sent him to train Galician troops. He resigned after they tried to cover up Susan's rape by that peacock prince."

"Good job that by Grey Fox," said Colonel Donnell without thinking, then cursed under his breath as he saw Asmara's ears prick up.

"Rape?" Irina bristled. "No wonder she is so scarred and wounded, and ran at this betrayal. We must find her. Bring her to me in Sarl, I will heal her. Richard? Go and get her, right now."

Asmara sat on a table, brought her feet up and sat cross-legged, ignoring the marks her boots left on the polish and the scowl from the general. She pulled a sheaf of papers from the leather satchel she carried and started scanning them. The king slumped into a chair.

"She's not with Devran," said the general, "because I brought him with us. He's helping the quartermaster."

"No," said Asmara, reading a letter without looking up. "Nor in his house. No sign of her with the players, either. First places that were checked." Colonel Donnell's eyes lit with interest and he edged over to read over her shoulder. She passed a letter to Colonel Donnell and shrugged at her father. "Sorry, not had time to read them all, lots of nothing in them."

Colonel Donnell read the letter. "Well, it seems the Church is not happy. The Venerable Reinand is causing a massive ruckus at Susan's disappearance and the archbishop himself is writing a letter of complaint to you, sir. Holds you responsible for the loss of a national treasure."

"So she isn't with the Church either, damn it to hell and back, where has the damn girl gone?"

"Church might be bluffing, of course Dad. But it's all moot any way. We've got an invasion to stop before we can find your girl."

--ooOoo--

Susan's story continues in *Mistress of the Gods,* due out in 2017. Her education continues at the hands of the Elves, where she meets their gods - or does she? Meanwhile, the king and the princess meet the Spakka and treachery in the north, before Susan returns to Harrhein and another attempt at becoming Queen in *Mistress of the Kingdom.*

These three stories compose *The Making of Suzanne,* a prequel to *In Search of Spice*, in which Susan becomes an advisor and confidant to Princess Asmara in her voyage to the fabled lands of Hind, and the sequel, *In Search of Solace,*

The next short story is set at the time of *Mistress of the Gods* includes the aftermath of one of the battles referred to in that book. A little extra for the reader.

If you enjoyed *Mistress of the King,* we would appreciate a review. This is the best thing you can do to help any author and helps to ensure more stories are forthcoming. You can write a review on Amazon even if you haven't purchased a book through there. Just go to the description of the book and you will see where it allows you to post a review. Thank you!

Keep up to date with the publication of new stories about Harrhein at https://www.facebook.com/harrhein

The Wagonmaster

Dedicated to the Royal Corps of Transport and one soldier in particular, whose recent death made me realise how little we appreciate the courage shown by some of the back up boys in any army. Gentlemen and Scoundrels of the Transport Corps of All Armies, I salute you.

Chad sprinkled the fine sand carefully over the bridge, his shoulders hunched against the chill wind. He was a medium sized, nondescript man with a regrettable tendency to being overweight. He debated whether to get some salt, but wasn't convinced he could persuade the quartermaster to let him have some. His wagon had slid going over the bridge earlier, and he was checking to see why and make sure it didn't happen to somebody else. It did not occur to him that he was being conscientious; it was just what you did.

He clucked his tongue in annoyance, as he found the crushed planking causing a skid to start, and the shiny polished wood which encouraged the skid to grow in the cold, icy weather. And to cap it all, the rails were weak. Weathered and old, he could see cracks in them. A good thump and a wagon would go straight through and into the creek below. Deciding it needed closer inspection from below, he moved to the front of the bridge where he could get down to the creek.

As he started to come off the bridge, he heard horses clopping up the road and saw a large carriage coming too fast up the road. The horses' necks were curved, indicating too tight curbs, and they were sweating. Chad recognised Sergeant Hicks driving the team, and sighed. The man was an idiot and a bully, and Chad had no idea how he had reached his rank. Still, he didn't want the horses hurt so he stepped out and flagged him down.

"Hold it, Hicks," he said, raising his voice above the querulous wind. "The bridge is unsafe when you've got the horses curbed like that. I'll lead them across for you."

To his astonishment, Hicks stood up on his seat. "Get out of the way, you fool! I have important people on board!" Hicks sent his horsewhip lashing in Chad's general direction.

Anger stirred Chad to action, and he caught the off horse's rein, bringing the carriage to a halt in a few steps, while he ran with the horse, hanging from the rein.

"All the more reason to take it carefully," he said, his voice calm with anger.

"Why, you young idiot," said the sergeant. "I'll have you on a charge, so I will. Report to the duty officer immediately!"

"What is going on?" A man stuck his head out of the carriage, and Chad vaguely noticed red hair and a large nose, but his attention was on Sergeant Hicks who looked as if he might try and whip him again.

"Nothing, Sire," said the sergeant, "just a drunk soldier. I'll deal with him directly."

'*Sire!*' thought Chad and looked in horror at his king peering at him owlishly from the carriage window.

"He doesn't look drunk to me," came the perfect tones of a well brought up young lady, and Chad found a young girl of perhaps twelve looking at him from the other horse. She was absently stroking its nose and considering him carefully from bright, calculating eyes. He took in the bright red hair and large nose and made the lightning calculation that this was the dreadful Princess Asmara who caused everyone problems. My word, she must have been out of the carriage quickly.

"What's wrong with my bridge?" The king asked with interest, climbing out of the carriage. "Show me."

"Your Highness," said Chad automatically and turned towards the bridge. The princess took the sack from his nerveless hand and inspected it as they walked. She looked at the area where he had scattered sand and then went and looked at the railings. The king followed her, while Chad tried to think of something to say.

"Doesn't look too dangerous?" asked the king.

"It is perfectly acceptable, sire, we wouldn't permit a bridge to get into a bad condition when you are visiting the frontier." Hicks had recovered himself.

"You said something about the curb?" asked the princess, looking at Chad with that disconcerting,0 direct look. He saw her eyes were green, but they had been brown just now and he was confused.

"Too tight a curb will make them flighty, ma'am," he said, in desperation trying to remember what you were supposed to call a child princess. "Then if the carriage slips on the bridge, they'll panic and pull the wrong way, making the skid worse. If the skid gets bad and hits the rail, it'll break and you'll end up in the creek."

"And the sand will stop the skid?" asked the Princess. Her eyes were brown again now.

"Not entirely, ma'am, but it'll help," he said, a slight tremor betraying his nerves.

"Hicks," cried the Princess without taking her eyes off Chad. "Why are the horses' mouths bleeding?"

"Ah, ah," stammered Sergeant Hicks, taken off guard. "From the bit, ma'am."

"You're not using a bloody gallic bit, are you?" said Chad, forgetting himself in a sudden surge of anger and then falling over himself to apologise. "Beg pardon, ma'am."

The king snorted with laughter and the princess waved her hand. Her eyes were now boring into Sergeant Hicks. "Sergeant, change the bits on the horses. Then take them across the bridge. Walk them over. If my cases end up in the creek you will be on the far frontier tomorrow. His Majesty and I will walk the rest of the way. You," she said, returning her gaze to Chad "will walk with us." She turned and walked across the bridge, the king smiling and walking after her. Chad trailed along, nervous and imagining what the sergeant major would say.

Within a hundred yards all nervousness had gone, and he was taking advantage of her sympathetic ear while he told her what he thought of the Royal Supply Corps. It tends only to be the officers who are nervous with their very superiors.

There is an invisible communication system in an army, which allows people to know when disaster is happening. Thus they were approaching the main fort just fifteen minutes later, when a pre-warned Sergeant Major Cuppold, Chad's superior officer, strode out of the gates in his best uniform. The Garrison Commander wasn't far behind him, but the Major was a clear winner in the damage limitation stakes.

"Major Cupper, isn't it?" asked the princess fixing him with her stare.

"Cuppold, Your Royal Highness," he answered with a slight bow, remembering they were not supposed to use court manners on the frontier. "Royal Supply Corps commander for this area."

"Excellent," she beamed. "We have been done a great service by your Wagonmaster. I am minded that he should be rewarded by promotion, perhaps to the rank of Sergeant." The princess might be young, but she had observed a great deal about soldiering and knew that Sergeant Hicks would take his revenge on anyone of lower rank.

"Regrettably that would not be a reward, ma'am," said the major diplomatically while Chad shuddered.

"Why ever not?" asked the princess, her grown up accent dissolving under her surprise so she sounded like the little girl she was.

"I first promoted Chad when I was a Sub Lieutenant, ma'am, and he lasted a week before he was busted back to private. We tried again the following year and that time he only lasted two days. We agreed then that he would be best never going above Senior Wagonmaster, which is what he is now and he's the best we have on the frontier."

Chad grinned. "I'll hold you to that, Sir!"

The king spoke directly to his daughter. "Valuable lesson for you, girl. Never over promote. Sometimes you need to promote somebody for them to find out they don't like it, which is one of the truly great things about the army. You can be busted back down to the rank at which you excel without loss of prestige for trying something else. And not everyone wants to be promoted." He looked at Chad. "You know exactly what to do and when, I would guess. And you like that certainty." Chad nodded.

"But we'll have to do something," exclaimed the princess. "Otherwise Hicks will be after revenge."

"Leave it with me, ma'am," said Sergeant Major Cuppold, grasping the situation. "Chad, I think we'll give you the Western Track, you'll re-supply the outposts as the thaw comes."

"Can I take Chloe, sir?"

The princess arched an eyebrow and a grin appeared, which flowed into a smile as the Major replied hastily.

"Take my best damn mare to boot, will you? Oh very well, but

I will send you two youngsters in the spring to lick into shape. Get your pack on her and come to my office in an hour, I will have orders ready for you."

*

Chad hunched his shoulders inside the leather jacket, thankful for the woollen jumper he had pulled on underneath it. It might be spring, but it was still bloody cold. With the lightest touch of the rein, he eased the wagon off the almost invisible track and onto the short grass of the high moorland. There was not much difference, and his offsider, a hulking youth with a cast in his eye, didn't notice at first. Then the map came out, and he squinted at it for a good ten minutes.

"Chad, shouldn't we be headed for the wood up the hill?'" he said in a worried tone, scratching the spot on the back of his neck.

Chad silently cursed the officer who had given the boy a map. "Not taking the main road. In wild country, best not to go the obvious way to avoid ambush. Never know when an Elven renegade band is going to come through." Chad had never heard of a band of Elves coming through, but thought it worked as an excuse. He preferred the open moorland and didn't feel like moving any fallen trees which the winter storms felled across the main track. However young Trev believed him, going white at the very thought.

"But Chad, we can't fight off a bunch of Elves! We can't fight anyone. A couple of weak crossbows and short swords won't frighten them."

Chad, who had once missed the barn door with a crossbow from fifty paces to lose a sizeable bet, agreed with him. "Why we are taking the open road. Nobody can sneak up on us." He pulled his hat down to forestall more questions and was helped by the rain, which slanted across the moor straight into his face, so he twisted sideways and took it on his shoulder with his back to the boy.

Chloe was the lead horse so he let her have her head, trusting her to find the safest way. He dozed in the damp rain, ignoring Trev, till the wagon bumped, nearly throwing him off. He swore under his breath, thinking it was going to be one of those days. Damn horse would sometimes find every bloody hole it could and unerringly run the wheel under his arse straight into them. Another jolt told him it was going to be one of those days.

It was one of those days for the next three, with Chloe getting more and more irritable. She even bit him twice and firmly kicked Trev when he hobbled her. The weather stayed closed in and Chad couldn't remember such a miserable, cold, wet trip. Finally, as they came round a hill, the clouds lifted slightly and the valley was laid out before them, glowing with subdued, clean hues of mauve and green. The fort lay a mile down the valley on the junction of two rivers, where the pass came out of the mountains. The best route through on the western side of the country, a route for the occasional raider.

Chad perked up and clicked at Chloe who picked up her pace for all of three yards in response. Trev was looking at the fort.

"Chad, why are the gates shut?" he asked, squinting at the fort.

Chad grunted, uninterested. He'd lost interest in Trev's conversation on the second day.

"Shouldn't there be horses in the paddock?"

Chad looked at the fort. It wasn't large, but containing a couple of acres with several houses and barns around a square. He could make out tiny figures on the high wooden walls, more than normal. The gates were indeed shut, but surely they would be seen any moment. He waited for the gates to open and somebody to come out to greet them, and prepared some stinging repartee in case one was Husk, an old crony.

Nothing happened, and something cold crawled through Chad's guts.

"It can't be," he whispered, the cold fingers of dread running up his spine and tickling his neck.

"What?" grunted Trev, who was thinking about a warm bath and wondering if they had a barmaid at the inn.

"They're under siege," whispered Chad, looking at the woods beyond the fort and seeing a couple of small trails of smoke coming up from cooking fires.

Trev sat up abruptly. "You're funning me," he said, stricken, staring at the hills around the fort. "Don't say that, Chad! You're scaring me, you are!"

"Oh fuck," whispered Chad, "we're dead men. They're elves." The reins were forgotten in his hands as he looked across the valley.

He could make out a shadow sign blowing from a lone pine on the hill. Abruptly, he threw up breakfast, just missing the side of the wagon and onto the dirt. The horses went on regardless.

Trev was whimpering. "Can we turn back, Chad? We can get away, mate, if we move fast?"

Chad could feel tears behind his eyes. "No chance. Once they see us, they can run us down. I don't know what to do! And without this food, the guys in the fort are dead."

"Oh!" Trev brightened. "They'll come out and rescue us, won't they Chad? Chad? They'll save us?"

"They're elves, Trev. If you ain't behind a wall, you're dead. Those arrows of theirs will take you every time. If they come out to rescue us, they'll die." Chad felt the tears start to run down his face, the bitter taste of death on his tongue. Why had this happened to him? There were no elves this far north. Patrols hadn't found any or he would have been escorted.

Trev broke, great sobs racking his body. "I, I heard what they did to you, how they killed you. Tell me it isn't true, Chad! I don't want to hurt like that. I want to be in the fort, Chad!"

Chad couldn't tell him it wasn't true. Elves liked bravery. He wasn't a brave man, he knew, and would always avoid a fight. Half the reason he was a haulier and not a soldier. Elves wouldn't like him, and they wouldn't like Trev who was equally scared. Through the mists of terror, a thought burbled through. The fort. They would be safe in the fort.

"We got to race them, Trev. We got to get in before they catch us."

"How the fuck are we going to do that? They've got bloody great longbows, kill us from half a mile away."

"We'll hide, mate," said Chad confident as it came to him. "Here, lend a hand."

*

"Sir! It's the relief wagon!" A sentry cried from the eastern rampart, unexpected and Sergeant Major Hollis hurried up the ladder to look over the wall. The wagon was coming straight down the hill, the horses going at a steady, even canter.

"Must've run into trouble, sir. Only one haulier."

Sergeant Major Hollis took this in and didn't comment. He knew how much his command needed these supplies, and that the elves would seek to cut them off. He acted swiftly.

"Sergeant Cochrane! Best archers to the southern and eastern walls, best crossbowmen to the corner." He shouted down into the compound, determined to give the wagon a chance. There were no woods to the east, just gently sloping moorland, but the woods came closest to the south and west, just out of bow range. The soldiers from the garrison were appearing from their bunks and duties, together with the few people who actually lived and worked at the outpost. All knew their lives depended on the relief wagon. There was barely a week's worth of food left and they were all on half rations as it was. The elves had been in the woods for three days, stopping all patrols and activity. They had arrived the day the first patrol had come and gone.

"Sergeant Cochrane, on my order, all crossbowmen will fire quarrels into the long stretch of woods in front of them. Repeat fire as fast as they can manage." It took the best part of two minutes to rewind a heavy crossbow for firing again, but they had the range for the woods. "Every crossbowman we have to the walls."

Soldiers were racing to the walls now, excitement rising and smiles across their faces. The chance of action raised morale, never mind if it succeeded. A soldier always thought he would succeed, even those who groaned and complained.

The wagon was several hundred yards away, and for a moment Sergeant Major Hollis wondered if it had been seen yet by the elves. He shook his head. Of course it had been seen, their eyes were far better than human eyes. Even now they would be making their way to the stretch of wood he had targeted, for from there the arrows would reach the wagon when it was about four hundred yards from the fort. He dare not wait any longer, for if he fired now he might injure some getting into position. But would it alert them to the wagon? He stopped the constant balancing, constant questions and doubt in the mind that is a commanding officer's lot and gave the command to fire.

The bolts hissed into the air and thumped into the woods. They were absorbed with barely a leaf fluttering, and no sign of any result. A constant rain of quarrels into the woods now began, and the wagon was coming into range. For a moment, the sergeant major thought he had succeeded, and then an arrow flew out of the very end of the wood, from a bush that no one would think could hold an archer. It arched high in the air and came down perfectly into the body of the haulier. There was a deep sigh as thirty breaths were released, but the wagon came on.

"What you goggling at, you sorry excuse for archers! Come on, hit that bloody bush! All around it! I want that fucking elf pinned like your aunt's sewing cushion or your bleeding sister in a tavern!" Sergeant Cochrane chivvied the crossbowmen back to giving covering fire.

The wagon kept coming.

More arrows came from the woods, oblivious of the covering fire from the crossbows, and the haulier was riddled and pinned to the seat, clearly dead. But the wagon kept coming.

"Why don't they shoot the horses?" asked the soldier beside the sergeant major.

"Elves respect horseflesh," answered the sergeant major absently, remembering a trip to their kingdom ten years earlier. "They don't hurt animals. Even so, I would expect them to shoot the horses rather than let us have them."

The wagon kept coming down the faint trail, now with heather on either side. They were barely two hundred yards away now, and beginning to pick up speed.

"Not too fast," whispered the major. "You don't want to hit a hole now. Corporal Jenkins! Ready the gates! Get them open so the horses know where to go. Shut them as soon as they are through."

Just as he turned back to the wagon, an elf came out of the heather, running at the lead horse. He groaned, knowing they were done.

The elf closed quickly, and tensed, ready to make the jump as the horse went by. He would swing up onto its back and turn the wagon away. At the last possible moment, the reins twitched, the horses turned abruptly, the wagon swung dangerously and the lead horse took the elf in mid-jump with her shoulder. He went flying and next moment the wagon bumped high as a wheel went over his leg.

The wagon sped up, the horses galloping now, and this time the arrows went for the horses. The near horse was hit three times, her scream coming out in a cloud of blood but, although she staggered, she kept going, the arrow deep in her lungs, as she swept through the gate into the yard, where she faltered, head down and blood pouring out.

The dead haulier screamed. "Noooo! Chloe! Noooo!"

The haulier fell over, and was revealed to be a sack of supplies in a jacket, with a hat tied on the top. Underneath it was a small space where the reins went, and a distraught figure struggled out, falling to the ground and running to the horse. Chloe was on her knees now, her life's blood pouring out, and she managed one last nudge to her master as Chad threw his arms round her, his tears falling into her blood.

*

"Brave man, your lad," said Sergeant Major Hollis several months later, over a beer in the officer's mess with Sergeant Major Cuppold. "Didn't turn a hair at being shot at by elves, but cried like a baby over his damned horse."

Cuppold swigged some beer to cover his thoughts at Chad being called brave. "So did the elves attack after that?"

"No, they pulled away once they knew we had food. Saved our bacon in more ways than one. Didn't let your wagon go back until we had a strong patrol to go with him, though. Thought they might lay for him, you know what they're like for revenge."

*

As the grey light of dawn crept through the saplings, Chad came up the hill with his wagon and stopped by a Company Sergeant.

"Still hot, Chad?" he asked.

"Should be, boss," replied Chad. "Got enough straw round the pots and some hot stones under 'em. Plenty of porridge to keep the lads warm."

The Spakka had launched a sudden raid in force down the peninsula, overrunning the border forts and were deep into Harrhein. Chad had been called up to help get hot provisions to the front line and was delivering porridge, hot and salty, to exhausted soldiers who had been retreating for the last two weeks. Now they came out of the wood and formed a queue at the back of the wagon. Chad pulled the straw and lids of the pots and started slapping porridge into the proffered bowls

"Good of you to get out of your pit, Chad," said a sergeant, an old friend. The soldiers always believed the hauliers lived a life of luxury with a warm bed and plenty of food.

"Wasn't going to, but your sister insisted and kicked me out!" he replied, although he hadn't even seen a bed in the last month.

"Oi! Just now you said it was my mother," said a corporal.

"Didn't you know he was your uncle?"

"Sergeant! Unload those pots, immediately." A crisp voice quelled the banter. "Wagonmaster, you are needed to collect some wounded." A brisk man jumped up onto the front of the wagon, and Chad suppressed a groan. One of those efficient bloody officers that get you killed before you know it, he thought to himself. And he's a bloody Pathfinder, no insignia to give away his rank.

"Of course, sir," he replied, none of his concern and resentment sounding in his voice. Damnit, it was thirty hours since he'd last had any sleep and this sounded like it would take another thirty. He whipped round to the horses, removed the feedbags and climbed up onto the front seat as the company sergeant shut and fastened the tailgate. "Which way, sir?"

"Down the track there and head north."

Chad moved the horses down the track, keeping them well left to avoid the deep mud. The Pathfinder noted this and nodded approval which Chad didn't see.

"We've about thirty miles to go, wagonmaster. You're Chad aren't you? Glad to have found you, you did a good job back out west a couple of years ago. In fact, couple of my lads were amongst the lot you saved, told me about it."

Chad didn't know what to say to that, and just grunted. He was thinking that the last he heard the Spakka were a lot closer than thirty miles, more like just over the bloody hill. The sky was lightening and they climbed a low hill. The Pathfinder had lapsed into silence. They didn't talk much as a rule, Chad avoided them when he could. Dangerous company. Sergeant Major Cuppold often tasked him with delivering to them in the middle of nowhere, far too close to the frontier, usually.

Chad eased up the hill, leaving the path to go through some low scrub and avoid the skyline. The wagon's high wheels were designed for just such manoeuvres. He eased the wagon through some trees and crested where they could see down the valley but not be seen. It looked like normal to him, and he had been down this road many times.

The Pathfinder slipped off the front of the wagon and jogged along beside it. Idly, Chad wondered if he actually was an officer.

"Keep following the track. Over the hill you will go through a deep gully, then across an open meadow and you will come to a stretch of forest coming down to the road ending in pines. Stop there, the wounded will find you. Don't come back the same way." He pointed along the road and gestured with his hands, not looking at Chad.

"You not coming with me?" asked Chad in surprise.

"You will be safer without me. You'll get through; they wouldn't let you through if I was along." With this enigmatic comment he faded off into woods and disappeared, ignoring Chad's stuttering response.

"Who's they? Who won't let me through? Where are you going? What's going on?"

Chad strained to see into the woods and find out where he had gone, without success. The horses kept on going and he couldn't decide what to do, feeling naked and exposed without the Pathfinder. He went down the hill and up the other side, his skin crawling the whole way, despite the sun coming out and warming his back.

Chad found the promised gully, which indeed he knew well. He hated it, in fact, always thought it was an ideal place for an ambush. With his shoulder blades shivering in anticipation of an arrow or, more likely, a thrown axe, he glanced up at the top of the gulley above him. And met the flat, implacable eyes of a Spakka staring at him.

The Spakka didn't move, and Chad kept going. He looked up into the trees, and realised that there were more Spakka there. Lots of them. All looking at him. Abruptly realising he was not breathing, he forced himself to take even breaths and tried to control the panic. The horses kept up a steady pace.

Ahead he could see a Spakka sitting on a rock and studying him as he came closer. As he drew level, he was looking him in the eyes, and another Spakka beside the rock moved. The seated Spakka put up a hand, and belatedly Chad realised he was stopping the other man from throwing an axe. The seated Spakka nodded at Chad, who nodded back automatically.

"Modig mann!" The seated man called, a great scar on his cheek gleaming white in the dawn's light, before he got up and vanished over the lip of the gulley.

Chad came out of the gulley into the sunlight and wondered how he was still alive. He was conscious of warmth, and realised he'd pissed his breeches and hadn't even realised. He breathed deeply, wondering if he was going to throw up, and was glad he'd missed breakfast.

By the time he reached the pines, he had himself back under control. He pulled up under the trees and unstuck himself from the seat, climbing down and going to check the horses without conscious thought. He had the left mare's foreleg up and was cleaning out the hoof when a voice made him jump, drop the hoof and allow the mare to tread on his foot.

"Now that's what I like - a man who cares for his horse when the woods are full of fucking Spakka."

He started when he realised that a man was looking at him over a crossbow from just a few feet away. He was lying under a bush and almost invisible.

"Who the hell are you and what are you doing here?" the man snapped.

"Uh, I'm Wagonmaster Chad, and I've come to take the wounded back. Are you injured?"

"You're funning me? Take us back?" A note of incredulity mixed with hope crept into the man's voice. "Chad you say? Heard of you. How many can you fit on that wagon?"

"Quite a few, I reckon. How many of you are there? And who are you?"

"We're the North Hallows Frontier Regiment, the Shield of the King." A note of pride crept into the man's voice. "We've 37 men here, all that's left of Lord Young's company. And every wound is in the front." He turned and called over his shoulder. "Sarge, stop digging your grave. We're getting out of here."

Chad realised that 37 men would take a while to load, so he filled the feed bags and put them on the horses. As he finished, a large man pushed the bushes aside and came out, looked at him and the wagon carefully. He had a crown embroidered onto his sleeve, denoting he was a sergeant. There was blood all over his tunic and he moved with slow deliberation.

"You are most welcome, Mister Chad," he said in a soft Northern burr. "Kindly assist in moving the wounded. Not many of us up to that."

"'Course," said Chad and followed him back through the bushes into a hollow, lined with bodies, it seemed. He gagged at the smell, of rotting flesh and dying men. A cawing came from above and he looked up to see there were a large number of crows in the surrounding trees.

"Waiting for tomorrow," said the sergeant, following his eyes grimly. "Come now; give me a hand with the Lieutenant." He went to a pile of clothes, which shook and sat up to reveal a boy. "We're getting out of here now, sir. Just get you on your feet, there's a good lad."

The boy smiled through a mask of blood and pain. "I've come as far as I can, sergeant. Up to you now. You take the walking wounded, leave me the rest. We'll manage. I know the land, remember. Raised here. Don't take the main road, go up through the Vale."

"None of that, sir. You know the men won't leave you." The sergeant spoke tenderly. "We've got a wagon now, we're all going together. Mister Chad has come to take us back, you remember, the hero of the elf raid two years ago."

Chad blushed, he'd tried to keep that quiet, and felt the boy's eyes inspecting him. "Plenty of straw in the wagon to keep everyone comfortable despite the jolts, sir. Shall we get you to the wagon?"

"That's very kind of you Wagonmaster. However get me a seat up front. I know the ways around here. You may have to tie me on, though."

Chad stared at the boy's right arm, which ended just past the elbow in a bloody, seeping rag. Looking around, he saw it wasn't an unusual injury.

"Spakka axes," murmured the sergeant. "About the only injury that isn't instantly fatal." He helped the boy to his feet and Chad busied himself picking up equipment and taking it to the wagon.

Soldiers filed out slowly and climbed painfully into the wagon.

Chad counted twenty eight on and it was packed. "Another seven? No trouble we can fit them in."

The sergeant looked at him for a moment, and then spoke to his Lieutenant. "I'm sorry, sir, but we have some who aren't going to make it. I will give them grace, but they would appreciate your words and face."

The boy flexed his left arm and looked at his hand. For the first time Chad realised he was missing part of the hand. "I can hold a sword, sergeant. I will do my duty."

"You can hold it, but you can't thrust properly. It wouldn't be fair, sir."

Abruptly Chad realised that they were going to kill some of the wounded. His gorge rose and he started to protest but couldn't find the words. He went back to the wagon while the boy staggered off with his sergeant.

He saw the guard who had first spoken to him, sitting on the straw in the wagon with a leg stuck out at an odd angle, blood soaked through the trousers and a horrific rent.

"What happened to Lord Young?" he asked.

"Spakka axe." The soldier grunted. "Split his fucking head in two." The soldier ruminated for a moment. "Good man, the Young Man. But his kid brother is something else. We'd all be dead if it wasn't for him. Not easy organising a retreat from axemen."

"Are there any of you that aren't wounded?"

"Went off with Lord Blackstair's company. They drove the Spakka back for a bit. How'd you get through, anyway? We must be about five miles behind the main Spakka army."

"I have no idea," said Chad with feeling. "A Pathfinder officer sent me down the track, and I went straight through the Spakka. They sat on the edge of the gulley and watched me."

"Where's your weapons? Were you holding them?" All the soldiers were listening to him, looking at him with eyes dulled with pain.

"Don't carry a weapon. Can't use the things. Me, I miss whatever I aim at with a crossbow, more chance of hitting myself or the horses. Safer without."

"You're a right mental bastard," said the soldier with respect.

"You wouldn't catch me walking through Spakka lines without a weapon. Did they do anything?"

"One of them was going to throw an axe, but another stopped him. When I went past he said something, sounded like 'mod egg man'"

"Brave," said the Lieutenant, climbing onto the seat, his face drawn and fresh blood on his legs. "He said you were a brave man. Spakka respect that. Hold to the low ground there, and go round that stump. You'll find a passable track, wont be too soft and the wagon will get through."

*

Chad would have liked to forget that trip. The smell was dreadful; he hadn't realised that blood smelt and now it was mixed with shit and corruption. The boy led them through back lanes and they never saw the Spakka. Most of the sickly sweet smell seemed to come from his arm. Every now and then the boy would hiss as they went over a bump, and once he bit off a scream when his stump brushed the side of the wagon as he tried to grab it with his missing hand. Some of the wounded became delirious, but the sergeant kept their discipline and they didn't cry out too loudly.

They stopped for a few hours to rest the horses, and Chad managed to get a bit of sleep. The soldiers slept in the wagon where it was warmer, only a few getting down. He noticed the Lieutenant going round and talking to each man.

They woke him after the second watch and he harnessed the horses and they went on through the night. He felt the Lieutenant's body like a block of ice beside him, and he shuffled closer, feeling his own body chill as he leaked heat into the boy.

Shortly after dawn they were coming down a track, the Lieutenant having fallen asleep at last, occasionally flopping his head onto Chad's shoulder. Chad saw two shapes beside the road and tensed before realising they couldn't be Spakka.

Coming closer, he saw a gaunt old man with a stern blond wife beside him. As they came up to them, a young girl came down the path that joined the track. Her dark eyes were huge, not looking at Chad as he came to a halt, but fastened on the Lieutenant.

The old man stepped forward and gently lifted the Lieutenant from his seat. The boy's head flopped backwards and Chad's skin crawled as he realised the boy was dead. The old man turned and walked away with his burden.

"Thank you for bringing us our son," said the old woman and she turned and walked away, followed by the girl, now openly weeping.

Unsure what to do, Chad looked back at the sergeant and saw him slumped down. All the soldiers had tears running down their faces, weeping quietly and openly. A big man at the back gestured to go on. Chad did so, the guilt rising up inside him. If he hadn't rested the horses and slept, the boy would have died at home. Maybe even lived under his mother's care.

"Lost his hand in the first action," said the sergeant quietly behind him. "Guarding the colour. Was always a killing wound. He just wanted to come home to die. Why he lasted so long. Thanks." This last was said gruffly, but murmured and echoed by the others. It made Chad feel worse, and a fake. He shouldn't have slept.

*

Chad sat on the rail overlooking the paddock and stared unseeing at his nephew, sitting beside him. The memories of twenty years in the Army flooded over him, the face of Old Lord Young as he took his son's body still haunting him fourteen years later. The princess had heard and sought him out. She commended him, but he had refused the honour of a medal presented by her in front of the garrison. That had annoyed her. The guilt had been too strong.

"No, Paul, I was just a haulier, taking stuff around for the army. I didn't kill anybody."

"What about women? Bet they all opened their legs for you, hey?" The boy grinned lasciviously, betraying his main reason for wanting to join the army.

A great emptiness swept through Chad as he remembered Maud, sweet smiling Maud. She'd laughed at his clumsy advances, touched his cheek and always been nice to him, whilst going off with the garrison soldiers. He'd married her, regardless of the belly swelling with another man's child, only to see her die in childbirth a scant few months later.

"Not what I wanted, lad." That was all he managed to say, wondering if he could ever share with anyone his feelings, how he would still see Maud's face on women as he passed them in the street, his heart raising with a lurch every time.

The boy looked at him with scorn, jumped off the rail and went off with his friends. Chad heard "Stupid old man" as the boy went round the barn and smiled ruefully. How could he explain his wars to a boy who though it was all about swords, and had no understanding of discomfort, of harnessing a recalcitrant team on a frozen morning with the leathers stiff and awkward.

He looked back into the paddock, and smiled at the beauty of this year's crop of horses. He had carefully nurtured the bloodlines, managing to get some of Chloe's relations from the Army when he retired five years earlier and took up horse breeding. It was a good life, he thought, and absently wished Maud was sharing it with him.

He climbed down from the rails, taking care not to jar his arthritic knee and turned to the stable, coming to an abrupt halt at the sight of an elf, standing just in front of him with a tube held to his mouth. The elf's cheeks puffed and a cloud of acrid black smoke engulfed Chad's head. He reeled back and sat down, coughing.

The elf sat down awkwardly on his haunches, a crooked leg off to one side. He looked at him with unblinking black eyes.

"Hello Fat Man," said the elf in perfect Harrheinian.

Chad looked up into his face and the years fell away, he was back in his charging wagon, looking out from under the dummy and right above the wheel as it went over the elf's leg. He heard again the sound of the bone breaking and he looked again into the same eyes, the same expressionless eyes that had looked up at him as the wagon broke his body and remembered again seeing the knowledge of who had caused the horse to turn into his jump flood into the elf's eyes.

"My leg didn't heal straight. The Shining Path, the Path of the Warrior, was closed to me. Thanks to you, Fat Man. I became a Shaman, a Medicine Man. I walk with the spirits and fly with the eagle. Black cap mushroom powder will kill you now, your heart will stop and all will think it is just age. For I am a peaceful elf now, with customers even in Harrhein. It would not do for them to think I had killed a Harrheinian Fat Man would it? Bad for business."

The elf smiled. He watched Chad as the pain rose in his chest, and his pulse started to race out of control.

"Eighteen years I have waited, Fat Man. Eighteen years I have followed you. I could have killed you before, but it was too obvious and I wanted you to know who killed you. But I thank you, Fat Man. You have made me a great Shaman. For seeking my revenge has given me great purpose. You are a brave man, a resourceful man, Fat Man. I am proud to finally kill you."

He watched as the pulse sped up and the seizure gripped the heart, watched the blood suffuse Chad's face, watched his eyes pop out and his sphincters release. Then he bent forward and touched his lips to Chad's forehead.

"Good bye, my Enemy, my Friend, my Maker. I shall sing your Benediction Song on the high hills overlooking the Western Trace, and I shall sacrifice your horse to you there." He spoke now in sibilant Elvish, turned and walked away.

*

Paul sat in the front row of the church, kicking his heels. Why did his stupid uncle have to drop dead like that? Now he was trapped in this damn church for the next hour and his mother wouldn't let him get off afterwards. He wanted to see the girl who was serving at the village inn, the only girl around this boring shit-hole of a village. The priest was droning on about Chad, clearly knowing nothing about him.

A noise at the back of the church made him look round. Soldiers were filing into the church, escorting a bishop. The bishop strode up the nave and looked at the priest whose mouth was dropped open like a mirror carp out of water.

"I am the Archbishop of Praesidium. If you please, good Vicar, I shall take over the service, for the memory of Wagonmaster Chad rings eternally in the Empress' hearing." The Archbishop looked at Paul's mother, Chad's sister. "The Empress shares your sorrow. She bids me to say that Chad has never been forgotten."

A large man in an indeterminate uniform strode forward. "Ma'am, there are not many outsiders remembered by the Pathfinders, but Chad was always there for us and we do not forget."

Another man stepped forward, a young man beautifully uniformed in shining blues and gold. "Ma'am, I am Lord Young, Captain of the Young Boys company of the North Hallows Frontier Regiment, the Shield of the King. Chad was our Shield when I was but a boy. The

North Hallows is honoured to be his pall bearers, as he bore us when my father and uncle died."

--ooOoo--

About the Author

Rex is English, but was born in Java, Indonesia and has spent many years in the Far East. He speaks Indonesian and Malay, with a smattering of other languages.

He has had an interesting life - as a youngster worked his passage on a container ship to Australia where he worked as a cowboy, gold-miner, door-to-door salesman and fruit-picker, before switching from Zoology to the Army to study at Sandhurst.

He saw active service in Northern Ireland and was Logistics Officer for Operation Drake in Indonesia. A country manager for an international tobacco trader at 25, he spent two years during the Cold War with MI6 before returning to the UK where he and his wife raised his two sons while working in marketing and publishing, with forays into NLP and personal development. Now they are adult, he and his wife have moved back to the Far East where he lives in Bali, travels, writes and researches.

He has always had a passion for writing and this was rekindled by telling stories he made up on the spot to his sons.

His hobbies are angling, reptiles, orchids, reading and hockey, though he fears that in his late 50's he is now a little old to keep playing the latter.

His wide experience and knowledge are interwoven into the tapestry of his writing.

If you have any questions for Rex, please feel free to use his Facebook Author page.

Mistress of the King

CPSIA information can be obtained
at www.ICGtesting.com
Printed in the USA
BVOW06s1926041216
469753BV00007B/57/P